GW01236788

The Curse
of the
Lonesome Mariner

Mark David Green

Copyright © 2012 Mark David Green

Cover page illustration by Anders Design

Proof read and edit by Storywork

Editing Services

This book is a work of fiction. No part of
the contents relate to any real person or
persons, living or dead.

The Curse of the Lonesome Mariner is
also available as an eBook from Amazon,
Smashwords (all other eReaders) or iTunes,
Sony, Kobo and Barnes & Noble websites.

www.markdavidgreen.co.uk

<u>Acknowledgements</u>

I owe a big thank you to a few special people
who helped make the writing of this book
possible:

To my mum and dad, Christine and Norman, for
the extra tuition in my early years.

To my grandparents, Cliff and Irene, for their
financial assistance.

To my wife, Nicky, for her love and support.

To three readers who very kindly gave me their
feedback on the first draft:
Valerie Woodward, David Martin and
Gillian Hough.

To Storywork Editing Services, for so much
invaluable editorial feedback.

To Mark Anders, for his fantastic cover designs.

And to Poppy, for just being herself.

One

I've always thought boatyards are magical places. They are full of hope and dreams and colourful characters, all looking for an escape from the drudgery of the system. There's no better place for putting plans into action.

I watched the diesel crane grumble into life with a cloud of oily smoke. Steel cables wound in, taking up the slack on two thick webbing straps which supported a newly polished sailing boat hull.

The crane's engine revved up, causing more noise and smoke. The boat wobbled, easing out from the support of a steel cradle to dangle free, an inch off the ground.

"Right-oh. Take her up," the baseball-capped Gaffer called out.

The engine revved harder, lifting the boat higher until it hung precariously in the slings, ten feet off the ground.

A lump gathered in my throat as I watched two yard guys walk with the boat as it floated past, one leading and holding a rope attached to the bow, the other following on behind with the stern line. Off to one side, the sun-bleached Gaffer kept a careful eye on the flying boat, instructing the crane driver with a series of precise hand signals.

The boat swayed gently with the motion as it passed the neat row of yachts stacked side by side on the gravel yard. Some stood on wood chocks and oil drums, while others with deeper keels sat higher, supported within steel cradles.

The crane trundled on past other sailors working on their boats, painting anti-fouling on fibreglass hulls, varnishing woodwork or climbing ladders propped against the hull, ten feet above the ground. Most acknowledged me with a friendly smile or nod and yet, I sensed a shift in mood and perspective. Mine, probably, but the atmosphere did seem different. Some boat owners came up to congratulate me on a job well done. Others looked on with a twinge of sadness, perhaps because their own boat had long since grown invisible roots, anchoring them to the boatyard.

I watched my home travel sedately away from her empty space on the gravel to the water, a distance of less than one hundred metres, but an emotional leap that spanned a generation. An old boy who owned a decaying motorboat near the harbour wall wandered over and began rolling a cigarette.

"Nice to see the old girl get her feet wet again. Bet you she never thought she would."

I nodded an acknowledgement to the old timer and walked with funeral feet to the edge of the quay. The yard guys all faced their Gaffer, adjusting the ropes until the boat hung over the water parallel to the quay wall. My eyes lingered on the name 'Jessica' painted in bright yellow on her stern, a smile twitching through tense muscles.

On the Gaffer's signal, the crane driver eased a lever, lowering the boat towards the seaweed-green water.

I watched her triple keels gradually dip through the glassy water, barely causing a ripple. I'd seen boats launched like this many times before. It always struck me that it might just keep going and sink onto the seabed, rather than sit peacefully on her waterline.

"She floats, always a bonus," said the old boy, appearing by my side. I watched him light his roll up and puff it into life.

"Enjoy your adventures on the wet stuff..."

The old salty seadog shuffled off, back to his unfinished project. I heard from someone that he'd started restoring his wooden motor boat twenty years ago, after his wife left him. I guess sometimes it's the thought of the voyage that counts, actually setting sail is a scary prospect.

The slings slackened off around Jessica, allowing her to float freely, seawater caressing her freshly painted waterline.

"Best check the seacocks, skipper," said the Gaffer, glancing at me. He held up his palm, indicating to the crane driver to hold the slings in position, just in case.

I hesitated before stepping aboard, trying to condense all the hard work, money, decisions, compromises... everything into this moment. So much *commitment.*

My stomach lurched as Jessica listed under

my weight. Such a novelty, I thought, a boat that moves…

A ripple of nervous energy tingled deep inside my chest. I climbed down through the open companionway into the cosy main cabin and lifted the locker covers, relieved to see a dry hull around each seacock. I poked my head outside and stuck my thumb up at the Gaffer.

*

I breathed in the warm afternoon air as I ambled back to the boat yard from the local shops, holding the oxygen in my lungs, absorbing a newfound energy. I couldn't help grinning as I strolled through the entrance, tingling with anticipation.

I walked past the boats stacked side by side, leaving the marina office and shower block behind. Through the car park, towards to the foot of the walkway where I paused, savouring the moment.

This end of the marina is hallowed ground, Harry, I thought. You've really done it! Lost in my own dreamy world of adventures and danger on the high seas, I didn't notice the police car. I descended down the slope to the pontoon berths and strolled past a line of boats all floating in a neat row.

The pontoon rattled underfoot, swaying mildly as I sped up, keen to see Jessica tucked into her berth. Halfway down on the right hand side, if I remembered correctly, partially hidden between two bigger and more expensive boats.

I slowed as I drew closer, surprised to see a policeman and a tall, well-built man with a chubby face and ruddy complexion wearing a suit and tie standing in front of Jessica's bow. My forehead creased into a frown, heart rate rising as I stole breath from my constricted lungs.

"Harry Straight?" said the suited man.

"That's me."

"Do you have a brother, Keith?"

I nodded.

"I'm Detective Inspector Randall. We've arrested Keith for... several offences, one of which is a sensitive matter."

"Oh, I see."

"We don't normally offer this sort of service to the criminal fraternity, but frankly sir, I'm a dog lover."

I switched my gaze between DI Randall and the uniformed policeman.

"I'm not sure I understand..."

I watched them both lower their heads. I dropped my eyes onto the pontoon, following a lead dangling from the policeman's hand.

A pair of large, unblinking chocolate-brown eyes stared back at me from behind the police officer's legs. Long black eyelashes framed the dog's small, expressive face. It had short brown and ginger fur with a white chest, a sausage dog body and long terrier-length legs. A hint of grey on its paws and nose suggested a dog rather than a puppy. Next to it lay a plastic bag. The dog's tail twitched apprehensively as our eyes met.

"Dog pounds are depressing places. Here..."

The policeman pushed the lead into my palm.

"Keith will probably make bail in a few days. Until then, the dog's all yours."

"I can't look after a dog, I'm setting sail soon. I've got to prepare…" I stammered.

"It's you or the dog's home, sir. Here's a note from Keith, he said something about a vet's appointment tomorrow."

The Inspector smirked and handed me a slip of paper, then patted me on the back and led the policeman away. I glanced down at the note.

Harry,
Been trying to get hold of you. Debs did a runner with my stash and the rozzers are taking me in. Do me a favour mate and look after the dog until I get bail. Couple of days, tops.
Cheers
Keith
PS. I found Dad's boat logbook in the loft, thought you might like it.
PPS. The dog's got a vet's appointment at Poorly Paws,
midday tomorrow.

I frowned and looked over towards the car park.

"What's its name?" I called out.

"Lacey," shouted the policeman as he climbed into the squad car. "And it's a he."

"Lacey?" I repeated, noticing the dog's tail flicker. "Isn't that a girl's name?"

"Apparently he's named after a rock band from Nottingham. Something to do with their mascot… Check out the undercarriage if you don't believe us…" shouted the detective inspector, before he slammed the car door shut.

I stooped down and stared at the dog's distinctly male genitals.

"Oh, right. I see…"

I caught a bemused expression in the dog's eyes as he backed away from me, so I reached out to let him sniff my hand.

"So, Lacey… What on earth am I going to do with you?"

Two

"You got any food, mister?"

I yanked my hand away, startled at the dog's barking. He wagged his tail, which I'd thought was supposed to be a good sign.

"It's okay, little one..." I began to say, as wash from a passing boat jolted the floating walkway.

The dog whimpered and splayed his legs on the pontoon's wood decking.

"Whoa, the world is moving! What's occurring?!"

I gently tugged on his lead, but the dog crouched lower, pushing back on his haunches.

"No way! That's water down there and this dog don't do the wet stuff!"

I couldn't help laughing, what a ridiculous situation! I crouched down next to the funny little dog and peered into his nervous eyes.

"Its okay, Lacey, you're quite safe. It's only... what the... you can't wee on the pontoon!"

I stood up, glancing around the marina wide-eyed, watching urine trickle across the teak walkway.

"Hey, don't shout at me, stranger. It happens when I'm anxious, alright!"

I flinched at yet more barking.

"You sure do make a lot of noise for such a small dog."

I offered my hand again, slower this time.

"Keith isn't a very responsible dog owner, is he?"

The dog allowed me to stroke his head as he whimpered, but kept a wary eye on me.

"Like you're going to be any better?"

"A few days, eh? Okay doggy, you'd best come aboard."

As carefully as I could, I scooped the small furry animal into my arms, picked up the plastic bag and carried them both towards Jessica. The dog cocked his ears and peered nervously at the water beneath the pontoon, whining constantly.

"Whoooaaa! Dogs aren't meant to fly!"

The dog twisted around, pushing against my chest, almost spilling out of my arms.

"Where's my proper owner…?"

"It's okay Lacey, nearly there…"

We lurched onto Jessica as I stepped awkwardly over the guardrails, the extra weight throwing my balance off.

"Whoa… don't let me gooo…!"

I sat down quickly in the cockpit. The dog's scrabbling paws scratched my arms, forcing me to release him as he began yapping again.

"What am I doing in a floating bathtub?!"

"Easy Lacey, it's a boat. A bit smaller than a house, but nice and snug."

The funny little dog crouched low on the cockpit seat and shot me an indignant expression. He took a tentative step, placed a paw on the slippery white gel coat, then yelped as his paws lost traction and he almost fell onto the cockpit sole.

"This isn't very dog friendly, mister."

I repositioned, shuffling over to remove the washboards and open the main hatch, my movement tipping the boat to the right. The dog glared at me, about to topple forwards, but instead he leapt for my lap, making me scrunch my eyes tight and wince as he trod on my groin. He pawed my clothing until I gave up trying to push him off my lap.

"Okay, okay. You can stay there, just move your paw off my…"

"Hey, Captain Nemo, get a grip or it's another paw in your tinkle-tackle, capeesh?"

I hunched over the bundle of furry trouble while I regained my composure. Damn you Keith! I struggle to look after myself, let alone this… creature.

The dog made a grumbling sound and burrowed deeper into my lap.

"Keep still, I'm comfy here."

I twisted my neck down to meet those big brown eyes.

"You're a pain in the behind!"

I tore myself away from his oddly hypnotic stare and picked up the plastic bag, emptying the contents onto the seat beside me:

A beige ceramic bowl with the name 'Rabbit' pressed into it. An old book with a grubby plastic wrap around its cover and a brightly coloured check-pattern knitted tea cosy.

Great.

I read the note again, then glanced down at the dog, snuggled into a ball on my lap, his head tucked in beside his tail. As the dog breathed in and out, he emitted funny grumbling noises.

"That's better, a stationary human hot water bottle. Lovely. This'll guilt-trip him into not moving for a while. It must be dinner time soon… Whooaa! I'm flying again…"

The dog scrabbled in my arms as I carried him down into Jessica's cabin.

"Noooo! I can't swim!"

I set the dog down onto the floor next to his rabbit bowl. He stared at me, unblinking, then flicked his eyes around Jessica's small cabin.

"Okay, this is weird. So we're under the water now. How's that work?"

Glug, glug, glug.

The dog flinched, jumping back as I poured fresh water into his bowl. He tentatively sniffed around the edge of the liquid, then turned his nose up and kicked his paws back, tossing his head.

"Water? Fish fornicate in water!"

The squawking bark echoed around the cabin. I glanced at my watch and leant down to show it to him.

"It's not dinner time, look… it's not even five-thirty."

We stared into each other's eyes.

Be strong Harry. Don't let it win…

"Not a chance mate! No one outstares a hungry dog!"

Blink.

"Bugger."

"Too right!"

"Okay, message understood. You're hungry. What have I got on board that's dog friendly...?"

The dog licked his lips as he craned his neck to watch me rummage in the galley lockers.

"The best I can do for now is a tin of tuna and some digestive biscuits. That okay?"

The dog barked and plonked his bottom down on the floor. His eyes followed my every move.

"Come on mister, starving dog here. Who knows when my next meal will be..."

As soon as I began lowering the food towards the floor the dog pounced, desperate to poke his nose in and get scoffing.

I don't think a Dyson could have hoovered up the food any quicker! He licked the bowl clean in less than ten seconds.

"Blimey, you're a hungry dog... didn't Keith or Debs feed you?"

Knock knock.

Bark, bark, bark!

"Harry?" said a doubtful voice.

I poked my head out through the hatch and smiled at Jim, a chubby chap in his late fifties, another longstanding tenant of the boatyard following an acrimonious split from his wife. Lacey jumped at the steep steps below me, barking furiously.

"I didn't know you had a dog."

"My brother's. Looking after it for a few days while he's away... on business," I added.

"Splendid, be good company for you. You ready?"

I frowned.

"Boat launch drinks. It's tradition in the yard. You're in the chair for the first round and we're all thirsty."

"Sure thing, just give me a minute…"

I ducked into the heads and glanced in the small mirror. My grey-blue eyes glanced back, their tiredness mostly concealed by my normally cheerful expression. I flicked a brush through my slightly dishevelled black hair flecked with grey and attempted a cheeky-dimples and sideburns smile, which I almost pulled off.

"Could do with a second shave today, Harry. You're looking a bit hitch-hiker-ish, but reasonably presentable… you'll do," I murmured at my reflection.

I checked my pockets for my wallet and phone and stepped up into the cockpit, turning to face the barking ball of fur as I lowered the washboard into place.

"Oy, pal, what's occurring?"

"I won't be long."

"Don't leave me alone in here. I get claustro-dog-phobic!"

I turned away from his unblinking eyes and slid the hatch almost shut, leaving a space for airflow. The barking recommenced, this time louder with a greater urgency.

"Noooo… don't leave me…"

I lifted one foot over Jessica's guard rail, then hesitated. What if the dog wanted a wee, or worse, a number two? Would it mess on the boat? Perhaps I wasn't being fair to him, first night on board and all that. I silently cursed Keith and slid the hatch open.

"Back so soon? Let's learn that lesson real early!"

"Come on then," I said to the excited dog, watching it skip around the cabin, bouncing across the opposing cabin seats.

*

I followed the dog towards the grassy patch in the corner of the boatyard, watching him stop to sniff around the boat cradles at regular intervals. Occasionally he'd stop to look around, see where I'd got to.

"Funny little thing, aren't you?"

I couldn't help chuckling as Lacey sort of half-squatted with one leg raised an inch off the ground while he peed and stared at me.

"Oh yeah, Harry. Here's the spot. Lovely."

Bizarre.

"That better?"

I shook my head as he trotted past making a strange whining sound, on the trail of some new scent.

"Laugh it up, sailor boy. Wait until I've been on the curry!"

Three

"I didn't know you had a dog. What a cutie," said Marion, the wife of Fred, a crusty old sailor who lived on his boat in the yard. Marion visited Fred at the weekends and he assured me they had the perfect relationship because Marion had the run of their comfortable house without 'a grumpy old git making it look untidy'.

I passed Lacey's lead to Marion and left her fussing over the dog while I went to the bar to get another drink.

"When do you set sail?" Jim asked, raising his glass to mine.

"Sometime soon. Just a few jobs to finish up, then I'll be off."

"No set departure date?"

I shook my head and took a gulp of beer.

"I tried it once, the big adventure. Got the boat in the water and onto a mooring buoy in the harbour. Know how far I got?" he said.

"Across the channel?"

"Poole Quay, then back here. It's not for everyone… there's no shame in realising that."

I looked away from Jim.

"I'll be okay."

"You don't seem convinced, Harry. What about the dog, is it going too?"

"No."

I glanced around the bar to make sure Lacey still held Marion's attention.

"My brother will collect him in a few days, after his holiday."

"So the plan is to port-hop down to Falmouth?"

"That's the general idea."

"What's waiting for you there?"

I paused to take a long slow pull on my pint.

"My father... and a long overdue visit."

"Oh, right. Sounds ominous."

"Lots of history and family issues." I attempted a weak smile then dropped my eyes back to my pint.

"And after that?" he said.

"I've not thought that far ahead..."

Jim sipped his drink, studying me.

"I'll be back in a jiffy, going to check on the dog," I said, scanning the room for Marion.

*

I sat back in Jessica's snug cabin and swirled a generous measure of brandy around the plastic tumbler. Lacey lifted his head from licking his paw and stared at me, his eyes following the glass, which I raised in a silent toast to him.

I looked around the cabin. Such a cosy home. My eyes rested on Lacey's plastic bag lying on the chart table. Something about it bothered me. I reached over and rummaged through the contents, pulling out the original log book for Jessica, which my father had recycled from work. The old Midland Bank ledger had a distinctive wraparound front cover with an overlapping tongue that secured it into a slot. I'd not seen it in years.

I flicked open the black, blue and red vertical column pages, fanning through them in my hands. So much history… mostly bad.

I tightened my hands to stop them trembling and backtracked to the opening page, casting my eyes over the first entry, made in long swoopy handwriting:

<u>9th day of April, Nineteen Seventy-Seven</u>
Launch Day. This sloop is named 'Jessica' by Elizabeth, the name she'd chosen for our daughter who surprised us by being born our second son. Champagne over the bow, good wishes and fair winds blessed. Baby Harry will start his sailing life early at barely two years old. Young Keith took the helm to bring us alongside the jetty, nicely done for a seven year old. He has a great sailing career ahead of him, I'm sure. Now the adventure begins!

My eyes rested on the date of the entry: thirty-seven years ago. How did I value the time, had I made the most of it?

I lowered the logbook and panned around the cabin again, this time picking out different elements of the many months of my hard work. Freshly sanded and varnished woodwork, new headlining, rewiring… the list went on.

I downed the rest of the brandy and replaced the logbook on the chart table.

"That's an emotional time bomb right there, Lacey."

The dog grumbled, his head slipping off my lap as I stood up and stretched.

"Oy, human pillow, come back..."

"Right-oh doggy, I'd better sort your bed out."

I found an old fleece which I used for painting, laid it out on the cabin floor beneath the companionway hatch and lifted him onto it.

"There, your bed, okay? Here's your water. Sleep well, little one."

I smiled at the dog, who stood there staring at me, his expressive little face looking oddly puzzled.

"You are joking, right?"

"Vocal little thing, aren't you?"

I turned away from the dog and made my way forwards to clean my teeth in the heads, then ducked into the compact bow cabin. I made a neat pile of my clothes on the opposite vee berth and then swung my legs up and into my sleeping bag. I lay there for a few seconds pondering. You're thirty-nine years old, I thought, there's no point dwelling on what happened...

I turned out the light, wriggled my feet deep into the sleeping bag and pulled it up around my hips and chest.

"What the hell...?!"

I yanked my toes away from warm fur and contrasting cold wet nose, my heart pounding, a cold sweat seeping through my pores. How did a rat get into my sleeping bag?!

The rat sneezed cold mist onto my toes, then scampered up towards me. I raced to get out of the sleeping bag, but the rat-dog stretched out and crawled up to meet me, its tail swooshing dangerously close to my midriff. I fumbled for the zip and whizzed it down just as the dog spilled out and made a lunge for my face, burying his cold wet nose into my eye socket and licking my cheek. I prised him away, spluttering as the little devil's tongue made contact with my mouth.

"Oy! This is my bed!" I yelled.

"What's yours is mine, amigo. It's first rule of human-pet ownership. Haven't you read the doggy rule book?"

"Lacey!"

I managed to grab the wriggling monster and carried him back into the main cabin.

"Right-oh, my hairy friend. This is your bed, okay? Through there, is my space. There's no room for both of us. Sleep well and I'll see you in the morning."

I pulled the bow cabin door shut, plumped up my pillow and climbed back into the sleeping bag, zipping it up to my chin. I settled into a snug position, closed my eyes and began to drift off.

Tip, tip, tip.

Scratch.

Scratch. Scratch. Scratch…

"What the…? Damn you, Lacey!"

I ducked my head into the sleeping bag, wrapped the end around my ears and squeezed my eyes tightly shut.

"There's no way you're coming in…" I mumbled.

Then it started barking.

"I'm lonely, so lonellllyyyyy…"

I gave in and opened the door.

"Hi Harry, what took you so long? You look bleary eyed… bad night's sleep? A hop, skip and little jump… there, that's better."

I shut the door behind the dog and banged my head on the roof as he jumped up onto the bunk while I tried to avoid his hot tongue.

"Waggy tail and licky face time?"

"Ugh! You've got to be joking…"

I tried to close access to the sleeping bag, but Lacey ducked his head down and flicked it over his head as he wriggled down my chest and tunnelled towards my feet. I rotated my body just in time to avoid a scrabbling paw in my delicate area and felt him spin round to get comfy beside my toes.

"You can't stay there, you'll overheat."

I unzipped the bag and shifted my feet to encourage him to vacate my bed.

Grrrrrrrrrrrr!

"Lacey, please. Come on, out."

"Not a chance, monkey chops."

We held eye contact.

Grrrrrrrrrrr. Ruf. RUF!

I lay there for a moment thinking, accompanied by Lacey's low throaty growl. After a few minutes contemplating, I drew the bottom zip up six inches, allowing the dog some air so he wouldn't suffocate. I tried to hunch my feet away from the odd sensation of his warm furry body, but he shifted position, taking up even more valuable space. I relented and eased my toes back down. How could one little dog be so demanding? Keith had better make bail, or else his bundle of trouble would be going to the dogs home…

*

I woke up to the sound of my own snoring, which seemed weird, because I felt awake.

I opened my eyes and glanced around the dim cabin, expecting the snoring to stop. But the steady rhythm continued. I frowned, my eyes drawn to the bottom of my sleeping bag, where a snout and small furry head poked out.

I nudged the dog with my toe, waking him with a discontented grumble. Lacey opened a sleepy eye and looked up at me. I felt his tail swish across the sleeping bag fabric. He stretched and pulled his elongated body out, then shook himself, hind legs wiggling comically.

"Watch out little one, you're a bit close to the…"

Plonk!

Lacey lost his footing on the narrow edge and toppled onto the floor.

"Whoa, who moved the bed?"

I burst out laughing, jerking my head up, banging it on the cabin roof again.

"Yeeoww!"

I swung my legs over the side of the berth and nearly tripped over the yapping, prancing dog.

"Ha! Sore head, Captain? What you need is some wake-up noise!"

I wandered in to the main cabin and flicked

the kettle switch on. The damn dog hadn't stopped barking.

"What?" I demanded.

"Food. Food. More food, then a walk. Chop chop, Captain."

I sat down on the cabin seat, blinking and stretching and yawning simultaneously, all while trying to fend off Lacey who stood on his hind legs on the seat, determined to paw my bare arms and lick my face. Silly me, thinking pets helped to relieve stress.

*

Something nagged at the back of my mind. I watched Lacey lay on his back on the opposite saloon seat, eyes closed, his head tipped to one side, paws dangling in mid-air. I'd already fed him and had taken him for a walk around the boatyard and into the adjacent park. So what had I forgotten?

I glanced at my watch: 11:46am.

Lacey suddenly twitched and leapt up. He jumped down off the seat and used his front paws to drag his bottom across the floor.

"What's the matter, doggy? You'll get splinters."

I couldn't help sniggering. The dog had a look of intense concentration, or was it discomfort as he scooted past my feet.

I reached down and picked him up, tipping him over in my arms. He looked a bit red under his tail.

"It's okay Lacey," I said, cradling him gently as he whimpered.

"That's alright for you to say, mister, you don't have chilli powder stinging your bum!"

"Oh bugger, that's it."

Holding Lacey close to me with one hand, I leant over towards the chart table and rummaged in the plastic bag for Keith's note.

"Midday vet's appointment. Damn! We're going to be late. Come on doggy, we've got to go..."

I carried Lacey off the boat and hurried along the pontoon.

"Hi Sheryl, have you seen Jim?" I blurted out.

"He's just popped out to the chandlers in town, probably be a while knowing him."

I thanked her and hurried away, mentally running through a list of options. I doubted the bus would get me to the vet's in time and no one else I knew with a car seemed to be in the yard. My gaze settled on my old Honda motorbike, a crazy thought occurring to me.

"Lacey, what are you like as a pillion passenger?"

Back on the boat, I rummaged through lockers, searching for my bike stuff and a small backpack.

"What do you reckon, Lacey, think you'll fit?"

I scooped Lacey up and tucked his body into the backpack, bottom first, then zipped him in. He looked at me with an indignant expression as I clipped the side straps under his front paws.

"So now I'm a Hell's Angel... interesting."

Lacey looked happy enough, so I lifted the pack onto my shoulders and craned my neck around so I could just see his nose out of the corner of my eye. Probably not one of my better ideas. What if…

I glanced at my watch as I picked up my safety helmet. The hell with it.

*

"Whooo-hooo! Faster!"

I couldn't feel the dog wriggling and only heard the occasional yelp over the engine, so I pressed on, careful to keep my speed down.

"This is fun, Harry! I can see so much better up here. Fan-dog-tastic! But where are we going? Through the traffic lights… past the library… over the lifting bridge… whoa there Captain, you're slowing down. Which means this is looking suspiciously like that place… no Harry, you wouldn't. We've only just met…"

I'd heard the location of the vet's mentioned in the boatyard because one of the others had to rush their dog there two weeks ago. I slowed down, indicating right.

I felt the backpack move. Tentatively at first, then paws pressed into my back accompanied by more urgent wriggling and loud insistent barking.

"Easy Lacey, we're nearly there."

I pulled up in a space outside the surgery, kicked out the side-stand and threw my leg off the bike.

"Harry you sneaky human! You can't bring me here, it's not playing fair!"

I wrestled the unstable backpack off my shoulders and lowered it to the ground, just in time to grab Lacey's collar to stop him wriggling out and legging it.

"It's okay Lacey. There's nothing to worry about…" I said in a soothing voice from beneath my helmet visor, but he'd become a frantic, yelping ball of energy.

"Nothing to worry about? This is the doggy death doctor!"

Lacey's claws scratched at the pavement as he desperately tried to run away. He gasped noisy elongated breaths as he strained against his collar.

"It's okay Lacey, they won't hurt you."

"That's easy for you to say, spaceman!"

I removed my helmet, shouldered the backpack and tried to coax Lacey towards the vet's entrance door. But no amount of gentle tugging on the lead would persuade him to come with me. I tried more pressure, but he sat back, crouched low and braced his front legs, almost pulling the collar over his head.

"No chance mister!"

I practically dragged the dog towards the vet's surgery, but soon gave up due to the disapproving looks from other pet owners. With a clenched-teeth sigh, I conceded and scooped him up. I held him tight to my chest, stroking behind his ears and talking softly to try and calm him down.

"Dogs don't come outta here... they don't come out!"

I carried Lacey into the reception, still whimpering and wriggling in my arms.

"Hi, this is Lacey. He's a bit nervous," I said to the receptionist, who nodded and smiled at Lacey, now a trembling bundle of fur.

"That's an unusual name for a male dog," she said sympathetically.

"Yeah, my human had a stutter, he couldn't say Lass... ss .. ss .. ey!"

I carried Lacey to a seat and placed him gently on the floor, but he wouldn't sit still. He ran on the slippery lino floor, paws skidding comically, straining against his lead as his collar bit into his neck.

Whooaarr! Whooaarr!

I couldn't handle his deep-throated gasps any longer and lifted him up onto my lap. I hooked two fingers under his collar, just in case.

"Gotta get out... gotta get out..."

Lacey began whining and trembling again in a ten second burst that built in intensity, then died off, the cycle repeated a few seconds later.

"He knows. They all do," said a woman next to me with a plastic cat basket perched on her lap.

"Knows what?" I replied, frowning.

The woman leant towards me, lowered her voice.

"What goes on here. Being *put to sleep*."

I studied the woman's sad expression as the realisation sunk in.

"They can't possibly know that?"

The woman flicked her eyes down at Lacey, then back to me and raised her eyebrows.

I felt another wave of trembling in my lap, so I leaned over the dog, gently hugging him.

"It's okay Lacey, it's just a routine check-up," said a soft voice from the edge of the room.

I sat up straight and looked over at the voice. The dog seized his opportunity and leapt off my lap, making a paw-spinning dash for freedom. The lead slipped out of my hand, trailing behind Lacey, whipping past the vet's slender legs. Lacey almost made it out the door, stopped short by the vet's well-timed foot stepping on the end of the lead. Lacey jerked to a halt, his hind legs pivoting out behind him. He lay there on the floor panting heavily, eyeballing the vet.

"Lacey, you know me. I'm not that bad."

"That's what you say, Doctor Death. I never saw Archie again!"

The vet crouched down and offered her hand, which Lacey sniffed suspiciously. Lacey seemed to sigh with a sort of acceptance as the vet stroked him.

The vet stood up and turned to face me. She looked to be around five feet five or six tall, a wisp of a girl in her late twenties or early thirties with mousey brown shoulder length hair, pulled back into a ponytail. She wore a light blue veterinary smock, brown trousers and a relaxed warm smile which accentuated her pixie-like cheeks and lit up her face without detracting from a professional business-like demeanour.

"Hello. Are you looking after Lacey?" she said.

"Yes, I'm Harry, Keith's brother. He's away… on business."

The vet nodded, the hint of a smile flickering on her lips.

"I'm Alice, Lacey's regular vet. Please follow me."

*

"How long is Keith away for this time?"

I glanced away from Lacey, stood trembling on the examination table. "Um, just a couple of days. In the short term."

"I see. Right, Lacey, let's take a look at you."

The vet gently lifted Lacey's eyelids, then felt behind his neck and front leg joints.

"And how has Lacey been?"

"Okay, I think. I've only been looking after him since yesterday."

I watched the dog flinch and make low throaty grumbling noises as the vet felt her way over his joints.

"He's in pretty good shape, considering his age."

I frowned. "How old is he?"

"Seven, according to his records. But that's misleading."

"How so?"

"Pet plan insurance premiums favour a lower age. Sometimes owners forget a few doggy birthdays. In Lacey's case, he's probably nearer to ten or eleven."

"Hence the saying, 'you can't teach an old dog new tricks'…?'" I muttered.

The vet glanced up at me and smiled.

"Yes, stubbornness or character… it's a fine line sometimes. Has Debbie left Keith again?"

I shrugged, watching the vet lift Lacey's tail, prompting him to growl and edge away.

"Whoa, easy Doc! You don't wanna go rooting around down there…"

"Okay Lacey, one more slightly unpleasant examination, then you're done."

The vet turned away and plucked a pair of disposable latex gloves from a box on her desk. The dog peered around me, following the vet's movements.

"Uh oh. Rubber gloves. Brace yourself!"

"Has he been dragging his bottom on the ground?" said the vet.

"Erm, yes, this morning," I replied, dropping my eyes.

The vet nodded, pulled some paper towels from a dispenser.

"Sometimes they need help with expressing their anal sacs."

"Oh, right."

I felt my cheeks flush, aware of the vet gauging my response.

"There are two glands, one each side of a dog's rectum. They contain a foul-smelling sticky liquid that's normally secreted to mark the animal's territory each time they excrete. It's the same stuff a skunk sprays as a defence against predators. Sometimes, if the dog's stools aren't firm enough to allow regular self-draining, the glands fill up and get uncomfortable. Hence the bum dragging."

The vet looked up at me. I nodded my head vacantly.

"So I need to manually drain the fluid. If you can hold Lacey firmly, please. As you can imagine, fingers prodding in that area isn't very pleasant. Ready?"

I repositioned to hold Lacey's front shoulders, his shuddering whimpers resonating through my hands.

"Oy, Doctor Death. Your fingers are not supposed to be poking my bottom!"

I held the dog tightly as he tensed and growled. The vet dipped her head behind Lacey's raised tail and homed in with her latex fingers.

"You're gonna get it, Doc, you're really gonna get it…"

"It's okay Lacey, its okay boy…" I said softly.

Lacey's body flinched again.

"Target acquired."

"We just need to apply a bit of pressure each side of the anus and…"

"Get ready to squeeeeezzze!"

The sound of a muted machine gun fired a three-second burst.

Pop, pop. Pop, pop. Pop, pop…

The vet leapt back from Lacey's posterior, a look of absolute *horror* frozen on her crimson face.

"Bullseye!"

A foul, gut-wrenching stench drifted across the examination table. The vet recoiled, her hand clamped over her mouth, red cheeks flushed with a hint of green. As she straightened up, I noticed blobs of grey gunk polka-dotted up her tunic, over her chest, shoulder, cheek, nose, ear and hair. Behind her, the spray pattern continued in regular dot intervals up the wall and onto the ceiling. Lacey shook himself and sat down on the table.

"Actually, that does feel better. Thanks Doc!"

The vet blinked rapidly, pulled a retching face, clearly struggling not to gag. Without a word, she hurried out of the examination room. The door swung shut behind her. I glanced down at Lacey, who turned his head around towards the gunk-splattered wall, as if to survey his handiwork.

"Good grouping. Give yourself a paw-pat on the back."

A sharp cold spike of nausea jabbed at the back of my throat as the disgusting smell drifted up to my nostrils.

I stood there at a loss what do. Lacey seemed unconcerned and lay down to nibble his paw. A few minutes later the door opened and the vet breezed back in. She wore a different colour tunic and it looked like she'd scrubbed her face and rinsed her hair.

The vet did her best to banish a frosty grimace as Lacey looked up from chewing his paw. His tail twitched tentatively with an adorable puppy dog *'who, me?'* expression. It was almost as if he knew he'd done something wrong.

"Right Lacey, that's you done," said the vet, reaching out to roughly fondle him behind the ears.

"Um… I'm sorry about what just happened… I wasn't expecting…"

"It happens sometimes. One of the downsides of the job," she replied quickly.

I took my cue and lifted Lacey off the table, then followed his wagging tail to the door where he whined to be let out.

"See ya, Doc. Thanks for the target practice."

"Thanks again," I mumbled.

"Please stop by reception on your way out, to settle up."

"Of course," I replied, unable to meet her eyes.

Four

I lifted up my laptop screen and opened a tin of lager.

"That has to go down as one of the oddest days I've ever had. Cheers for that, Lacey."

I glanced over my shoulder and raised the beer tin towards Lacey, who licked his lips.

"Not a chance," I said.

I took a long swig of lager and began typing my password, unable to stifle a dark chuckle as the image of the vet's mortified fluid-splattered face flashed through my mind. Poor girl.

I felt something dig my side, heard a soft whine. Lacey sat beside me looking up. His paw jabbed me again.

"I'm thirsty."

"This isn't for you. There's your water, down there."

I eased Lacey's nose away.

"Come on, spoilsport. Just a snifter."

He pawed me again just as I took another swig, jolting my arm and causing beer to dribble down my chin.

"This is *mine,* understand? If you continue to be a pest I'll be forced to…"

Footsteps scuffed on the pontoon outside the boat. Low voices and bursts of radio static floated across my subconscious, all unthreatening background marina noises. Until Lacey began barking.

"Who's there? You'd better be dog friendly cos this canine don't take no crap!"

"Harry Straight?" a forceful sounding voice called out.

I slid the hatch open and poked my head out.

Half a dozen guns pointed at me from the pontoon, the weapons clenched purposefully in black-gloves.

"Hands! Show us your hands!" shouted the voice.

I stared at the gun-toting figures and froze. Down in the cabin, Lacey leapt at my feet, yapping.

"Hands, now!"

I slowly lifted my arms.

"Drop it, drop the weapon. NOW!"

I opened both hands, allowing the near-full beer can to slip from my fingers. The blue-clad figures visibly stiffened, straining to point their weapons closer to me, their eyes bulging and fixated.

The tin thudded on the deck, spraying frothy beer all over the cockpit. The figure nearest to me rapidly closed in, his machine gun clasped tightly into his shoulder, trigger finger poised.

"Don't move!" he shouted, stepping onto the side of the boat without using his hands to hold on.

Before I could open my mouth to say 'be careful', I felt the boat tip under his weight. He lost his footing with the motion, made a valiant attempt at yanking his other foot over Jessica's low guard wire, but the inertia tumbled him forwards. His first foot slipped away and he fell face-first onto the cabin roof, then bounced backwards off the guard wire. His machine gun clattered onto the deck beside me, his legs kicking up water as he dangled precariously between the pontoon and the boat, immersed up to his waist in seawater.

"Get down! Get down on the floor!" other high-pitched voices shouted at me.

I stepped awkwardly down into the cabin and inadvertently stood on Lacey, who yelped and nipped my ankle. The pain collapsed my leg, sending me crashing down the steps onto the cabin floor. The bloody dog pranced around barking, echoing around my throbbing head.

"What the hell…?"

I felt the boat rock again as several heavy bodies climbed aboard, accompanied by more shouting. The washboards slid up. Shards of sunlight pierced through the gloom, making me wince and cover my eyes.

I felt a boot push onto my neck.

"Stay down!" the voice shouted.

Something leapt over my head.

"Incoming…!"

I heard a screech, coinciding with the pressure on my neck easing.

Coughing, I clutched my sore neck and squinted up into the sunlight to see Lacey's jaw clamped around the policeman's groin. The little dog dangled in mid-air, his legs kicking and body twisting as the policeman thrashed around trying to wrench Lacey off his manhood.

"Aaaahhhrrr!"

Panic rushed through me – what if they shot the dog, or worse, me? I threw my hands out to try and prise Lacey's jaws open, at the same moment as the policeman bashed his head into the teak hatch surround, crumpling him into a heap over the chart table.

I gathered the salivating, wriggling dog into my arms, pulled him tightly into my chest and sat back on the floor, scooting backwards as far away from the unconscious policeman as possible. My hand closed around Lacey's nose, muffling his barking, my heart pounding with adrenalin. I snatched short gasps of air and stared at the red dot hovering on Lacey's head. I glanced up at the open hatch into the barrel of a machine gun and a pair of cold, hard eyes.

"Don't move a muscle," said the machine-gun-toting policeman, his voice firm but less aggressive than his colleague.

I held my breath.

"Are you alone on the boat?"

I nodded.

"Have you seen your brother today?"

I gasped for breath, shook my head.

"Do you have any weapons, other than that dog?"

Another shake of my head, pulsating now with a machine-gun-quick cadence.

The policeman slumped over the chart table groaned and moved his head.

"Okay. Very slowly, I want you to stand up and come outside without letting go of the dog.

Do you understand?" said the policemen crouched in the cockpit.

I nodded again and rolled forwards onto my knees. The gun barrel eased back to allow me to slowly step up into the cockpit. I glanced around at several other weapons, adding to the collection of red dots dancing in a tight cluster on my chest. My legs began to wobble and shake, threatening to give way as nausea tugged at the back of my throat.

"Sit down there. Hold onto the dog. Do it now."

I sat down in the cockpit opposite the policeman, my whole body shaking. Lacey continued to try and wriggle free, growling through my hand clenched around his snout.

"Let me at 'em, Harry, it's playtime!"

"Identify yourself," said the policeman sat opposite me.

"Harry Straight."

"Keith's brother?"

I nodded.

"Have you seen him today?"

"No. Are you here because of the vet?" I blurted out.

I glanced between several pairs of eyes and noticed the grip on their weapons relaxing.

"We're here because your brother has done a runner."

"Oh."

"Feisty dog you've got there, sir," said the policeman, a stern edge to his voice.

"Yeah, I should have shot the little sod…" said a woozy voice from the cabin.

"You very nearly did, Matthew. Fortunately you saved both of us a ream of paperwork. Get yourself to the medic."

The first policeman hobbled up into the cockpit, rubbing his head. He threw me a filthy look.

"Not bad for an unarmed pet-loving civilian," said the policeman crouched down opposite me. He removed his official looking baseball cap and clear wraparound glasses and sat down, the machine gun at his side clanking on the deck.

"Is that a compliment or a warning, officer?" I said, making a show of stroking Lacey.

The policeman's chiselled features relaxed into a tight lipped smile. He removed a glove and offered his hand for Lacey to sniff, but quickly withdrew it when Lacey growled through bared teeth, still clamped shut under my hand.

"Got yourself a real Jekyll and Hyde there. Unpredictable. Dangerous."

"It's not my dog, it's… it's… unfortunate. I'm looking after him for a friend. You can't blame him for trying to protect me. It's not every day we get ambushed by commandos brandishing automatic weapons…"

The policeman held eye contact for long time, then glanced over his shoulder, tipped his head at his colleagues. The other gun-toting figures lowered their machine guns.

"*Semi-automatic* weapons. Cuts down on accidental discharges and collateral damage," he said, leaning forwards, elbows resting on his knees. "We'll be keeping an eye on you, Harry Straight. If you see Keith, or have any contact from him, you call us. Before we have to call on you. Because next time, it might not be the same congenial outcome. Do you understand?"

I felt a shiver tremble through my neck. I nodded meekly, my throat dry, making it difficult to swallow. He leant in closer. I could smell tobacco on his breath.

"Otherwise…"

He pointed his first finger at Lacey, cocked his thumb and mimed a gun shooting him in the head. I watched slack-jawed as the policeman mouthed blowing smoke away from his imaginary finger gun.

"Enjoy your boat sir, lovely hobby," he said, twirling his finger in a small mid-air circular motion.

I sat there watching the policemen leave, one of them supported between two colleagues as he stumbled along the pontoon. I released Lacey from my death grip, ensuring that I kept two fingers hooked under his collar as he pranced around the cockpit, barking.

"Come on you gutless pussies, I'll take you all on! This dog is just gettin' warmed up!"

Oh brother, what have you got me into?

Five

"Beer, lovely!"

I lifted my head from my hands and turned to stare at Lacey's wagging tail as he slurped at the froth seeping from my dropped tinnie.

"Thirsty boy, eh Lacey? Hold up, I'll get you some water…"

But I couldn't move, my limbs had stuck rigid. Lacey yelped as he pawed at the can, trying to reposition it onto its side so more frothy liquid trickled out. He held one of his front paws off the ground at an odd angle as he chased the beer, trying to lap it up before it disappeared down the cockpit drain.

"Ouch! Beer. Ouch! Lager. Doggy dangles… I prefer ale, Harry. The bubbles in lager make me fart. Ouch, damn paw!"

Some kind of sixth sense snapped my stare away from Lacey as I became aware of marina curtain twitch syndrome. Vague movements from other boats drew my gaze. Fellow sailors made a poor show of finding excuses to be on deck. Some stood tall making exaggerated stretches, others began washing their boat deck, all snatching glances in my direction. I looked back at Lacey, nudging the empty beer can around my feet, his limping more pronounced now.

I sighed, hung my head and fished my wallet out of my pocket, rooting around for the vet's bill.

I pulled my mobile phone from the other pocket and began to dial.

"Here we go again."

*

"Whoa yeah! Faster, faster! Ears, we have lift off! Oooowwweeelll!"

I heard Lacey howl, muffled though my safety helmet, but I didn't feel him struggling to get out, so I twisted the throttle further and weaved through the traffic.

I prepared myself for the same tug of war outside the vet's front door, but to my surprise Lacey trotted along beside me, limping in a sort of Mexican body wave rhythm. He actually looked enthusiastic as I opened the door to the surgery.

Lacey tried to hop up over the step, but he misjudged the height, yelping as he hit the side and sat down, holding his paw up.

"Arrhh, elephant arse! Thanks a bunch of bazoobies, Harry."

I reached down to pick Lacey up, nudged the door open with my elbow and shuffled inside. Alice the vet and Rose the receptionist glanced up from leaning over the reception desk.

"Hello again," said the vet, folding her arms as she straightened up.

"Hi. We had a bit of, um… an accident."

Lacey whined and lifted his paw, right on cue. *"Poorly poochy…"*

The vet raised her eyebrows at Rose, then

45

disappeared through the door behind reception and reappeared by my side.

"Can you pop him gently down, please."

Lacey stood on three paws, his tail twitching, looking at the vet who crouched down, studying him. Lacey took a step forwards, overbalanced, head-butted the vet's knee and fell over.

"Is that alcohol I can smell?"

"Um... well, it's kind of a long story..."

Lacey's little paws waggled in the air as he rolled onto his side, tongue lolling from his mouth.

"Oops."

"Your dog is drunk again."

"Like I said, it's a long... what do you mean, *again?*"

"Follow me," said the vet, gathering Lacey up in her arms, cradling him like a baby.

The vet closed the treatment room door, still holding Lacey.

"Exactly how many *hours* have you been looking after your brother's dog?"

I felt my cheeks flush. I looked away from her piercing eyes.

"Erm, maybe twelve..."

"Twelve hours."

She shook her head, passed Lacey to me.

"Here. You'd better hold him, he's not capable of standing on his own."

Lacey grumbled as I held him against my chest. I thought I caught a mischievous glint in his eye.

"Uh oh. Lager fart."

The vet leaned in to examine Lacey's limp leg. My nose twitched. An evil smell enveloped us.

"Silent but deadly…"

"Ugh, not again! You are such a wicked dog! Or was that your irresponsible owner?"

The vet recoiled, pinching her nose.

"Ha, good one!"

I could have sworn the pesky dog sniggered at me. The rank smell hung there between the vet and me. After a long pause, I chuckled.

"Got yourself a real handful there…" said the vet, trying not to giggle. "I'm not sure I want to know, but what happened?"

"My brother… has a lot to answer for."

The vet nodded, observing me carefully as her features iced over.

"We'll need an X-ray to confirm, but I think it's broken. I'll take him to get it checked out. You can wait in reception."

*

I sat jigging my leg, arms folded, head hanging over my chest, trying to avoid the scrutiny of Rose from behind the reception desk. Twelve hours of trouble. Nice one Keith. But then I relented, as I always did when I thought about my wayward elder brother, recalling the reason I could never think badly of him for long. I lifted my head as someone sat down beside me. I glanced at the vet, minus the dog.

"You see Rose, our lovely receptionist?" she said.

I looked over at Rose, who smiled sweetly at me, one elbow propped on the counter, palm under her chin. She waggled the reception telephone in her other hand.

The vet leaned towards me, her voice low but firm.

"The first speed dial number is the local police station. The second is the RSPCA."

I swallowed, my mouth like sandpaper.

"I think I'll be okay, thanks. You're not that scary."

"Nice try, buster. What happened to Lacey's leg? And don't even think about bullshitting me."

I held her gaze, fighting off the now familiar apprehensive twinging deep inside my chest.

"Honestly, I doubt you'll believe me."

She raised her eyebrows, turned to face Rose.

"Okay, okay. The police dumped the dog on me yesterday because Debs has left Keith, who's been taken into custody. I didn't want to look after Lacey, I'm off on a sailing trip in a few days. But there was nowhere else for the dog to go. So I agreed to help because it's only for a day or two and we settled down on the boat. Next thing, I have a squad of SWAT police surround the boat, yelling and pointing machine guns at me. Fifteen stones of aggressive heavily armed policeman and a tippy boat don't mix, resulting in one of them falling into the harbour. In a state of shock, I dropped my afternoon treat, a very tasty tin of European lager and fell backwards into the cabin, whereupon I accidently stood on the dog, which bit me on the ankle. A second angry policeman stood on my neck and crushed my windpipe into the floor because he was convinced I had another concealed beer can *weapon.* Unfortunately for him, Lacey locked his jaws around his testicles. In the confusion – there were lots of aggressive voices shouting and more guns pointing at me – the police officer on the boat banged his head and I had to prise Lacey off his groin in order to save Lacey – and probably me – from being shot. When the situation calmed down, Lacey lapped up the remains of my beer which was swilling around on the cockpit floor."

I pulled up my trouser leg and rolled my sock down.

"Here's Lacey's teeth marks, see? Do you really think someone could make up something that implausible?"

I searched her features for some compassion.

"Do you?" I asked again.

"No."

I breathed a sigh of relief and sank back into the chair.

"But you're a Straight man, I'd expect nothing less."

She stood up, walked to the reception door and locked it. Then she turned to face me, her arms crossed.

I alternated my gaze between her and Rose, who held the telephone to her ear, speaking into the mouthpiece.

"Oh come on, is that really necessary?"

Detective Inspector Randall unfolded his arms, stretched them above his head, then clasped his hands behind his neck. His professional fixed stare bored into me.

"We heard about you, Mister Straight. News travels fast around here, especially when it involves an SO 19 cock up. Elite squad of armed police disabled by an eccentric sailor and his feisty rat-dog. You can't make this stuff up."

DI Randall placed his palms on the table and leaned forwards with an earnest expression.

"Two of them needed medical attention."

He began counting off his fingers.

"Elite wild west copper number one: bruised knee, dislocated shoulder, cut lip and a change of clothes due to an impromptu swim in the harbour. Hot-shot-shooter number two: concussion, grazed cheek and…"

The detective's mouth twitched as he struggled to contain his amusement.

"…partial tear to the scrotum due to around ten kilos of dog dangling from his balls."

He erupted into a deep belly laugh. I sat there patiently, waiting for the right moment.

"Yes, well I'm sorry about all that, most unfortunate and not really my fault… but, um, do you mind me asking… what are you going to charge me with?"

The detective managed to squeeze out a few more words before he became completely incapacitated with hysterical laughter and had to wipe tears from his eyes.

"Charge you? I'm bloody congratulating you!"

*

Double déjà vu.

I sat down in a corner of the Poorly Paws reception and glanced around at the other pet owners, then flicked my eyes towards the desk. Rose viewed me with mild amusement. Other animal nurses and vets peered around the reception door, eyeing the curiosity that I'd become.

I heard the patter of claws on the vinyl floor and looked up to see Lacey being led in by Alice, the vet. Lacey wore a plaster cast on his front right leg and a clear plastic loudhailer-shaped cone on his head, all of which gave him a comical straight-legged hobble and lampshade-head judder every third step. He wagged his tail and scurried over to me. I made a show of welcoming him with enthusiastic stroking and smiled at the frosty looking vet.

"He still seems pleased to see you, despite having sobered up."

The vet handed me Lacey's lead, then folded her arms.

"I had to give a character reference so Lacey wasn't taken away."

"Oh right. Thanks."

"She means *put down*," said Rose. "Alice fought Lacey's corner. You owe her a big thank you."

"Yeah Harry, that's the long sleep death potion hocus-pocus. I'd never have forgiven you."

I turned to face Rose, who stared at me from behind the reception desk without any warmth whatsoever. I felt the colour drain from my cheeks. A cold bead of sweat trickled down between my shoulder blades.

"I see. Thank you, I… I do appreciate your…"

"We're thinking dinner and a bottle of wine ought to cover it," said Rose, a wicked glint in her eye.

I glanced at the vet, sensed her stiffen.

"There's no need for that. I hate having to put down a healthy animal, so I persuaded the police that Lacey wasn't a danger to the public. What all this means is because I vouched for Lacey and indirectly you, Mister Straight, you have to convince me that *today* will never happen again. If you can't, I won't release Lacey to you."

"You have that authority?"

"I do. So think very carefully about what you say next."

I looked down at Lacey, stretched out on the floor, trying to poke his mouth around the plastic cone to nibble the plaster cast. He flicked an eye up at me.

"Don't make a dog's dinner of it, Harry, comprende?"

I looked away from Lacey. Several thoughts flashed through my mind:

> 1. Problem solved. Leave the dog with the vet. She'll find him a nice home.

2. What would Keith think if I abandoned his dog? I still owe him.

3. I haven't thought about that other thing in the last few hours, so maybe the dog is the distraction I need.

4. The vet is actually quite an attractive lady…

I swallowed and scanned through my imaginary list again.

"It's fair to say that life hasn't been boring since Lacey was, erm… entrusted to me. It's my duty to look after him, which of course I will, and…"

Rose cut in, mimicking my voice. "And I think it's only fair that I take you out to dinner, Alice, to repay you for your kindness. During the course of a pleasant dinner and a bottle of decent wine, I will demonstrate my competence in the care of Lacey. Would that be acceptable?"

I opened my mouth to intervene, but Rose switched voices to impersonate the vet.

"That indeed would be acceptable, Mister Straight. I'll see you outside this building at eight o'clock tonight. Please ensure the pub is dog friendly so you can demonstrate your intention to consider Lacey in everything you do from now on."

Rose clapped her hands and stepped around the reception counter, ushering the vet back into the building and me and Lacey out of the front door.

"Good, that's all sorted. Off you both go. I don't want you cluttering up my waiting room – there's not enough room left for a police squad.

Go on, shoo. And Harry, change your shirt, okay petal?"

I stole a glance over my shoulder at the vet, caught her bemused and embarrassed expression as Rose shut the door between us.

Six

"You do realise, Harry, that if it rains really, really hard, this lampshade is going to fill up with water and I'll drown in my own private goldfish bowl."

I squeezed the grumbling dog into the backpack, trying not to make eye contact with him. The clear plastic loudhailer pushed his ears up and forwards, so they looked like devil horns.

I zipped up the backpack sides and clipped him in, the plaster cast poking straight out, parallel with his nose.

"Okay, we're all set. Nice salute, Lacey. All hail the Nazi-lampshade-dog."

It must have been the tension of the morning, an adrenalin overdose perhaps, but I couldn't stop giggling.

"Oy, space cadet, it's Superdog to you, all right sunshine? I fly through the air, paw outstretched to save humankind, again…"

I lifted the rucksack onto my back, fastened my helmet strap and fired up the motorbike, still grinning at the stupid dog.

*

"Mister Straight. Can you step into the office please," said Barbara, the boatyard owner's wife. I noticed her nostrils flare as she waited for me to lock up the bike; warning sign number one.

"Of course, just a jiffy."

Lacey trotted behind me on the lead, not entirely successfully. He coped with the plaster cast pretty well, adopting a stiff-legged body-roll trot, but every time he stopped to sniff anything, the edge of the plastic lampshade caught the gravel, threatening to pivot him into head-butting the ground. Passing close to boat support cradles and other objects also caused spatial awareness issues, as the side of the plastic cone banged into everything he passed too close to.

The steps up to the first floor office caused Lacey similar problems, forcing me to carry him. Barbara started on me as soon as I entered the office, before I had a chance to participate in the usual small talk pleasantries; warning sign number two.

"Never in the sixty-three years my family has owned this boatyard have we ever, *ever* had armed police stake out a yacht, wave guns around and intimidate the other berth holders. It's totally unacceptable. We have our reputation to think of."

I stood there holding Lacey, knowing better than to try reasoning with Barbara until she'd finished her rant.

"You need to leave. Tomorrow."

"Tomorrow? I need another week to stock up and finish my boat jobs. Please Barbara, it wasn't my fault. My brother…"

"Your brother. Your dog. *Your* responsibility."

"But I'm paid up until the end of the week."

"We'll reimburse you in the morning, when you leave."

My shoulders sagged and I trudged out of the office with Lacey still cradled in my arms.

*

"You need a proper drink. Come on, I'm buying," said Jim, over a fortifying cup of tea in the boatyard café.

"I'd love to mate, but I need to use the bike later."

"One won't hurt."

I shook my head, sorely tempted, almost able to taste a cool mouthful of beer. I glanced down at Lacey, sat by my feet, staring up at me, licking his lips. I smiled at him and offered my open, empty palms. He sniffed them optimistically.

"I'm hungry."

"Sorry little one, I've got nothing for you."

"Come on stingy."

"Ooh Harry, he's so lovely. I've cooked a spare bit of bacon, would he like it?" said Cathy, the café owner. Lacey wagged his tail and whined.

"Would I like some bacon… do cats throw hissy fits?!"

"Sometimes I wonder how much he understands. Looks like a 'yes please' from Lacey. Thanks Cathy," I said.

"Come on Harry, what about that pint?"

I watched Cathy tear the bacon into several pieces which Lacey accepted enthusiastically.

"Thanks Jim, but I have to sweet talk the vet into letting me keep the dog."

I stood to leave, waiting for Lacey to eat the last piece of bacon.

"I thought you didn't want the hassle of taking the mutt with you?"

"I know mate, but I owe it to Keith to look after him," I said, tugging gently on Lacey's lead.

"After all the trouble he's got you into?"

I hesitated, wondering if I should explain. Maybe some other time. I shrugged at Jim and led Lacey out of the café.

*

"I'm not sure this is really me."

I peered down at the bouffant lilac flowers on the shirt held up to my chest.

"Chicks love bright, pastel colours. It's a reflection of a gentleman's creativity and broadmindedness in the bedroom," said Jim, winking at me.

"It's not that sort of date. We were both ambushed by the receptionist."

"You get both of them? Fantastic, this gets better and better!"

I shook my head in dismay.

"This is the only shirt you've got?"

"The only clean, mildly inoffensive one. You know how it is with boat work…"

I glanced down at the shirt again and sighed.

*

The vet didn't see me at first. She stood outside the surgery looking a bit self-conscious. I nearly didn't recognise her, dressed in normal clothes. She'd styled her hair, applied a small amount of makeup and wore a simple yet elegant summer dress.

"Phwoar, Harry, the devil dog doctor is a hottie! I'd wolf-whistle if my paw wasn't in plaster."

I parked up the bike and lifted Lacey off my back, then turned to face the vet and removed my crash helmet.

"You've got to be kidding…" she said.

"Um, yeah. Bit of a dilemma. Bring the doggy and risk a telling off because of the bike, or leave him with a friend and get accused of abandonment. This felt like the honest way to play it."

"I see."

The vet crouched down to stroke Lacey.

"You look different, with proper clothes on…" I began to say, then stopped myself.

"Ouch Harry! Not exactly a smooth operator, are you?"

The vet glanced up from tickling Lacey's tummy.

"Today has been the most surreal day ever," she said, standing up and smoothing her dress down. "And this is… unexpected. Rose is so naughty, setting this up."

"It's the least I can do."

An uncomfortable silence crept up on us. I tried to think of something to say, but she beat me to it.

"Nice shirt."

I unzipped the rest of my bike jacket and peered down at the flamboyant design.

"I borrowed it from a mate. Most of my clothes are covered in anti-foul paint."

"Let me guess. Your friend is mid-to-late forties, short, tubby and recently divorced."

I nodded.

"Figures. Shall we go?"

I locked my bike helmet to the front wheel and pocketed the keys, then patted the fuel tank, my hand resting there for a moment.

I caught an amused look from the vet.

"Irene is an old friend. Do you mind if I leave her here tonight? A mate will collect her tomorrow."

"Of course," said the vet, a hint of caution in her voice.

"I'll take Lacey home on the bus later," I added quickly.

We walked in silence towards the local pub, which apparently had a dog friendly garden.

"The detective said you live on a boat."

"I do. Called Jessica. She's a Falmouth Gypsy, which is a small sailing sloop, twenty-four feet long. I've been restoring her for the last eighteen months."

"That sounds like a lot of work. How old is the boat?"

"She was built in the Nineteen Seventies. Around the time…"

I checked myself. This wasn't a conversation I wanted to get into.

"…I was born. How's Lacey doing, do you think I should pick him up?"

We both looked down at Lacey, hobbling along on his fractured leg.

"He looks happy enough. Have you owned a dog before?"

"No."

"So your brother has dropped you in it, living on the boat and all."

"Yup, a bit."

We crossed the road to the pub and made our way through the car park to the beer garden.

"Red or white?" I asked, tying Lacey's lead to the picnic table leg.

"Red, please. And don't forget a bowl of water for Lacey."

I nodded and walked off to find the bar, returning with two menus, a bottle of mid-priced red and two glasses.

"I thought Lacey could share mine," I said, maintaining a poker face.

"I wouldn't recommend that…"

"No. I'm kidding. Be right back."

I left the vet stroking the grumbling dog and headed for the bar.

"Red wine's for Chi Wawas. Beer is a proper dog's drink… bring me a half-pint of Old Thumper, Captain."

I returned a few minutes later with a large salad bowl full of fresh water. I think the barmaid assumed I had a full size dog, maybe like a Rottweiler. It must have been Jim's loud shirt.

"You expect me to swim in that? I had a bath last year."

"Tell me about your plans for the boat," said the vet.

"I'm heading west for the summer, port hopping. Final destination, Falmouth."

"That sounds lovely. It's a very pretty coastline."

The vet raised her glass.

"To summer sailing and man's best friend. That's you, Lacey."

We chinked glasses. The vet dropped her eyes to Lacey, who lay by her feet, watching us with one raised eyebrow.

I sipped the wine, enjoying the warm sensation as the alcohol began working its woozy magic.

"What's waiting for you in Falmouth?" she asked.

"I'm taking Jessica home to see my father. Our first meeting for over twenty years."

I swilled the remainder of the wine in my glass, watching it slowly drift down the sides.

"Oh. Did you fall out?"

"Something like that. How am I doing so far, doggy doc... do I get to keep the pooch?"

The vet took her time replying.

"Jury's still out, Harry," she said in a neutral tone.

*

"Is Lacey a regular visitor to the surgery?" I asked after my second glass of wine.

"Every few months. He's not in bad shape..."

We both glanced down at Lacey's whining, his paw pressed onto my leg.

"What's up, little one?"

"You're stuffing your face with sausage and mash and my stomach is rumbling. So take a wild guess, Romeo."

"Food probably. When did you last feed him?" the vet asked.

"Before we came out. I made a special trip to the shops for proper dog food."

"Maybe he could have a small treat, to help him bond with you."

I eased the last forkful of sausage away from my mouth and glanced down at Lacey's large tongue lapping at his jaws.

"Yeah, don't be selfish, Harry."

Lacey pawed me again, whining even louder. I reluctantly picked the sausage off my fork and offered it to him.

"There, friends for life. Or at least the next few minutes… So, Harry, twenty years is a long absence. What happened?"

I finished off the last of my wine and glanced at the empty bottle.

"He was… *difficult*, back then. We had a disagreement, properly fell out."

She nodded, waiting for me to continue.

"It's tricky… lots of things were said in anger, by both of us. Things that can't be taken back, or easily forgiven."

I took a deep breath and glanced away, not focussing on anything in particular.

"The first of August is his seventieth birthday. So I'm going to sail down there."

"To wish him a happy birthday?"

"To try. He has dementia. The last time Keith visited, my father barely recognised him."

"Sounds like it's going to be an emotional journey…"

"Yes. Yes, it will be. Would you like another drink? I could really use one."

I got up, barely waiting for a positive reply before I hurried away, a familiar sick sensation rising from the pit of my stomach.

*

I lifted my head from the toilet and flushed away an unpleasant reminder of the past and the future. I splashed cold water over my face and cupped a handful to rinse away the acidic taste in my mouth. I turned away from the mirror, unable to look myself in the eye.

"Large brandy please and another bottle of the Chilean red," I said to the barman, flapping the front of my shirt to try and cool down.

*

"Sorry about that. Families, eh? Tell me about yours."

I plonked myself back down in front of her and opened the bottle of wine.

"I'm an only child. Mum and Dad live in Dartmouth, all pretty normal really."

I nodded, topping up her glass.

"No testicle-munching pets?"

She laughed.

"Me, or my folks?"

"You. Being a vet, you must like animals."

She sipped her wine, holding eye contact with me.

"I have a golden retriever called Holly. She formed part of the break-up deal with my ex."

"Oh, right. Sorry to hear that."

"Don't be. He was a lazy, long-haired animal. The ex, not Holly. Are you sailing on your own?"

"No."

"Oh. Someone going with you?" she asked in a conversational tone.

"Sort of. Four-legged variety. If the doggy doc signs me off as sane."

"So you can sail Jessica single-handed?"

"We'll find out tomorrow…"

"I can't tell if you're joking."

I took another glug of the wine, floating in woozy happiness.

"Nor can I."

I started to chuckle.

"What?"

"Earlier today… Lacey, swinging his legs in mid-air, teeth clamped around the policeman's scrotum. Man's best friend!"

My laughter became hysterical, forcing a giggle from the vet.

"Sorry, private joke. You had to be there, eh Lacey?"

The vet smiled politely and waited for me to regain my composure.

"Thank you for a lovely dinner, Harry. I should probably head back soon. I have an early start in the morning."

"Of course."

*

We ambled back towards the surgery, stopping occasionally to release Lacey's lampshade from catching on the footpath paving stones.

"So… what happens now?"

"I thank you for a pleasant evening and point you in the direction of the nearest bus stop."

"Yes, of course. But I was referring to this little monster," I said, jangling Lacey's lead.

"Oh. Well, I am a bit concerned about you taking him on the boat. What if he falls in?"

"Don't worry Doc, they have pet lifejackets."

"They do? Okay. Good."

"You humans are so bad at this… find out if there's any jiggy-jiggy on offer!"

"Lacey's getting impatient."

"Yes, little bugger. Thank you, Alice. It's been a nice way to finish off a bizarre day," I said, offering my hand, which she shook in a business-like manner.

I smiled and turned to walk away.

"Harry."

"Yes, hello."

"The bus stop is the other way."

"Right-oh."

I turned around and led Lacey past the vet, who stood with folded arms, the hint of a smile twitching on her lips.

"Alternatively, I have a couch. If you like…"

"Game on, Harry! The couch is a hop, skip and a jiggy-jump away from her bedroom!"

I looked down at Lacey's nasal noises, then I smiled at Alice.

"Um… thank you, that's a lovely offer. But it's probably best I make my way home. In case the boat's been impounded…"

"I whip up a mean scrambled egg breakfast."

"Harry! We're talking fifty shades of fun time here, buddy! What are you waiting for?!"

"Ordinarily that would be fantastic… but I couldn't possibly inflict a dawn armed police raid on you. What would the neighbours say?"

"Suit yourself."

I hesitated for a moment, then dropped my eyes and walked on.

Seven

Bang! Bang! Bang!

The noise echoed around the tiny bow cabin, piercing my skull. I groaned, peeled my parched tongue off the roof of my mouth with a 'cluck' sound and forced an eyelid open, recoiling from the shards of sunlight filtering in through the overhead hatch.

"Harry Straight. This is your marina wake-up call!" shouted Barbara, her shrill voice stabbing the back of my eyes. I buried my head under the pillow.

BANG! BANG! BANG!

"Bugger off!"

"I heard that! You've got half an hour before the bridge opens. I'll see you in the office in ten minutes, or else Bruce will cut your lines and cast you adrift."

I rubbed sleep from my eyes and squinted at my watch. Something furry wriggled and stretched by my feet. The warm bulge climbed up my body inside the sleeping bag, its paws tickling. I fumbled for the zip, still in a daze.

"Wakey wakey, hung-over human!"

"Ugh, dog breath kisses!" I spluttered, trying to squirm away from Lacey's enthusiastic greeting.

"Speak for yourself, dustbin lips. It's a gooooood mooooorning! Feed me. Feed me.

Feed me!"

The dog jumped onto the floor, head-butted the cabin door open and hobbled to his empty bowl.

"Harry, really. What would the vet say? Need a reminder… time to GO LOUD!"

"Arrrrrrr, Lacey, shush!"

"Won't! Food! Food! Food!"

"How can a small dog make so much damn noise? Okay, okay. Message understood."

I squeezed out of my sleeping bag and stumbled into the saloon to fill up Lacey's water bowl. That done, I opened a tin of dog food.

"What sort of day is it, my four-legged fiend?" I said as I slid the main hatch open and recoiled from Barbara's face, looming two feet in front of me.

"Six minutes! Then it's chop chop, bye bye," she yelled.

"Morning Barbara," I muttered, enjoying her appalled reaction at my appearance.

"Strong coffee. Then my office, pronto. And clean your bloody teeth first!"

*

I stood at the reception desk, fidgeting like a naughty schoolboy as I watched Barbara count out a hundred pounds in notes. I felt Lacey paw my leg and reached down to pick him up.

"You do realise that you're making this poor injured dog homeless, don't you? I thought you were an animal lover, Barbara…"

She pushed a selection of coins across the counter and laid a receipt in front of me.

"Sign and date here."

I transferred Lacey onto my left arm, leant over the desk and scribbled my signature.

"They do say there's no such thing as bad publicity. I'd have thought you'd welcome the extra exposure," I said.

"Armed police are not good publicity."

I pocketed the cash and turned to leave, cradling Lacey in my arms.

"Good luck with your Dad," she said.

I half-turned.

"It's nice to see Jessica back on the water where she belongs. You've done a good job restoring her. You should be proud of yourself."

I felt my jaw slacken as the hint of a smile threatened to turn up the corner of her thin lips.

"Cheers," I stammered as I opened the door and shuffled out, my stomach sending queasy ripples up my spine.

*

"This isn't the send-off you deserve, Harry. We had something planned… it's not right to leave like this," said Jim.

"She's probably done me a favour, I've got to push off at some point. You know what everyone says about this place… it has some sort of Death Star magnetic power."

Jim glanced around the other boats moored up and nodded, a wry smile on his lips.

"Will the dog be okay?"

"I've just promoted him to first mate, with extra rum rations. He'll be fine."

I finished preparing the mooring lines, made my way to the stern and knelt down by the engine instruments.

"Here we go. Fingers crossed."

I closed my trembling fingers around the key and turned it.

Neeeerrrr ver-room!

The engine clattered into life with a cloud of oily black smoke. Seawater spat out from the exhaust, making Lacey sneeze and bark simultaneously.

"Where are you? I'll take you, sea monster… come on and show yourself!"

I stroked Lacey, easing him away from the stern cleat, then took a deep breath to try and calm my racing heart.

"Ready to cast off?" said Jim, untying the bow line.

"Go for it."

I slipped the stern line and coiled it up by my feet. Lacey sniffed the rope suspiciously, wobbling on his feet as Jessica began to reverse away from the berth.

"Whoa… bathtubs don't move, Harry!"

"Nearly forgot, Jim. Here…"

I passed the motorbike keys across the three foot gap.

"For Irene. She's at the vet's, with the helmet. She's all yours."

Jim stared at the keys in his hand.

"The vet?"

"The motorbike!"

Jim grinned, pocketed the keys and raised his hand.

I glanced anxiously around me to make sure we'd cleared the other boats, then swung the rudder over and eased the throttle forwards, steering away from the marina.

"I'll post your shirt back," I said to Jim.

"It's yours, for luck. Cheers for the bike, Harry, I'll look after it. Don't forget... all the girls love a sailor!"

I glanced over my shoulder, waved one last time to Jim, then dropped my eyes to follow Lacey's fixated stare at the water rippling away in our wake.

"Now the adventure really begins, eh shipmate?"

I took a deep breath, my dry lips stretching as I forced a smile, exaggerating the sensation of wind on my face as the boat chugged along beneath me.

Two hundred metres ahead of us, the Twin Sails lifting bridge began to gracefully rise, allowing us enough time to tag on behind a motor boat and follow it into the holding area to wait for the lifting of the second bridge. I eased the throttle back, an uneasy thought occurring to me: what now?

Eight

I dunked a ginger biscuit in my tea and sucked the liquid from the pulp, crunching the remaining dry quarter, luxuriating in the flavour and texture.

"Ouch!"

Lacey pawed my arm, his cheeks puffing as he whined and licked his lips.

"Oy, gobble guts. Where's mine?"

I broke a corner off another biscuit for the dog and attempted to retrace my thoughts, trying not to get distracted by Lacey's messy open-mouth crunching. So many years since Jessica had last been on the water. Only one season in commission when... that night...

I shuddered, my thoughts interrupted by the continuous ringing of the old bridge bell, indicating an imminent lift. Several other boats cast off the waiting pontoon, jostling for position as the green traffic lights flashed and the bridge slowly began to rise. I wondered how different Poole Quay had looked the last time Jessica had been here...

I glanced to my right as we passed under the old lifting bridge, doubting the Sunseeker factory had been there thirty-seven years ago. The new marina, five hundred metres straight ahead, certainly hadn't. Visiting yachts back then would have tied up alongside the quay.

I felt a mild panic attack shudder through me,

overheating my skin, despite the cool breeze.

"Deep breaths, Harry, relax…"

I watched the quay slip by on my left side and instinctively brushed my hand across my chest. A familiar angry, adrenalin-fuelled defiance washed over me. The past and future are set… here and now, that's all that counts, I reminded myself.

"I think we'll stop here, Lacey. It's an expensive berth, but it's an important part of the journey. And I'm guessing you could do with a walk, right?"

I glanced down at his twitching tail.

"Lacey go walkies?" I asked, as much for my benefit as his.

"What a stupid question, even for a numpty like you, Harry. Let's go!"

I stroked the excited dog and adjusted course towards the entrance to Poole Quay Boat Haven.

"Shall we see if they've got space for a small boat?"

"Forget that Harry, have you seen how many pubs there are?"

*

I'd walked the quay several times during my life, trying to get to grips with what happened all those years ago.

"You know Lacey, this is the first time I've arrived here by boat. It's different somehow… maybe we'll stay here for a few days."

The second time you've been here, I corrected myself.

Lacey stopped to sniff around a bollard, allowing me time to survey the quiet bustle and relaxed holiday atmosphere. He tugged on his lead, prompting me to amble on, following Lacey's wagging tail and inquisitive nose.

"Ahh, what a cute puppy. What's that thing on his head?" said a young-sounding voice.

I turned to see a girl of about seven walking with her mother.

"I think it's to stop him chewing the bandage on his leg."

"Can I stroke him, mummy?

The girl let go of her mum's hand and skipped over to me.

"Kirsty, wait. Remember?"

The girl nodded at her mum and stood still. "Is your doggy friendly, please?" she asked me.

I smiled at the girl and glanced over at her mother.

"I'm looking after him for a friend, so I'm not sure. Shall we see?"

I crouched down and called Lacey. I held my hand out, mimicked by the young girl.

Lacey hobbled over, wagging his tail. He sniffed my empty hand and transferred his attention to the girl, licking her fingers.

"Vanilla, my favourite!"

The girl giggled and pulled her hand away.

"The doggy can smell your ice-cream," said the mum.

"What happened to its paw?" asked the girl.

"Someone stepped on it… by accident," I said quickly.

"That would be my responsible pet owner, eh Harry? Belly rub…"

Lacey rolled onto his back, the plastic collar scraping on the pavement as he waggled his paws in the air. Such a floozy!

"He's gorgeous. How old is he?" said the mum.

"Um, I think about ten."

"Really? He looks like a puppy."

I nodded. "It's his daily Botox regime. Costs me a fortune."

"What's the writing on his hurt leg?" asked the girl, pointing to Lacey's plaster cast.

I peered at the underside of the bandage, then picked up Lacey and cradled him like a baby to get a closer look.

"That looks like a telephone number," said the mum, leaning in. "Dog Doc," she read aloud, which preceded the numerals.

Lacey flicked his eyes between the two of us and tried to lick our faces. The mum giggled and tickled Lacey's tummy.

"I'd say you've pulled," murmured the mum as she pulled away.

"But you didn't get to nuzzle her muzzle, did you Harry?"

I put the grumbling dog back on the ground. Lacey shook himself, then wandered off.

"Missed your chance there, Harry. You need to wise up to womankind…"

"Oh, looks like we're off. Nice to meet you both… bye," I said, letting Lacey lead me on.

The mum shot me a cheeky wink as she clasped her daughter's hand.

"There goes your second sympathy shag right there… you're gonna need some serious help, fella…"

"You're an impatient little dog, aren't you," I said in response to Lacey's yapping.

Every few steps I caught a glance of the phone number written on Lacey's plaster cast, prompting me to wonder when Alice the vet had written it.

*

We turned around just before the lifting bridge and began to wander back towards the marina.

"If you're going to be a proper first mate, we'd better get you a lifejacket," I said, waiting to cross the road opposite the chandlery.

"We're about to enter an Aladdin's cave for every sailor, Lacey. There's many a marital argument started in these places and plenty of credit cards lost for eternity. You're the money monitor, okay? Make sure I don't spend too much."

Lacey hobbled into the chandlery, his wagging tail and injured dog routine drawing lots of attention. I could almost hear the discounts tripping off the sales assistants' tongues.

"The carry handle on the top would allow you to fish the dog out of the water by hand or with a boathook. Shall I demonstrate, sir?"

"Yes please," I said, smiling as the manager grabbed the carry handle on the pet buoyancy aid and lifted Lacey off the ground. Oh dear, if looks could kill!

Lacey dangled beneath the red lifejacket which looked like an old style body warmer. His tail hung limp between his legs, head down, indignant eyes gazing up at me.

"You're frigging joking, Harry. This is so Nineteen Eighties."

"Sold to the dog in the funny jacket. Come on shipmate, back to the boat," I said as I paid up, minus an adorable doggy discount.

We left the shop, Lacey still sporting his fashionable lifejacket, lampshade and plaster cast. Actually, reluctant saunter is a better description of Lacey's doggy grumbling three-step.

"You humans are soooooo predictable. What is it about dressing up a furry animal that's so amusing?"

"You are a vocal little mutt, aren't you?"

We walked on, Lacey drawing amused glances. Despite my best intentions to circumnavigate the row of pubs on the quay until later on in the evening, Lacey had other ideas. We got as far as the Jolly Sailor on our stroll back to the marina before he sat down and refused to budge.

"Come on Lacey, this way."

"Nope."

"Are you tired?"

"Tired, thirsty, hungry. But mostly thirsty. Humiliation is dehydrating."

I tugged on the lead, but he glued himself to

the ground and I couldn't budge him. With a sigh, I squatted down.

"What's the matter?" I asked, stroking his head, preparing to pick him up.

"We're going this way. Follow me."

I watched the crazy dog stand, shake himself and walk away from the harbour. He took up the slack on the lead and leant against it, pulling me towards the pub.

"You're not supposed to be encouraging me…"

"Stop stalling Captain, it's your round."

The anticipation of a cold pint toyed with my taste buds, drawing saliva into my parched mouth. Mineral water would have been more sensible, but…

"Okay, Lacey. Lead the way. Where would you like to go?"

"To an empty bench outside the Jolly Sailor. Don't dawdle."

I tied Lacey's lead around the table leg and ducked inside, leaving him basking in the afternoon sunshine. I'd probably earned a drink, I reasoned, given the stress of the last twenty-four hours.

*

"There, fill your boots little one," I said, placing the water bowl by Lacey's feet. I sat down and raised the glass of ale to my lips, barely taking a sip before I felt something prod my leg, accompanied by high-pitched whining.

"And how am I supposed to drink, Einstein?"

Lacey dipped his head towards the water, his nose pinged away by the edge of the lampshade catching on the ground, leaving his tongue air-licking over the top of the bowl.

"Oh, I see the problem. Here, let me help."

I tipped the water bowl up inside the lampshade lip.

Slurp, slurp, slurp.

"Right, I'm done. Let me at the frothy stuff."

"More, or enough?"

I lifted the bowl higher, but he flicked his head away and pranced backwards, barking at me.

"Water is for wimps. Let me at the hops!"

I chuckled at Lacey's yapping, my eye drawn back to the phone number on his paw.

"When did she write this, Lacey?"

I lifted Lacey up onto my lap to inspect the handwriting, which seemed to please him. He twisted and shifted round to sit upright facing forwards in my lap, enjoying his vantage point.

"Cheers Lacey. And cheers to Alice the vet."

I lifted the pint to my lips and took a gulp, aware of Lacey's beady eyes following the glass as I placed it back on the table.

"Maybe it's an emergency call-out number, just in case you take a bad turn. What do you think?"

I instinctively reached for my pint, took another swig and rested the glass on my knee.

"Sooooo cute!" cooed a female voice.

I glanced up, aware of liquid slopping over my leg. Lacey had his nose buried in the pint glass, the lip pressed into his forehead. He lapped up the beer and exhaled through his nose at the same time, causing beery froth to expand up the glass, over his snout and settled on his eyebrows. I tried to pull the glass away, but he followed it, determined to drink as much as he could.

I wrestled the glass away and placed it out of reach in the centre of the table.

"Harry, you beer-tease! I'm almost finished."

I pulled the yapping hound back from jumping up on the table, aware of the attention of several other drinkers.

"Such a honey! What's his name?" said the same throaty voice, an octave lower than before.

A woman in her early thirties leaned across the table to stroke Lacey, revealing a flash of her cleavage. I hastily averted my eyes, conscious of a muscular tattooed man drinking with his mates at an adjacent table who kept looking over at me.

"His name's Lacey," I said, trying to shrink back into my seat, away from the woman.

"Ahh, such a beautiful name. What happened to his foot?"

"C'mon Harry, let me finish!"

"Shh Lacey… do you want to go walkies?"

"It's right there, calling out… Lacey, drink meeeee… it's not like you're gonna want it now I've slobbered in the glass…"

"I think he wants your beer, love," said the woman, reaching over for the glass, which she held up at an angle to Lacey's nose so he could dip his tongue in and lap up the rest.

"I'm not sure that's such a good idea…" I said.

"Aww, he's lovin' it."

"Oh yeah, atta-girl! Keep this up and you're coming home with us later…"

I watched slack-jawed as Lacey polished off the dregs of my beer. He didn't even spill too much. And that's pretty much the last thing I can remember…

Nine

The grip tightened around my neck, hands squeezing air from my windpipe. I stared up at the powerful tattooed forearms, muscles flexing, cigarette-stained teeth clenched behind thin, scowling lips…

I woke with a start, gasping for air. Wispy details of the dream slipped away, sinking rapidly into the depths of my subconscious.

I'm awake, thank God, I realised. But if I'm awake, why am I still choking…?

My fingers reached up, desperate to prise the hands away from pressing into my throat…

But my fingers didn't find human fingers, instead the flesh felt soft and… hairy.

Huh?

"Lacey!"

The dog grumbled as I lifted his long tummy off my neck. Through blurred, gummy eyes, I saw his tongue darting towards my face. I turned away from his wet nose and stale dog-beer breath, but he lost his balance and head-butted me.

"Yeouch!"

I shoved Lacey aside and pushed up on my elbows, remembering to stop short to avoid the bow cabin's low roof. I scrunched my eyes shut, tried the old quick-blink acclimatising technique.

That's odd, I'm not in my normal place.

I glanced around the main cabin, not normally seen from this low angle.

That's weird… the seat cushions from each opposite berth lay beneath me on the cabin sole… why would I rearrange everything?

Lacey stretched out across my tummy and crawled down my legs into a sort of yoga 'salute to the sun' posture, then sat up. He turned to glance over his shoulder at me, his tail twitching.

"I'm feeling a bit wobbly…"

Lacey swayed and fell over onto his back, kicking his legs up in the air as he slid down into the gap between me and the other body.

"Whoopsie."

I rubbed my face, encouraging my eyes to fully open.

Interesting choice, Harry, sleeping on the floor. Quite comfortable actually, but the question is, why?

The groan next to me didn't sound like Lacey. In fact, the scrunch of bleached blonde hair and black roots looked decidedly human…

"Morning," she mumbled, rubbing her eyes.

The other person rolled over towards me and smiled through smudged makeup.

"Hi," I replied, watching Lacey twitch and wriggle around so he could stagger to his feet and crawl up between us to lick the woman's face.

"Good effort, Harry, she's pretty decent."

"Ugh, Lacey, you need mouthwash."

Using the convenient distraction, I lifted the unzipped sleeping bag laying over me to check on my clothing situation.

Naked below the waist. Oh dear…

"You insisted on keeping your tee-shirt on," spluttered the woman, trying to dodge Lacey's kisses.

"Um, yeah… I do that sometimes."

"Kinda kinky actually, being partially clothed. There ought to be a government health warning on this cute dog."

"Oh? What sort of warning…" I replied, my head beginning to pound.

"This dog will seriously damage your relationship. He's just so irresistible."

I watched her cuddle Lacey.

Think Harry! Try to fill in the gaps…

The woman lifted up the corner of the sleeping bag, searching for something.

"And you're not bad either, Harry," she said.

The soles of my feet began to tingle, the nervous warning sign I get walking too close to the edge of a cliff.

"Ah-hah, there you are."

The woman reached down to her feet, grasped something, then arched her back and slipped her knickers back on, wiggling her hips as she pulled her skirt back down over her thighs.

"Who's Gwen?" she said, in an offhand sort of way.

"Um… my ex-wife. Why?"

"You called out her name… last night."

Lacey groaned and stretched out between us. *"Harry, rookie error buddy!"*

"Oh. Sorry about that," I said, shifting my gaze from her to Lacey.

She shrugged. An uncomfortable silence began to develop.

"This um… relationship you mentioned… whose do you mean?"

"Mine, silly. Wayne will be wondering where I've got to."

I gulped, staring at her.

"Oh. I didn't realise you were…"

"Yes you did, Harry. You just don't remember the conversation. Can't say I'm surprised, after the amount you drank. Quite the boozer, aren't you?"

"Did we… you know…"

"Yes. You were magnificent."

"Right. Okay. Did we… take precautions?"

She laughed and sat up, looking for her bag. She rummaged inside it.

"Several precautions, judging by this empty packet," she said, tossing a condom box onto the bed. Then she asked, "Do you mind if I smoke?"

"Sure. Outside though. Gas on-board boats and naked flames don't mix."

I watched her step up through the open hatch as I desperately tried to fill my memory blanks.

"Would you like a cup of tea, um…?"

"…Sharon," she replied. "Lovely, thanks. Milk and two sugars please."

I found my pants and trousers, dressed quickly and made the tea. I also fed Lacey, troubled by something nagging at my woozy brain as I watched him scoff the lot.

"He's missing his plastic lampshade," I said.

"It's probably still at the pub. He started knocking glasses over. You got fed up and removed it," she replied, blowing cigarette smoke above her head.

I passed Sharon her cup of tea, then lifted Lacey into the cockpit. He hobbled around to Sharon, leaning against her. I sat down opposite them. Sharon stroked Lacey and studied me through the cigarette smoke.

"You're still trying to remember what happened."

I nodded sheepishly.

"This doggy… he likes his beer almost as much as you do," said Sharon.

"It's a family trait."

"That'll be Keith's influence."

I perked up from my hangover slouch. "You know him?"

"Wayne does. That's why he thought you were alright to leave me with while he went off to meet his mates. Same problem as me, Harry. With a cute dog like this, how could you possibly be a bad person?"

"I'm not a bad person."

"I know that, Harry. You were very considerate last night. But Wayne… he might not see it the same way, now we've been properly acquainted…"

I shrank back in my seat, my chest squeezed by invisible tattooed hands.

"So after this little monster drank your beer, I bought you another. Figured it was worth it, for the comedy value. You repaid the favour with the next round, celebrating the launch of your boat.

One drink led to another and I'm afraid I just couldn't help myself. I'm not usually so… spontaneous, especially with older blokes, but you and this adorable dog are very easy on the eye."

I spluttered my tea. She took another pull on her cigarette.

"I'm not sure what happens now. You know, after…" I said.

"What do you normally do?"

I looked over her shoulder at the harbour.

"With my wife? Make the tea, cook breakfast perhaps."

"Before her, you know, other lovers."

I shook my head, glanced back at her briefly then dropped my eyes.

"None before her and you're the first since I got divorced."

"No marriage break-up one night stands?"

"No."

"So you're a womble?"

"A womble?"

"Yeah. You've only had one ball-ache woman."

I shrugged, and ruffled Lacey's fur, making him grumble.

"Harry, mate. We gotta sort this out… a one count is abysmal!"

"Didn't you ever get curious, about being with other women?" Sharon asked.

I shrugged.

"I got married at nineteen. I guess I've had a sheltered life…"

"Blimey. That's amazing."

Sharon blew more smoke, studied me for a moment, then leaned in, cupped my face in her hands and kissed me. She held her lips pressed to mine, then eased away.

"Mmm. You are a rare and special breed, Harry."

She sat back, looked away from me as she finished her cigarette.

"So, um… what now?" I asked.

"Depends on who saw me come back here. You were a pleasant surprise, Harry. But honestly, you're not really my type. I mean you were, last night, obviously. But it's probably best we put this down to a one-off. You go your way and I'll go… *oh shit!*"

Sharon knelt down on the cockpit floor and peered around me. I half-turned to follow her anxious stare. Wayne, the same tattooed ape from last night, marched purposefully down the quay, heading for the marina entrance.

Bloody hell!

"Time for me to make my excuses…"

Sharon crouched low, ducked down into the cabin and reappeared a moment later with her shoes and handbag.

"Harry, it's been lovely. You were a real gentle man."

"Will you be okay?" I asked.

"Technically I'm separated, so yes, I'll be fine. But Wayne is the jealous type and ex-military. So you, Harry…" she glanced at the quay, keeping a wary eye on Wayne, "…had best get going."

Sharon stepped off the boat onto the pontoon and slipped her heels on.

"Right now?"

"Unless you want to be torn limb from limb… goodbye Harry, last night was lovely. Good luck with your journey and look after that cute doggy."

"Oy, you slapper!"

I stared at Wayne, his fist raised, shouting obscenities. My heart rate accelerated rapidly, pounding inside my chest, echoing behind my sore hung-over eyes. Wayne started running towards the marina entrance.

Lacey jumped up, front paws resting on the cockpit coamings, barking near my ear.

"Yo, giro! This sailor's just nailed your floozy and made her scream, twice! Oooowwwll!"

I winced at Lacey's noise, desperately trying to put the order of our exit into action.

"Think, Harry! Ropes, engine, cast off. No, start engine, ropes… engage reverse gear… keys. Where did I put the keys…?"

I jumped down into the cabin, leaving Lacey barking in the cockpit.

"Oy! Crayon features. We'll take you, and your dribbly dick mates!"

I grabbed the keys off the hook by the chart table and raced up the steps into the cockpit.

"I don't want to go, not ready, too much to do… damn and bugger!"

I fumbled the right key into the ignition and kept an eye on the shore as Wayne climbed over the entrance gate and sprinted along the pontoon, closely followed by one of the marina staff.

"Please start, please start, please…"

Ner, ner, ner, ner, nerrrrr… verROOM!

"…thank you big man, thank you!"

"You're a 'kin dead man!" shouted Wayne as he slowed to round the main walkway, then raced along our pontoon, brushing Sharon aside as she held her arms out, trying to block him.

"Leave him, Wayne!"

"I'll be back for you, Shaz!" he yelled, now barely thirty metres away from me.

Adrenalin throbbed through my veins, making my body shake like the biggest sugar rush ever.

I left the engine revving hard in neutral, climbed over the guard rails onto the pontoon, yanked at the stern mooring rope and tossed it aboard. I hurried to the front of the boat to untie the bow line.

"You're 'avin it now, you cheeky little sucker!" yelled Wayne.

"Bugger! Focus, Harry. Rope, untie, cast off. You might just get away with…"

Clank, cough. Clank, cough. Clank… brrrr.

The engine spluttered and died.

I turned, wide-eyed, to see Wayne begin to slow so he could take the last corner, now no more than five seconds away from battering me.

Four seconds.

Three.

Two…

Ten

"You're a dead man!" yelled Wayne, spit frothing from his mouth.

Think Harry!

Engine start…

No time.

He's big, he's angry. He's going to kill me…

You certainly pushed the boat out this time, Harry…

Wait: Push. The. Boat.

Yes!

Lacey pranced and postured on the bow, howling and yapping as Wayne overshot the turning, barely three metres away.

"Come on you piece of stilton lard, we can take you!"

Wayne lunged, his hand swiping at my head, the inertia of trying to make a sharp right turn causing him to stumble. His leg crumpled, sending him crashing down onto the pontoon into an uncontrolled sliding tackle, buying me a few more precious seconds.

Desperately trying to control my heaving chest and rasping breathing, I threw the loose rope on board and gripped the pulpit, pushing the small boat away from the finger pontoon.

"I'm gonna smash your head in… rip your 'kin balls off…" shouted Wayne between gulps of air, pushing himself up from the pontoon, legs driving him towards me.

"Lick my tail, you elephant-chipmunk-cheek gigolo juggler!"

I gritted my teeth, pumping my legs, willing Jessica to gather speed through the water. With my last step before fresh air, I pushed off hard, like a long jumper leaping from the take-off board. The boat cleared the end of the pontoon and I managed to heave myself up onto the bow, gasping for breath, the gap between me and the pontoon's angry muscle-man widening.

One metre.

Two metres.

Three…

"I've seen your face, arsehole!" bellowed Wayne, between wheezing gulps of air.

I glanced back at him, crouched down on the pontoon, his red face contorted, eyes boring into me. I looked away and stumbled back to the cockpit, pushing the tiller hard over to the right, willing the stern to come round, away from the moored boats behind me.

The engine turned over for a few eternal seconds, then fired and settled into a lumpy rhythm. I pushed the throttle ahead before the engine had a chance to die again and steered Jessica away from Wayne's panting, venomous threats.

My hand shook on the tiller as I yanked it to the left to bring us round parallel to the breakwater, heading for the marina entrance less than fifty metres away.

I couldn't suppress a grin, then a laugh. I

could still taste the cigarette smoke in my mouth from Sharon's kiss, triggering a series of flashbacks, igniting something primeval and instinctive deep inside me.

"Woo-hoo!" I yelled as I steered Jessica out of the marina entrance.

"That was exciting, eh Lacey!"

I ruffled his ears, but he barely turned to acknowledge me, still fixating his barking on the marina.

"He's getting away, Harry! We can take that poodle poo!"

Lacey's little body tensed as he yapped, sinewy muscles poised.

"I'll take you for a walk soon boy, on the beach at Studland, okay?"

"Studland, as in land of the studs? You humans are strange."

My face began to ache from grinning so much. Who'd have thought I could attract a younger woman? Any woman, in fact…

I eased back on the throttle, reducing our speed.

"What a beautiful day, Lacey."

Jessica's bow pushed through the green glassy water, parting irregular ice cube patterns that dispersed in our wake. I took a long deep breath of fresh, salty air and sat down beside Lacey to steer past Brownsea Island on our right hand side, following the deep water channel towards millionaire's row on the Sandbanks peninsula.

Did life get any better than this?

We stopped off at the floating fuel barge, not far from the harbour entrance. The cheerful fuel guy handed me the pump nozzle and stroked Lacey through Jessica's guard wires.

"First time filling her up?" he said.

"Yes, how'd you know?"

"You look like you're enjoying yourself. No sailor likes diesel."

"I think there's something satisfying about being self-sufficient."

I heard Lacey whine. I glanced over my shoulder at him pawing my leg.

"Self-sufficient? You speak for yourself, Harry the stud. I need a wee."

"What's up Lacey? I won't be long…"

"He can come aboard if he wants to. There's a bucket to sluice down if he needs a pee," said the fuel guy.

"Lacey go wee-wees?" I asked in a low, self-conscious voice, noting his waggy tail.

I retrieved Lacey's lifejacket from the main cabin, still messy with the duvet and cushions strewn on the floor from my bedroom antics. Lacey tried to fidget out of the straps, but I managed to clip him in, then lower him onto the fuel barge.

I kept a watchful eye on Lacey as he sniffed around, edging cautiously up to the water's edge before finding an agreeable spot. He squatted down, a comical fixated expression of concentration on his face.

I finished filling the tank and carried the nozzle back onto the barge, watching Lacey skip away as the fuel guy tipped a bucket of seawater over the deck beneath his paws.

"Not a natural seadog, this one," he said.

"No, he's still learning the ropes," I replied, smiling at Lacey rolling over so the fuel guy could tickle his tummy.

"I bet he's popular, with the ladies."

I shrugged and fought to suppress a grin, but couldn't.

"You'll have to rent him out to lonely sailors," he said, chuckling with a deep, resonating belly wobble.

I followed him into the wheelhouse to settle up, wallowing in a strange sense of fulfilment from my nocturnal activities, despite my memory blanks of the sensuous details…

*

The fuel guy cast off our lines and I steered away from the barge, lining up Jessica's bow with the harbour entrance between Shell Bay on our right and The Haven Hotel at Sandbanks on our left. The chain ferry trundled across the gap between the two points and we tagged onto the line of other boats, all heading towards the Swash Channel and the open sea beyond.

"Imagine being tied into that life, eh Lacey? It's a different perspective from out here."

Lacey's ears twitched, but he seemed more interested in wandering around the deck to find the sunniest spot. We managed to time our exit with the chain ferry unloading cars on the Shell Bay side and eased through the entrance with the last of the ebb tide under our keel. I couldn't have timed our exit from Poole better if I'd tried.

I rubbed my aching cheeks. Have I ever smiled this much? If I had, I couldn't remember when.

Safely through the harbour entrance, I sat down on the cockpit coaming, staring out at the shallow curve of Shell Bay, now giving way to the much larger Studland Bay and Old Harry Rocks beyond. Golden sandy beaches lined the base of gorse-clad sand dunes which, on a sunny day, sheltered nudists.

I chuckled and turned to face Lacey.

"See over there? 'Old Harry Rocks'. I'm famous!"

"So I saw last night… for about ten seconds. You pop stars, no staying power…"

Lacey yawned and stretched out, grumbling as he settled. I shook my head and watched the sun twinkle on the Swash Channel swell, chopped up from the wake of boats entering and leaving the harbour. I turned to glance over my left shoulder. Bournemouth Bay and the seaward side of Sandbanks opened up behind me, the horizon dotted with exclusive apartments and hotels.

Lacey trotted over to me and nuzzled up, shifting his body to lean against me. I reached down to stroke him as we motored on with the sun warming our backs.

"How about a walk on the beach, Lacey?"

His big brown eyes stared up at me, his tail twitching.

*

The anchor chain rattled through the stainless steel bracket, shedding rust particles. I felt the chain slacken in my gloved hands as it touched the seabed and I started counting off the correct length. Lacey paced the deck, whimpering as I made off the chain.

"Are we stopping? Is it Lacey fun time?"

"Let's blow up the kayak, shall we? Hope you've got plenty of puff," I said to him.

Lacey followed me back to the cockpit, watching intently and whining as I rhythmically stepped on the foot pump.

"A big shoe? Or is it a banana?"

"You're an excitable little thing, aren't you…?"

I clipped the paddle together and lowered the kayak alongside the boat, blocking Lacey's attempts to dive into it.

"Easy boy, me first."

I gingerly lowered myself into the kayak, clinging onto Jessica's gunnel. I barely had time to straighten my legs and lay the paddle alongside so I could offer my free hands to help Lacey, when he leapt into my arms, tipping my balance.

"Whoa, Lacey…!"

He hit the water first with a splash and high-pitched yelp.

"You bastard! I fudging hate water…"

"Yeeeeaaarrr… bloody hell its cold!" I shouted, flapping my arms and kicking my legs to counter the shock of falling in.

Lacey doggy-paddled frantically beside me, his plaster cast knocking on Jessica's slippery hull. I reached up to hold onto the gunnel with one hand and used all my strength to lift up under Lacey's tummy, pushing his anxious paws under the guard rails. His claws scratched my knuckles as he climbed aboard, the salt water smarting.

"Nice one Lacey!" I spluttered.

Lacey shook salty water off his saturated coat, his tail vibrating and collar rattling.

"What'd ya do that for, numpty?"

"Lacey, stop barking. You're not helping," I blurted out, stuttering as my teeth chattered.

Retrieving the floating paddle, I swam to the upturned kayak and flipped it over. No sooner had I got back into it than Lacey perched back on the gunnel, preparing to jump into my unprepared arms.

"Lacey, stay!" I said in an assertive voice, to no avail.

I just had time to cling onto Jessica's guard wire to brace myself before Lacey launched himself at my lap.

"You are so impatient!"

"Ha! Dogs don't wait for anyone. Get used to it, monkey chops."

Lacey shuffled round in my lap until he faced forwards.

"Come on, let's go. I'm freezing my doggy-danglies off."

I tried to shove Lacey down towards my feet to give me more space to use the paddle, but he hunkered low on my lap and refused to budge.

"So that's it. You're staying put?"

"This dog don't dance."

I gritted my teeth and squeezed the paddle in my fists, staring skywards. Lacey craned his neck around and tried to lick my face. I looked down at him and sighed heavily.

"You're such a stubborn dog."

I pushed gently away from Jessica and took a few tentative strokes, having to hold the paddle with straight arms to avoid bopping Lacey on the nose. The things I did for my brother…

*

"The beach, yippee!"

Lacey leapt off my lap as soon as the kayak scraped to a stop on the sand. He scurried through the ankle-deep water and took off along the beach, his comical straight-legged bum wiggle accompanying his joyful barking as he chased down a cluster of seagulls.

"I wonder if you like to chase sticks…?"

I scanned the beach for driftwood, but barely had a chance to pick up the nearest stick when Lacey zoomed past and snatched it from my hands, holding it aloft in his jaws like a trophy. I managed to grab it but he held on, clamping his jaws tightly around it as I lifted him and the stick into the air.

"You're a crazy dog," I said, watching his legs

dance as he dangled below the stick, growling and eyeballing me.

"Hah, you can't bark properly, because you'd have to let go!"

I tickled his tummy, feeling the weight drop off the stick as he fell onto the sand, then I hurled the stick along the beach. Lacey bolted after it.

I took a deep, satisfied breath and turned to look back at Jessica, resting on her anchor in the sparkling bay beneath the cliffs.

You're a lucky fella, Harry, I thought, drinking in the fresh salty optimism.

Eleven

I closed the sailing almanac and tucked my passage notes under the front cover.

"Early start in the morning, Lacey. Tides will be in our favour."

Lacey lifted his head to yawn, then lay back in the sunny cockpit and stretched out. I stroked his side to which he made a sort of appreciative soft grumbling sound, then shut his eyes.

"I must have run twenty miles, Harry. What's your excuse? Oh yeah, bedroom Olympics…"

"If only I had your energy, Lacey…"

"Believe me Harry, you've already given a gold medal performance earlier this morning."

I looked away from the dog and stood up to scan three hundred and sixty degrees around our anchorage. The white chalky cliffs tapered away from Old Harry Rocks, gradually sloping down towards Studland beach. Past the harbour entrance, Bournemouth and Boscombe beaches trailed away eastwards towards Hengistbury Head and the hazy outline of Christchurch Bay. Beyond that, the faint shape of the Isle of Wight's cliffs at St Katherine's point and The Needles, south of which a vast expanse of shimmering salt water adventure and danger lay waiting.

"Westwards-ho Harry me old mate," I said,

mesmerized by the sparkling expanse of sea. "Let the adventure begin…"

*

Later that evening when the sun had set behind the cliffs, I stretched my legs out on the port saloon berth, tucked a pillow behind my back and opened up Jessica's boat logbook. Lacey jumped up and sat on my lap, yawning as he twirled round and lay out on my outstretched legs.

"Human hot water bottle, lovely."

"Don't mind me, will you," I said, peering over the logbook at him. I shook my head, playing down the smile twitching on my lips.

Good pet discipline, Harry. He knows who's the boss. I cast my eyes back to the logbook and flicked through the entries.

That's odd…

The pages curled from the back, going forwards. I flipped the logbook over and opened the last page, puzzled to see neat circular handwriting that hadn't been there a few days ago.

This is a new section – 'Harry's Hoes' – for all female guests to record their adventures aboard the good ship Jessica. God bless all those who shag in her.

July 21st 2013 – Poole Quay
Dear diary, please forgive me. It's been thirty-

*two years since my last confession. I'd been
out on the quay with a girlfriend, when I saw
the cutest dog you could imagine. Lacey had
a plaster cast on his leg, plastic lampshade on
his head and wore a funny little lifejacket. Oh,
and he'd just stolen a slurp of Harry's beer. It
was one of those knicker twanging moments
in life when you think, why not?
Here are the facts about Harry:
He's a bit shy getting down to business (wink,
wink…) but once there – wow! The dog will sit
there looking at you while you're in some
interesting 'legs akimbo' positions. But don't
worry, not many animals kiss and tell, so your
naughty stuff is safe with Lacey. Oh, you may
have to nudge him away from certain areas
that smell interesting, so watch out for a cold
wet nose sniffing around your nether
regions...
Good luck girls, enjoy!
Sharon (Harry's 'number two'!)
PS. Gotta love this little boat x*

I laughed out loud and read the entry again,
then lowered the logbook, still chuckling. Lacey
shifted on my legs, opened a sleepy eye and
gazed at me. I reached out and stroked his
head.

"You're trouble with a capital 'T', Lacey."

He wagged his tail, stretched out, emitting a
doggy mumble.

*"I didn't see you complain last night when
Sharon used your tinkle-tackle as a lollipop…"*

I turned the logbook over, my smile dispersing as I thumbed through the pages to find the next entry my dad had made.

7th day of May, Nineteen Seventy-Seven
Day 1. Straight family circumnavigation of Great Britain. Falmouth lighthouse left to port at 09:05 hours. Breezy force 5 south-westerly. An hour into the flood tide; long smooth sea state. Four persons on board: Captain Anthony, First Mate Elizabeth, Able Seaman Keith and infant Harry. Intended destination: Fowey.

I lowered the logbook, my hands gripping the sides.

"I should probably let sleeping dogs lie, eh Lacey?"

Lacey moaned and slid gracefully off my legs onto the cushion as I eased myself up and leaned over the galley to rummage through a locker.

"Who does that..."

I gripped the galley fiddle, dropped my head and screwed my eyes tightly shut, forcing several long deep calming breaths into my lungs.

"...to a baby?"

The brandy cork pulled off with a comforting suction 'plop'. I poured a decent measure and raised the glass towards the logbook, laying open beside Lacey. I shut my eyes as the brandy warmed its way down my throat, savouring the tingling, dulling sensation.

The electronic alarm drew me away from the dream, its imagery distant, yet tantalisingly close, if only I could decipher what it all meant.

I'd had the vague sense of floating, weightlessness that felt neither hot, nor cold. A hollow twinge in my stomach…

Loss? Bitterness…?

Regret.

I eased my legs out of the sleeping bag, away from Lacey's warmth beside my toes. I shuffled into the saloon and pulled the curtain aside, peeking out through the condensation as the first rays of sunlight stretched out across Bournemouth Bay.

Another dawn, another day.

*

"This time Lacey, I have a plan."

I lifted Lacey up onto my shoulder, his front paws clinging to my back as I held his body tightly to my chest.

"I'm not a morning dog, Harry. Can't we have another hour in bed?"

I ignored his groans and carefully stepped down into the kayak.

"See, much better than your leap of faith," I said, shifting him onto my lap where he sat sniffing the fresh morning air.

I paddled across the flat calm water, that magical changeover between the sun and moon reflecting in the water, occasionally obscured by wispy mist hovering in sporadic patches.

We nudged right up the beach on the high tide with barely an audible swoosh of water lapping on the shore. Lacey yawned, his reluctance to leap onto the beach requiring me to lift him onto the wet sand.

"What a beautiful morning, Lacey," I said, turning to gaze at Jessica, sunlight glistening on her deck.

I dragged the kayak up the beach, kicked off my flip-flops and began to amble along the tide line, searching for a suitable stick for Lacey.

Hang on, where's the dog?

Lacey sat in the kayak, his head just visible above its side.

"Come on, Lacey, walkies!"

"Not on your knobbly knees, humanoid."

I stopped walking, called him again.

No joy.

I shook my head and strode back to the kayak.

"Are you shivering? Come on, walkies. You'll soon warm up…"

"It's bloody cold! This dog don't get outta bed for less than a cup of tea and a decent breakfast. You're not learning, are you Harry?"

We both stood our ground, holding eye contact.

Deadlock.

I dropped a hand into my pocket, watched his eyes follow the movement.

Ah-hah, gotcha.

"Ooh, what's this Lacey? What's this?"

I withdrew my hand, pretended to put something in my mouth, faking a chewing motion.

"Mmm, that's lovely."

I turned and walked away from the kayak. Out of the corner of my eye I noticed Lacey lick his lips then hop out of the kayak to scamper after me. I glanced around and broke into a run, closely followed by the yapping dog.

"Come here, you sneaky poodle-person. What's in your pocket?"

*

"What better way to start the day than a walk on a deserted beach followed by a cup of tea and a bacon sandwich?"

I tipped some extra milk into Lacey's weak tea and placed it on the floor beside his rabbit bowl, which contained chopped bacon and dry dog food. He pounced on the food, devouring it enthusiastically, allowing me a precious few seconds to bite into my sarnie without him pestering me for more.

"Weymouth, here we come…" I mumbled between bites.

*

I hauled down on the main halyard, lifting the mainsail up the mast, watching it sag lazily in the light breeze. Once tensioned and tied off, I sorted out the other lines and sat down on the bow, each foot resting on a cleat beside the anchor locker, ready to pull up the chain. Lacey plonked himself down next to me and leaned his body onto mine.

"That's not particularly helpful, Lacey."

But he wouldn't budge, so I began to pull on the chain, doing my best to flick my elbow out so I didn't knock into him. The chain rattled through the roller as I dropped the slack into the locker.

With the anchor securely stowed, I eased the mainsheet, unfurled the genoa and then pushed the tiller away, filling the sails with the gentle breeze. Behind us, the rudder made a gurgling sound as we began to make way.

We poked our nose out around Old Harry Rocks, revealing the town of Swanage in the next bay and the open sea beyond. Lacey took up his familiar position curled up by my side, sharing warmth.

For now, everything felt right in the world.

Twelve

The wind freshened as the forecast had predicted and two hours later, Jessica had heeled over by twenty degrees, her sails filling with a near-perfect twelve knots of breeze, pushing her along at a decent pace. We still had four hours of ebb tide with us, perfect for an early afternoon arrival in Weymouth.

I marvelled at how effortlessly Jessica slipped through the water, her freshly anti-fouled hull no doubt helping, another testament to all my hard work.

"Look after your boat and she'll look after you… not unlike a good woman," I said, mimicking one of the old boys in the boatyard.

The distant mobile phone ringtone roused me from my thoughts, its insistent tone obnoxious in the peace and tranquillity aboard Jessica. I tied off the tiller and stooped down into the cabin to retrieve my phone from the chart table.

"Hello."

"Mister Harry Straight?"

"Yes, who is…?"

"Detective Inspector Randall. I trust you're looking after that ball-breaker dog of yours?"

"Of course, Inspector."

"Good. Your brother, Keith. Have you heard from him since we last spoke?"

"No."

"Okay. You're clear what you need to do if he does get in touch?"

"I am."

"Excellent. Some more information has come to light. I'd like to ask you a few questions."

"That's a bit tricky, Inspector. I'm currently sailing to Weymouth."

"I see. I understood you'd be in Poole for a few more days."

"That was the intention, Inspector. Unfortunately your colleagues messed that up for me. You remember, the ones with guns?"

I waited for the Inspector's reply, listening to the background office bustle and regular tapping sound which sounded like a pen drumming on a desk.

"Keep your phone on. I'll send a colleague to meet you, around three this afternoon?"

"Fair winds and tide permitting, I should be there."

"Thank you for your cooperation."

The Inspector hung up, leaving me to ponder what else he wanted to ask me.

*

The Isle of Portland loomed large and grey on our left, its imposing stone breakwater shielding the old Navy harbour and Chesil Beach causeway from view. Stretching out on our right, Weymouth's esplanade and two-mile-long crescent-shaped beach joined with chalky white cliffs topped with lush shades of greenery.

I checked my watch, mentally calculating our passage time.

"Just over six hours, Lacey, not bad for a little sailing boat."

I fired up the engine and furled in the genoa, motoring with a taut mainsail until just off the harbour entrance where I turned head to wind, engaged neutral and pulled the mainsail down.

We pushed on into the narrow entrance under reduced engine revs towards The Cove, an area with a visitors' pontoon for smaller boats. Seagulls swooped and squawked overhead, circling around the commercial fishing boats and tourists eating fish and chips on the pretty quay. We passed the lifeboat station and I turned Jessica left, away from the lifting bridge towards the old town by Brewers Quay.

"Plenty of space, perfect," I said to Lacey, who pattered around the deck, whining at all the new and interesting things to see.

With only three other boats moored up on the pontoon, I steered easily alongside.

"I suppose we'd better take you for another walk, me old shipmate," I said to Lacey, removing his lifejacket.

*

Lacey roamed along the quay, hobbling and swaying to counter his stiff plaster-cast leg.

"I bet it's an odd sensation being back on land, after the movement of the boat..."

I watched him stop to sniff the fresh fishy air,

necessitating a quick sideways step to regain his balance.

"You been tampering with my water?"

I let Lacey take me where he wanted to go. We crossed the lifting bridge into the new part of town, heading towards the pedestrian shopping centre.

A middle-aged passer-by crouched down to stroke Lacey. He glanced up at me.

"Reminds me of a friend's dog..."

I nodded, watched him stand up and walk on, a distant expression etched into his weather-worn features.

Lacey tugged on his lead. I let him continue our magical mystery tour.

"A pub? Really Lacey, we're going to have a talk about your drinking problem... come on, this way, I want to do some shopping first."

Lacey wagged his tail and jerked against the lead, heading for Finn's, a tatty and rough-looking biker's pub.

"Seriously?"

"They're friendly in here, dog's honour."

I shrugged at Lacey's whining and followed him into the pub, my eyes darting around the gloomy interior.

"Is it okay to bring the dog in?" I asked the large barman.

He flicked his eyes over me, resting his gaze on Lacey. His expression softened.

"Lacey, right?"

"Erm, yeah."

"He want some water or his usual?"

"Maybe both, if that's okay."

He nodded. "And what about you, mate?"

I watched the barman pour half a pint of Guinness, then he disappeared out back and returned with a plastic container half-filled with water and an empty Tupperware dish.

"I'll have a pint of the same please," I said, tipping my head at the Guinness pump.

I looked down at Lacey.

"Your usual, eh? Regular are we?"

Lacey stared back at me, unblinking. I paid for the drinks and carried Lacey's two bowls to a corner table.

"Bet you he goes for the Guinness first," said the barman.

Lacey wagged his tail and tried to jump up at the bowls before I'd put them down on the floor.

"Hurry up Harry, don't keep the thirsty animal waiting…"

I placed the bowls at Lacey's feet and watched him bury his nose in the Guinness froth. I walked back to the bar and scraped the change into my pocket.

"What happened to his foot?"

I glanced up at the barman. He'd shifted his stance to lean forwards, clenched fists resting on the bar. I took a gulp of my pint, tried to drop my voice an octave.

"We had a bit of a scuffle, with erm… the *rozzers*. Big guns, small angry dog. The pig trod on Lacey, broke his foot. So he bit him in the balls, did Keith proud."

The barman relaxed his posture, a thin smile creasing his lips as he slapped me on the shoulder, making me slop beer over my hand.

"Proper dog. What they do you for?"

"Me? Possession of a deadly beer can… thought I might be hiding Keith."

"Yeah, I heard he'd taken cover. Be lucky, pal."

"Sure, you too. Cheers."

I dropped my eyes back to my pint, switched hands and shook away droplets of Guinness. The barman turned to serve another customer, so I took my opportunity to slink away to the corner table.

I flicked my eyes around the pub, Weymouth's answer to a rock and roll boozer. Lacey drew my eye to the floor, his wagging tail and broken leg hobble heading away from me as he nudged the now-empty bowl across the bare floorboards.

The cool Guinness slipped down easily, washing away the salty tang from the sail over. I toyed with the glass, savouring the taste as I quietly toasted myself.

"Cheers Harry, your first passage completed. The old girl did you proud."

"Do you want some more, doggy?" said a husky sounding voice from the other side of the pub.

I lifted my head from scrawling in the boat logbook and twisted round in my seat. A gothic punk woman in her mid-thirties poured clear liquid from her glass into Lacey's Guinness bowl.

I watched Lacey dip his nose in, then pull back, sneeze and start barking, kicking his paws behind him, like a sort of sporadic and frustrated moonwalk. The rest of the gothic woman's group laughed at Lacey's reaction.

"Sorry dog, I had a heavy one last night. Need to rehydrate…"

"Don't tease me with that bubbly sugar water crap. I want a proper drink!"

The goth lady laughed, reached down to stroke Lacey, but he kept barking.

"If you want to buy the dog a proper drink, love, it's half a Guinness," said the barman.

"You're joking," said the goth woman.

"I never joke about alcohol, especially cos he'll drink most of you under the table," he said, placing a half-pint of Guinness on the bar.

I watched the attractive goth approach the bar, pay for the drink and pour half of it into Lacey's bowl. She drank the rest herself. Lacey nudged the bowl up against the table leg, chasing down every last drop, before reverting to his comical moonwalk-prancing and vocal frustration.

"Don't be stingy, crow lady!"

Amusing as Lacey's war dance looked, I ambled over to quieten him down.

"Is he being a pain?" I asked.

"Not at all. He's a right little character," said the goth girl, meeting my gaze.

"Come on, trouble," I said, kneeling to scoop Lacey into my arms.

I carried Lacey back to my table where I sat down with him on my lap, careful to push my pint of Guinness out of his reach.

"I'm Gertie. Buy me a drink? I'd offer to get

the first round in, but technically, I already have," she said, sitting down opposite me.

Gertie reached out to stroke Lacey.

"I'm not sure I'm staying for another," I said.

"Not even a quickie?"

I shot her a quizzical look.

"Um…"

"Do you play Monopoly?"

I frowned.

"You know, take a chance card. Despite all this…" she made a circular motion in front of her face, "…I'm the sanest person I know. In fact, when sober, I'm capable of some very intelligent and stimulating conversations."

I watched her face soften when she smiled, contrasting with her dark makeup.

"What sort of stimulating conversations?"

"Pint of Kroni and we'll find out."

I held eye contact with her for a few seconds.

"Why not. Do you mind looking after the dog for a minute? Please don't let him have any more beer."

"Sure."

I lifted Lacey up and passed him to Gertie.

"You're in for a treat," murmured the barman as he placed the drinks in front of me.

"How so?"

"Gertie is a fussy girl and normally you wouldn't stand a chance, but that dog is a fanny magnet."

"Oh, right. Cheers."

I pocketed the change and watched Gertie for a moment. She sat massaging Lacey's ears, making his eyelids droop.

"I think you've found a friend there," I said, setting the glasses down.

"He's gorgeous. Thanks for the drink…"

She offered an outstretched hand.

"Harry," I said. "And this bundle of trouble is Lacey."

We shook hands. Lacey yawned and repositioned on Gertie's lap.

"You guys, so polite. Get a room already."

"Is he alright?"

"I think so. He grumbles and groans, but I reckon it's his way of letting me know he's comfortable."

"Okay, good. So, Harry. Have you ever had any sexually transmitted diseases?"

I choked back a mouthful of Guinness.

"Which one do you want?"

"Good answer. So much better than a blabbering long-winded avoidance."

"I'm hardly going to say yes."

"True. I like to start with sexual history and work backwards from there."

"Backwards?"

"Yeah, you know, brothers and sisters, family stuff like that. Kinda boring and not relevant until later on. First off it's all about attraction and compatibility, right? I mean, if any of that's missing, what's the point progressing any further."

"Safety first?"

"Honesty first. Any interaction between two people needs to be based on truth. The ground rules can follow later."

"You've lost me."

"Okay, so it's all about understanding the opposition. For example, if I thought you were a lying toe rag who'd do the dirty behind my back with my best mate, then that's fine."

"It is?"

"Sure. So long as I know. Then it's my choice on what basis to get involved. Let's face it, if the person in question has a gorgeous body and *take-me-to-bed* smile, but is a complete shitbag, I'm going to be wary of anything long term. But I'd still consider a one-off liaison… life's too short, you know…"

I returned her smile, took my time in replying.

"That's a novel take on human characteristics. You ever had any?"

"Shitbag boyfriends?"

"Sexually transmitted diseases."

She glanced down at Lacey, made a show of stroking him.

"Redirection, catching me unawares. Nice work Harry, especially since you didn't answer the question yourself."

She tipped her head up from being hunched over Lacey and shot me a mischievous look.

"I've never had a sexually transmitted disease," I said.

"Nor me. Been tested a couple of times, just in case. Frightening experience, everyone should try it."

I nodded, my head fuzzy with the intensity of our conversation. I took several mouthfuls from my pint.

"You look like you were married."

"I was, for a long time."

"Figures. Did you get bored?"

I shrugged. "Towards the end, when we were already on the slippery slope of not getting along. More unsettling than boring by that stage, though."

"Maybe I'll try it later in life. I think marriage should be part of retirement planning. Anyone childless, whether through choice or circumstance, should get hitched in their fifties. They can enjoy a single life when they're young, healthy and energetic, then settle down so they can look after their partner into old age. No one would ever get divorced."

"Interesting… what about couples with kids?"

"Same rules, but they should stay single after a break-up. Why shackle yourself again?"

I pretended to consider her views while I planned my escape.

"It sounds a bit clinical. What about love… where does that figure?"

"Love is for wimps," she said, draining her drink. "Another?"

Despite my instinct to head for the door, I found myself nodding at the mention of another drink.

"Why not."

"And the pooch?"

She passed Lacey to me.

"He can have some of mine," I replied, noticing Lacey licking his lips.

"Deal. Back in a tic."

Gertie leaned across the table to stroke Lacey and kiss me on the lips.

Oh dear, I thought, that's me buggered.

I flinched at my mobile phone vibrating in my pocket.

"Mister Harry Straight?" said a clipped female voice.

"This is he."

"Detective Constable Best. DI Randall asked me to meet you today in Weymouth at three o'clock. Are you available to answer some questions?"

I glanced at my watch: 2:55pm.

"Um, sure. I'm in Finn's. The pub."

"Your boat would be better sir, less public. I've checked with the Harbour Master and I'm waiting in Cove Street, adjacent to your vessel. Would you meet me here at your earliest convenience?"

"That sounds like you want to meet me right now."

"Yes sir."

I glanced at the bar where Gertie stood ordering drinks, her back to me.

"I'll walk over."

I quickly downed the rest of my pint, gathered Lacey into my arms and snuck past Gertie, heading for the door.

*

Lacey began growling as soon as he spotted the detective.

"Watch yourself Harry, I smell bacon!"

"You've already picked her out, eh Lacey? She must be a cat person," I murmured, smiling and offering my hand to DC Best who returned a business-like acknowledgement, but didn't accept my hand.

"Good afternoon Mister Straight. Please lead the way."

"Of course. Come aboard."

I led her down the ramp onto the floating walkway next to Jessica.

The detective accepted a cup of tea and I sat down in the main cabin opposite her.

"The reason I'm here is to ask whether your brother gave you anything before he disappeared."

"Such as?"

"Something unconnected to the dog."

I shook my head. "Nothing important springs to mind."

"Can you describe everything that was in the bag please. Item by item."

I scrunched my forehead, picturing the bag's contents, trying to think if there was anything that could compromise Keith.

"I'll do better than that, I'll show you."

I pointed to Lacey's rabbit food bowl on the floor of the cabin.

"That's the first item, right there. The other is…"

I opened up the plastic bag and removed Lacey's knitted body warmer.

"Mind if I take a look?"

I shrugged and sipped my tea, watching her silently examine the colourful dog warmer. She traced her fingers over the stitching, scrunching the wool in sections. I turned away and glanced out of the open companionway, tracing the outline of the old buildings and the overcast sky. Falmouth beckons, I thought. A few things to sort out along the way before seeing the old man…

"Why are you making this trip?" she asked, handing the knitted material back to me.

"To see my father and finish a journey. He built this boat himself. Before I began restoring it, she'd been laid up for over thirty-five years."

"What happened?"

I looked away, took a moment to compose myself.

"Long story and not relevant to Keith disappearing. What did he do?"

"I can't say. It's… delicate."

She stood to leave. I stared at her, processing what she might really be saying.

"No way, not Keith. He's a loveable rogue, not a pervert…"

"It's nothing like that, sir."

She hesitated, studying me, then sat back down.

"Keith's name has been attached to a number of investigations. Stolen goods, smuggling duty-free cigarettes and alcohol, high-end burglaries, that sort of thing. But we never had enough to charge him."

"Hang on, I thought he jumped bail?"

She shook her head.

"No. He wasn't charged. That was a ruse to get us national police cooperation. He's wanted because of some compromising photographs."

"What sort of photographs?" I asked, the corners of my lips turning up.

"Get out of jail free photographs…"

My smile grew as I watched her sit back and fold her arms.

"Of whom?"

"All I'll say is that someone much higher up the food chain doesn't want them plastered over the internet. DI Randall and I have been tasked with bringing Keith in, so we can negotiate."

"Like I said, my brother is a loveable rogue…"

"There's more. Keith is also a witness in a very high-profile prosecution case."

I felt a cool shiver prickle the hairs on the back of my neck.

"Keith's no snitch, Detective. He'll never agree to take the stand."

"No, we know. And therein lies the problem. He's trying to buy his freedom from appearing as a witness by using the photographs as blackmail. If he's forced to testify, he publishes them."

"I don't get it. What does he gain?"

"His anonymity. Keith knows some very unsavoury characters. If he testifies, he's a wanted man. He knows they'll hunt him down, no matter what protection we can offer. So if he disappears, doesn't take the stand, he's in the clear. But we need this conviction, he can help take down a big organisation. There's a huge amount of pressure from up on high to make sure we nail these guys."

"So you need to find Keith, offer him cast-iron

guarantees with some sort of witness protection, new life, whatever. In exchange for his testimony and the photographs?"

"Exactly."

"Forgive me for saying this, but you don't appear to be in a strong bargaining position."

She held my gaze.

"There's another problem. The organisation Keith is due to testify against is aware that we've been in contact with him. So they're looking for him too, to make sure there's no risk of him talking. And these people, they're not bothered about collateral damage in order to protect their interests. It's essential we get to your brother first. So you need to let us know if you hear from him. It's the only way you'll be able to protect him."

I took a long, deep breath.

"By shopping my brother to you lot?"

"Yes. Make no mistake, your brother is a dead man running."

She stood up and handed me a business card.

"This is my phone number. You hear anything from Keith, you ring us. He's in a strong bargaining position because of those photos, they'll buy him a comfortable new life."

I took the card and watched her climb up the companionway steps into the cockpit.

"I hope it works out with your dad. Enjoy Weymouth, it's a real circus town in the summer," she said as she stepped off the boat.

Thirteen

I took Lacey for a walk to clear my head. I wasn't really concentrating on which direction we went, allowing Lacey to lead me alongside the harbour, past the RNLI station towards the Nothe Fort.

What a mess. No wonder Keith had legged it, I'd have done exactly the same.

"You've got it easy, Lacey. A nice uncomplicated life."

I watched Lacey trot along, tail wagging, ears poised, sniffing here and there, the leg cast hardly interrupting his tempo.

Where are you, Keith, I wondered. Are you safe?

I glanced over my shoulder, looking for anyone who seemed out of place, my imagination running wild. What if Debs didn't leave of her own accord… what if she'd been abducted, or 'disappeared'…?

My mobile phone vibrated, accompanied by its two-tone text message alert. I fished it out of my pocket and stopped walking to squint at the screen:

> So easy rider, how's shipmate Lacey getting on? Has he made you walk the plank yet? Dog Doc

Lacey tugged at the lead, on the scent of something interesting.

"Come on Harry, there's squirrels to chase…"

I smiled as I replaced the mobile phone in my pocket and walked on, watching Lacey bounce up the steps leading to the Nothe Fort. His plaster-cast leg flicked sideways up the steps, followed by a comical bottom-wiggle as his hind legs followed. It took me more time and effort to climb the steps than my furry friend.

"Hey Lacey, you fancy a drink later? My shout."

*

We settled at a corner table in the Red Lion, a cosy traditional pub opposite Brewers Quay, staggering distance from the boat.

I lifted Lacey up onto my lap and glanced around the lifeboat photographs and rustic wood cladding. Not the sort of place Keith would have frequented.

I took a sip of my pint and toyed with the mobile phone.

"How shall we reply, Lacey?"

"Forget the phone fiddling, amigo. Where's my drink?"

Lacey craned his neck up to lick my face, whimpering. I tickled his ears, noting his gaze follow my pint back onto the table. I ignored his pleading eyes and lip-licking as I read the vet's message again. I wondered about the best way to respond.

After a moment or two, I began typing a reply:

Now in Weymouth after beneficial weather window. Lacey making friends with the locals. Still teaching him how to make a decent cup of tea. Harry.

Fairly safe, I thought. Non-committal yet friendly. Right now, complications I could do without.

"Hey sailor, why'd you run out on me?"

I glanced up to see Gertie pull out a chair and sit down opposite me.

"Am I really that scary?"

I shuffled in my seat and attempted a smile.

"Sorry, I had to meet someone. Kind of important."

"Sure you weren't running away? You left in a hurry."

"No, of course not."

"Okay... so I had to drink your pint and mine and Lacey's half. Would have been a shame to waste it. This means I can no longer be considered capable of stimulating sober conversation. You'll probably get more sense out of Lacey than me."

Gertie reached out to stroke Lacey.

"He's quite the drinker, Harry. Not unlike his owner, I suspect... you have that look."

"Meaning?" I said, a bit too quickly.

"It's a hint of quiet desperation, which could be confused with boredom, of life in general. But my guess is that you're resigned to your fate and you can't wind down properly without a few drinks. Am I right?"

I stared at her for long enough to realise my jaw had dropped open.

"Thought so. Me, I like the escapism of drinking. I compare it to putting on my makeup; it's toned down during the day at work. But when I put my war paint on, I can become somebody else for the night. Yet you don't wear a mask, Harry. Why?"

"You've lost me."

"You haven't given me any flannel about yourself. So you drink not to become someone else, but to forget something…"

She studied me intently. I looked away.

"You want a drink?" I asked, pushing my chair back and lifting Lacey down onto the floor. I slipped his lead under the table leg.

"I'm getting a sense of déjà vu, Harry. Are you going to leg it again?"

"And leave the dog? I had to meet someone, honest. You drinking or not?"

"Guinness, thank you. Have one yourself and don't forget Lacey. He's been drooling."

Gertie unclipped Lacey's lead and lifted him up onto her lap while I headed for the bar.

*

I joined the queue, my thoughts drifting.

What are you doing with your life, Harry? Same old question, eh. Give it another couple of drinks and the answer won't matter… ten seconds into the future and no past…

I arrived back at the table to find Lacey

cradled in Gertie's arms, three paws dangling at ninety degrees, the fourth pointing skywards.

"He's practically comatose," I said.

"Lacey is a sweetheart, Harry. I bet he helps attract the ladies."

"Such a confidence boost, knowing you're sitting here with me because of a cute dog. Does wonders for my self-esteem. And you ask why I drink…"

"I sense irritation, Harry. Did your hot date stand you up?"

"Not exactly. I met a policewoman."

"Stripagram?"

"No, the real deal."

"Oh really. Been a naughty boy?"

"My brother is… helping them with some stuff. But he's gone missing. They thought I might be hiding him on my boat."

"Are you?"

I laughed, the image of Jessica's compact cabin flashing through my mind. I caught her puzzled expression.

"It's a size thing. You'd have to see the boat to understand. There's not enough room to swing Lacey, let alone harbour a stowaway."

"Ooh, that sounds like an invitation, Harry. I bet it's cosy for two shy consenting adults… ah, I almost forgot…"

Gertie lifted her shoulder bag up and retrieved Jessica's logbook.

"Because if this is anything to go by…"

She slid the logbook across the table.

"…you come highly recommended."

I stared at the logbook, confused.

"You left it in Finn's. I wouldn't have bothered coming to find you had you not forgotten it."

"How did you know I'd be in here?"

Gertie flicked open the front cover.

"Boat name *Jessica.* I checked at the harbour office, they told me where you'd parked up. And here is staggering distance…"

"Oh," I said, still staring at the logbook.

"So what's this boat like inside?"

A bark from Lacey broke my trance.

"Harry, this is it fella! Strike three… what are you waiting for?"

I sat back and raised my glass, considering Gertie as I drained the last mouthful. A flashback to Sharon teased my recollections.

"It's snug."

"Probably gets lonely sometimes, for one man and his dog… I'm going for a smoke. Get you another drink when I come back?"

I placed my empty glass on the table and nodded.

"I'll take Lacey out for a wee at the same time, if you like. Promise I won't dog- nap him."

I hesitated and glanced through the window, realising I'd be able to keep an eye on both of them.

"Okay."

I watched Gertie and Lacey weave their way through the busy pub towards the door, then checked my mobile phone, remembering a message alert from some time ago:

Glad safe arrival. Shipmate Lacey is

excused tea making duties until his cast comes off – vet's orders! Watch out for his irresistible charm on those Weymouth girls... Dog Doc x

Signing off with an 'x' – a friendly way of concluding the message, or something else? Hmm... you need to be careful with tanked-up texting, Harry. That way lies trouble...

*

"The next round says he ends up at the feet of the woman in the red dress," I said, holding Lacey over a Tupperware bowl which contained a few mouthfuls of Guinness.

"I'm going for the bald guy to my left. Lacey's bad leg will push him over that way."

"C'mon you guys, stop teasing me, thirsty canine here!"

I gently lowered the whimpering dog to the floor and released him.

"He's off!" screeched Gertie.

Gertie and I watched Lacey lap up the Guinness. He stuck his nose in the corner of the square container, pushing it across the floor, chasing down every last drop of liquid. His little legs hobbled awkwardly, the plaster cast banging into the container, pushing it towards the bar.

The Tupperware knocked into someone's foot, causing a change of direction. Lacey repositioned his body, manoeuvring the container faster now without the weight of liquid.

"Way to go, Lacey!" whooped Gertie.

I watched Lacey close his jaws on the side of the bowl and lift it above his head, right under the bald guy's table.

"Next round's on you, Harry."

Gertie rattled her empty glass on the table. Lacey left the empty container and picked his way through the drinker's legs towards us. He looked a bit cross-eyed and wobbly on his paws as he tried to lick the froth off the end of his nose.

Other drinkers stared at the floor as he weaved around their feet.

"Well done Lacey, that's telepathy, eh! This could be an expensive night for your daddy."

Gertie scooped Lacey up onto her lap and cuddled him, just as the dog started hiccupping.

"Uh oh. Uh oh. Uh oh…"

"Line 'em up, Harry," said Gertie, slapping my bottom as I passed her on the way to the bar.

*

I suppose natural progression dictated that we'd end up on board the boat after such an entertaining evening… "For a nightcap," Gertie had suggested.

I had to carry Lacey the short distance to the boat and it's quite possible that Gertie carried me some of the way, I can't really remember.

Our newly invented drinking game had struck a chord in the pub. We'd set Lacey off with a

splash of Guinness in the container and many of
the drinkers had taken bets where he'd end up.
In fact, I think I came out with more money that I
went in with, a first for me.

I poured a measure of brandy into two mugs
and handed one to Gertie. She smiled a woozy
thanks and sat down opposite me in the small
cabin.

"It's lovely Harry, but where do you sleep?"

I leaned forwards and pointed to the vee
berth at the front of the boat, just as she did the
same, banging our heads together. I turned to
face her, my vision blurred, head spinning, our
noses only a few inches apart.

"It's kind of compact for what I had in mind…"
she said in a husky, gravelly voice. "How about
you bring the hooch and the pooch and come
over to my place?"

Fourteen

I carried Lacey across the lifting bridge to the newer part of town, where Gertie led us into a shared flat above a coffee shop in the high street. I sank down onto the sofa, aware of Lacey jumping up next to me.

"Uh, Gertie, is Lacey okay on the couch?" I called out.

"Course he is, little darling," came her muffled reply from the depths of the kitchen.

Lacey snuggled up next to me, quietly grumbling as he closed his heavy eyelids and sighed deeply.

"Be careful human, Gertie has a wacky way about her…"

I felt the couch sag as Gertie sat down on the other side of me. She handed me a generous measure of brandy and chinked her glass against mine. We each took a sip and sat there for a moment, only Lacey's doggy murmurings interrupting the silence.

"You humans, so much unnecessary foreplay…"

I placed my brandy glass on the coffee table and draped my hand over Lacey's back, stroking him. I sank back on the couch and allowed my eyes to close.

"Harry, it's been an enjoyable evening, but do you want to have some real fun?"

I forced my eyes open.

"Follow me, sailor," she said, taking my hand to lead me into the bedroom.

*

"Do you like to be tied up?"

"Um… not sure I ever have been," I said, my voice slurring.

"A Gertie bedroom virgin. Awesome."

Gertie guided me to sit down on the edge of the bed. She leaned in and kissed me, her tongue darting into my mouth.

"Shuffle up the bed, my lurver," she said, coming up for air.

Barely able to keep my eyes open, I wiggled up the bed as instructed and peered through near-closed eyelids at the open bedside drawer and the pair of handcuffs she dangled between each thumb and first finger.

"They look serious," I mumbled.

"Relax Harry, this'll be fun."

I heard a metallic ratchet sound, felt the cold metal close around my left wrist which she secured to the metal headboard.

"I'm not sure this is really for me, Gertie… no offence…"

"It's a control thing, I agree. But just go with it Harry and trust me."

Click, click, click.

The second set of handcuffs closed around my right hand. She pulled my hand above my head and snapped the cuff shut around the bed frame.

"Good body, for a man of your age, Harry," she said.

I flinched as she ran her fingers down my chest, pelvis and thighs.

"Shoes, off."

I felt her tug on my laces, flinching at the odd sensation around my big toe as she pulled off each sock with her teeth.

"Good luck down there, missus. Harry's feet are guaranteed to make you pass out…"

"Shhh Lacey. I'm seducing your dad, I need to concentrate…" said Gertie, munching on a mouthful of my fragrant sock as she stood up and looked down at me, hands on her hips. She flicked her head, tossing the sock over her shoulder.

I couldn't help myself, I began to giggle.

"Nice party trick… what happens now?" I said.

"Role play."

I frowned, craning my neck off of the pillow, trying to see what she'd removed from her drawer. Gertie opened her hands, stretching the elastic eye mask between her fingers as she closed in on me.

"Ooh, it's all gone dark."

"That's so you can't see me change…"

"Change into what?"

I could hear the concern in my own voice.

"Someone else, Harry. A *really* fun person."

I felt the bed give as something landed by my head and began licking my face. Lacey's cold nose pushed under the mask, trying to find my eye socket.

"Ugh! I hope that's you Lacey, because otherwise I'm seriously worried about your transformation, Gertie…"

"You won't be mistaking me for your dog when we get going, Harry my love."

I tilted my head away from Lacey and managed to peer under the mask with one eye. Gertie sat at the dressing table, doing something with her makeup. I craned my head as far as possible, watching as she opened another drawer and removed a large round biscuit tin.

Lacey whined and bounced across the bed towards Gertie.

"Fan-dog-tastic, I'm ready to eat my own paws!"

"Sorry Lacey, no biscuits in here…" said Gertie, popping the lid off the tin.

I strained to try and tilt my head further to peer inside the box, officially getting slightly concerned at how weird things were getting.

"Boy oh boy Harry, are you in for a dog-ass surprise…"

*

The same sensation as floating, yet different… I peered through a haze, trying to separate fantasy from reality… unlike previous incarnations of the same dream, this sensation felt much more vivid. The liquid I floated in seemed actually… *wet.*

I tried to wipe the liquid off my cheek, but I couldn't move my hands.

I flinched as another squirt of cool liquid splashed onto my lips and dribbled down my chin.

Eyes… eyes, open.

Darkness. The mask had been replaced properly.

Am I still dreaming?

The sensations felt real, despite my brain swimming in alcohol.

Maybe that's it… I'm awake but still drunk.

But it didn't feel the same, something wasn't right. I flicked my tongue over my lips.

What is that liquid I can taste…? Wait, it's turning warm… huh?

I felt my lips begin to tingle.

It's not warm, it's hot. It's really, really hot… tastes like…

"Wakey, wakey!"

…chilli oil. What the bloody hell…?!

Loud circus music blasted out into the room.

"Aaaaarrrhhhh!"

I felt something behind my head. Her fingers yanked the mask off, forcing me to scrunch my eyes shut to douse the bright light.

"Surprise!" yelled Gertie.

Only it wasn't Gertie behind the light. I stared into the face of my own private horror show. A bright red plastic rose spat more chilli oil, narrowly missing my eyes.

"Yeeeaaaaarrrrrr!"

A frizzy luminous green wig, big round red nose, ghostly white face, blood red lips and full-on scary clown makeup loomed over me. But it didn't stop there, oh no.

I dropped my panic-stricken eyes away from her manic cuckoo-clown face to the rest of her outfit. A bouffant white shirt beneath a brightly coloured waistcoat, ballerina tutu, red fishnet stockings and holy shit, the real frightener: a big black strap-on penis, behind which I could see wisps of overgrown fluorescent orange pubic hair.

"Aaaaarrrhhhh!" I yelled again.

"It's time to get really naughty!" Gertie-the-clown screeched, pulling a high-eyebrow wide-grin wacko pout.

"Whoopee, playtime!"

Lacey barked close to my ear, then I saw a ginger and brown flash leap across the bed over my groin, jaws open. A pair of teeth clamped around the clown's strap-on willy, Lacey's long body bouncing down, hind legs kicking on the bed, bungee jumping off Gertie's groin.

"Lacey! Get off Gertie's big Bertie!" she shrieked, pulling back from the bed. The elastic around Gertie's groin stretched as Lacey tugged in the opposite direction, growling through his clenched jaw.

"Mine! Mine! Mine!"

The rising crescendo tempo of circus music drowned out Lacey's closed-mouth yapping. He crouched down low and sprung back up, simultaneously wrenching his head to one side, ripping the elastic.

Ruff, ruff, ruff!

Lacey dashed around the bedroom on a victory lap, the big black strap-on penis held aloft in his mouth.

"Woo-hoo!"

"Lacey, bring it back!" yelled Gertie, lunging for the jubilant dog.

I'd have laughed my head off if I hadn't been in such a predicament.

Gertie wrenched her wild-eyed focus away from chasing Lacey and turned her attention back to me.

"Don't worry Harry, we'll get to that part later... let's get you naked!"

She ripped my shirt open, spilling buttons on the bed, then grabbed my belt buckle. I kicked my legs out, but she straddled my thighs, pinning me down, despite my bucking bronco attempts to throw her off.

"The more you struggle, the more I like it!" she shouted, grabbing hold of my pants and trousers together, yanking them down my legs.

"Get off me... this isn't fun!" I yelled, trying to back away from the vivid orange bush that danced between Gertie's thighs every time she moved.

"Tut, tut. That tee-shirt has got to come off!"

She tried to tear the cotton away from my shoulders, but couldn't.

"Looks like I'll have to cut it off, yippee!"

The Gertie-clown 'thing' leapt off the bed, opened a drawer and wielded a pair of scissors like a dagger.

"Hold still, my lovely..."

"No, please Gertie you can't, it's..."

"Prepare for a night you'll never forget!"

"Gertie please, I'm begging you, don't. I need to explain..."

I sucked my stomach in as she pulled the tee-shirt taut, snipped the collar then gripped the material in each hand and tore downwards, ripping it off my chest.

"Aaaaarrrhhhh!" she screamed, and clamped her hands to her eyes.

Gertie peeked out from behind her fingers, gasping, the loud circus music still blaring out. She backed away from the bed and stood up, turning to face the wardrobe, her whole body shaking. After almost a minute without moving, she reached out and switched the music off.

"I'm sorry, I didn't know," said Gertie in a quiet, flustered voice.

She turned to face me, unable to pull off a sympathetic expression through the clown makeup.

"What happened?"

"You don't deserve to know. Please untie me. Give me back my dignity."

"It was supposed to be a bit of fun… something different after your boring married sex life."

"How do you know it was boring? Now unshackle me, please."

"Okay, okay."

Gertie began rummaging through a drawer.

"They're here somewhere…"

I watched Gertie spend several minutes searching her bedroom until she turned to face me and shrugged without making eye contact.

"I can't find the keys."

"I'm not playing games, Gertie. Set me free."

"I'm being serious. I've lost them."

Fifteen

Gertie made me wait until after she'd removed the crazy clown outfit, got dressed and reapplied her normal gothic makeup before she called a friend to help. At least she pulled the bed covers over me, tucking the sheet under my chin so only my head, arms and cuffed hands could be seen.

"I'm sorry, I really am," she repeated again and again.

She even tried to kiss me, but I turned my head away. Only Lacey broke the frosty mood, by refusing to hand back his new strap-on stick.

"Lacey, please stay there," pleaded Gertie.

Lacey bounded onto the bed, stepped over me and sat down beside my head, wagging his tail, the big plastic penis still clamped between his teeth.

"Lacey, stay!"

"No way ho-say!"

Lacey dived under the covers, wielding the strap-on willy, flicking the sheet over his head. After another fruitless game of tug, Gertie finally managed to wrestle the penis away from Lacey's jaws by bribing him with a slice of cheese.

*

Help arrived in the form of several of Gertie's

girlfriends, who burst into fits of giggles as they paraded into the bedroom. They held a meeting at the foot of the bed, discussing the best way to free me.

"Fire brigade?" suggested one of the girls.

"Dynamite?"

"Just leave him there, we could use him as a sex slave…"

Several of them took photos with their mobile phones. Fortunately Gertie salvaged the last shred of my dignity by insisting no one lifted the duvet to 'inspect the crown jewels'.

After some discussion, one of the girls rang her boyfriend, who turned up an hour later armed with a toolkit.

"You alright mate? Daft question, eh. Good job you're not local, you'd be laughed out of town."

"Yeah, cheers for that."

The boyfriend turned out to be alright. He cut the chain with a hacksaw, then left the room so I could dress. He returned to carefully saw off the bracelet part of the cuffs.

"One of my mates ended up with Gertie, but he stayed strangely silent. Do you mind if I ask… what's she like in bed?"

I rubbed my sore wrists, free at last.

"She's very… entertaining," I replied.

"Good, good. She gave you the full treatment then?"

"Oh yeah, I had the full performance."

I thanked the guy and yanked the bed covers back to reveal Lacey, stretched out on his side.

He opened a lazy eye at me, grumbled as he stretched out.

"You stopped clowning around now, oh masterful one?"

"C'mon Lacey, time to run away from the circus…"

Lacey jumped off the bed and followed me into the lounge where the girls clapped and wolf-whistled me.

"Ooh, such a cute doggy… no wonder you invited him back. He's such a honey."

I caught an apologetic look from Gertie as we headed out the door.

Lacey and I walked slowly back to the boat through the drizzle. I kept my head down, staring at the pavement, avoiding eye contact with the night-time crowd. I heard some comments about that cute puppy, but I kept on walking.

*

I lay awake in the tiny bow cabin, staring up at the stars through the open hatch.

Lacey had already settled in his usual spot at the bottom of my sleeping bag, his head poking out of the bottom. He snored lightly, his furry warmth comforting, curled up next to my toes.

I felt a few splashes of rain and lowered the hatch until only a small air-gap remained.

Damn you Gertie… why did you have to be so… weird?

*

I woke the next morning to the sound of heavy rain drumming on the fibreglass roof, miserable yet comforting from the cocoon of my sleeping bag.

Lacey grumbled as my feet tickled his tummy and he stretched out, arching his back and pointing his paws. I lifted my head off the pillow and strained my neck to look down at his upside-down head.

"How's your hangover, Lacey?"

His tail twitched within the confines of the sleeping bag.

"I want a coffee and you need a walk, so it's time to brave the rain."

"You go for me. This dog doesn't do wet weather..."

He yawned and held unblinking eye contact with me.

I fumbled around in the sleeping bag for my mobile phone.

"Four text messages, Lacey. Busy night."

Knock, knock, knock.

"Harry, are you in there?"

Lacey twitched, wriggling onto his front, ready to pounce up and bark. I managed to reach down just in time and closed my fingers around his jaws. I raised a finger to my lips as I held his confused gaze.

KNOCK, KNOCK!

"Harry? I'm really sorry for what happened."

A shuffling sound outside, then the boat tipped towards the left and an envelope slid in through the gap under the hatch, landing on my head.

Lacey's body tensed. He tried to make a dash for the envelope, but I kept my hand around his snout. The boat bobbed back upright as Gertie stepped back onto the pontoon.

I waited until her footsteps faded, then picked the envelope off my head and held it at arm's length as I released Lacey. But he leapt up and snatched it from my hand then dived onto the floor, thrashing his head side to side.

"Lacey!" I hissed, hurrying out of the sleeping bag.

I wrestled the soggy paper from his salivating mouth and held it up high, dodging his attempts to jump up at me. I removed the hand-scrawled note and dropped the envelope onto the floor.

Lacey pounced, tearing and shredding until he'd scattered a pulpy mess on the cabin floor, buying me enough time to read the crumpled note.

Dear Harry (and Lacey)
No more clowning around! Sorry to put you through that. I didn't know… (how could I?) It was fun up until that point though, right? What happened to your stomach? Is it painful? I'm sorry I freaked out. I think I understand now why you drink…
Do you fancy getting together again?
I can handle it, if you can. No circus stuff though, that only comes out when I'm really drunk, which by the way is your fault (both of you) for being such a laugh.
Here's my number… call me!
Gertie

PS. I tried to stop the girls posting your photo on their Facebook pages. At least the duvet covered your important bits.

"Let me have it, spoilsport!"
Lacey sat on the floor, wagging his tail, barking at me. I dropped the note, watching him trap it under his paws and rip it with his teeth.

"It's time to move on, Lacey," I said, leaving him shredding paper as I sank down behind the chart table to plan our escape.

*

I immersed myself in the therapeutic analysis of tidal predictions, studying charts and making passage plan calculations. Sailing around the notorious Portland Bill wasn't to be taken lightly, conditions needed to be right.

"Early to bed tonight, Lacey. Four o'clock alarm, we leave at dawn."

Lacey started whining.

"Bring me a cup of tea, I'll see you at nine."
I glanced down at him, lying on the opposite seat.

"That means no booze for either of us until we're safely across Lyme Bay…"

"No booze, no breakfast… what sorta ship you running here, Captain?"

Sixteen

Leaving Weymouth would be a significant undertaking. Once safely round Portland Bill, we'd have approximately forty miles of open water across Lyme Bay. Due to my intention to sail straight across, we'd be as much as twenty miles offshore and out of sight of land. I began making a checklist of provisions to buy and safety precautions to put in place.

Just as I plugged in the rechargeable handheld VHF radio, I remembered the unread text messages on my mobile phone.

All of them from the vet, I noted.

That's odd.

I read the first message, then tabbed up to see the communication chain between us, hoping it would make more sense:

> Text Msg. 20:03
> Lacey has progressed from tea making to Guinness drinking. He told me it was medicinal, for his broken leg. He's getting lots of attention from a slightly scary local lady. Harry

So far, so good.

> Text Msg. 21:38

How much Guinness? Alcohol isn't
good news for small animals! Dog Doc

She seems a bit tetchy. Bad day at work?

Text Msg. 22:57
Don't worry, he's on halfs.

Maybe I shouldn't have been quite so
honest…

Text Msg. 23:16
Are you being serious? You're drunk.
I'm going to bed. Look after Lacey –
properly! DD

…and stopped messaging her…

Text Msg. 00:52
No dunk doc, Gert sa hi, who want
bandy? Pooch hoch, fun. Bye

…because I got the impression she might be
getting a tiny bit annoyed…

Text Msg. 00:54
I'm in Dartmouth this weekend and will
check up on Lacey. Be warned, I can
still remove him from your care so
LOOK AFTER HIM PROPERLY! No
more messages, it's late – GRRRR!

…meaning I should probably have called it a
night…

Text Msg. 02:14
Maad clwn killi sase & cffs. Btch! 8 nch dck Hlp! H

…before it got to this stage.

Text Msg. 02:18
What planet are you on?! It's past 2am. I have to work in afew f****** hours. You f****** idiot!

Oops.

I glanced down at Lacey, unable to stifle a snigger.

"That's another fine mess you've got me into, Muttley…"

*

The alarm echoed around the tiny cabin, which amplified its synthetic tone. I groaned, stretched and eased out of the sleeping bag.

Coffee. Walk dog. Wake up…

Lacey tried to glue himself to the inside of the sleeping bag, so I had to prise him out and carry him ashore for a walk. I ignored his muttering complaints and lowered him onto the ground.

"Harry, it's brass monkey's chunkies out here…"

"We've got a long trip ahead, Lacey. You need to go for a wee."

Lacey sat down, shivering. Despite my insistent tugs on the lead, he refused to move.

Damn dog!

I picked him up and carried him to the nearest patch of grass.

"Okay, I get the hint! But you humans don't understand. I can't wee and poo on demand, it has to be the right place, see. So don't rush my movements."

Thankfully Lacey began sniffing around the grass, eventually settling on the right spot.

"I'm on the job, Harry. You happy now?"

*

"Harry, this ain't cool baby."

"For a small dog, you sure make a lot of funny little noises. There, that should keep you warm."

I stood up to admire Lacey's brightly coloured wool body warmer beneath his lifejacket. He stood there looking miserable, his tail between his legs.

"You're not serious. I can't be seen dressed up like a lap dog poodle. Ugh!"

The engine fired first time and settled into its familiar rumble, setting Lacey off barking.

"Shhh!"

"Shush yourself! It's bloody NOISY!"

Bugger. So much for a quiet departure.

I slipped the bow and stern lines, pushed the tiller over and steered Jessica away from Weymouth's lifting bridge. The street lights faded in the first light of dawn, breaking ahead of us to the east.

We motored past the collection of commercial fishing boats and pleasure craft moored up alongside the quay with the sun rising over the horizon, promising to banish the cool nip in the air.

I stood tall at the helm, grinning as I steered Jessica towards the harbour entrance. Once clear of the stone breakwater, I raised the mainsail, then turned south, setting a course to the left of Portland Harbour's sea wall.

"It's been nearly forty years since you first passed through this tidal gate, Jessica… I bet it's nice to be back on the water, where you belong…"

*

We left the hulking grey Portland stone breakwater behind and began skirting the cliffs, staying the recommended 'biscuit throw' away, as the pilot book had suggested.

The rising sun cast thin shadows across the deck from Jessica's rigging shrouds, the heat seeping through my layers, warming my soul. Lacey stretched out beside me, pressing his paws into my side, his head pointing towards the sun.

I checked my watch, recalling my notes on the best time to round Portland Bill and the hazards the passage presented.

    a) Converging tides
    b) Nasty overfalls
    c) Lobster pots, which could get wrapped around the propeller

I smiled wryly as I mentally checked through the risks, the thought occurring to me that despite the potential danger I faced at sea, given recent events, I might actually be in more jeopardy on land.

"Our speed's increasing, Lacey. The tide is really kicking in now. Are you ready for a nautical roller coaster ride?"

"I'm sunbathing… no communication allowed."

"First lobster pot… left turn, Lacey."

We weaved our way through the pot markers, careful not to drift too far out and risk the wrath of the converging tidal streams. I nervously checked our position and the depth gauge, my senses heightened.

"Seven knots, Lacey, and building…"

This is exactly what you need Harry, I thought, being right here, immersed in the moment…

The lighthouse edged into view as we began to round the underside of Portland Bill, into a deepening swell which helped push us along at 7.8 knots. I caught glimpses of white horses to my far left, prompting me to adjust course, hugging the coast to avoid getting sucked into the overfalls which had pummelled many an unsuspecting boat and skipper.

"Hold your nerve, Harry. Stay tight on the right, head north for a bit longer…"

I glanced at the instruments. Compass: northwest. Depth: 7 metres. Speed: 6.7 knots and falling…

The vast open expanse of Lyme Bay opened up ahead of us, as Portland Bill's notorious frothy, lumpy overfalls fell away in our wake.

"This is living, eh Lacey? Eight hours or so, next stop Dartmouth."

*

Forty miles farther west brought a more spectacular coastline compared to the softer rolling landscape between Poole and Weymouth, where one headland flowed seamlessly into the next with minimum gradient change between.

Making our final approach to Dartmouth after the open sea, without landfall close by, the coastline had undergone a glaring transformation. The rugged cliffs had sharper peaks, lending a stark angular hardness that completely fitted its 'Jurassic Coast' label.

I watched a gap begin to open up between Dartmouth's imposing jagged entrance and the giant Mew Stone rock to our right.

The engine spluttered into life, gurgling seawater through the cooling system, spitting it out in a constant and reassuring cycle.

"Engine seems fine, Lacey. Must be allergic to irate tattooed ex-husbands…"

I checked our course, making sure we left the Mew Stone cardinal markers well to our starboard side as we began shaping our course for the gaping jaws of the black rocky entrance. Lacey began pawing me and whining.

"Nearly there, Lacey. Can you see Dartmouth

Castle? It's up there on the left. On the opposite bank is the town of Kingswear, home to the steam railway. This is a real treat, sailing in here. I'll take you for a long walk as soon as we moor up, okay?"

"That's all nice to hear, Captain. But my bladder is the size of a pregnant milking cow and I need to pee, pronto."

Lacey continued to paw me, so I sat down and helped him up onto my lap, hoping that would placate him and buy me some time before I could take him for a walk.

We rounded One Gun Point, marking the entrance to Warfleet Cove, prompting me to line up Jessica's bow with the castle ruin above Bayard's Cove. After making a right turn, we steered due north until the river widened, revealing Dartmouth town on our left and Kingswear to the right.

Pastel-colour houses clung to the steep valley sides in neat terraces, overlooked by the vast Royal Naval College, high up on the Dartmouth side just before Old Mill Creek. We'd lucked out with our timing to see the steam locomotive pulling vintage coaches out of Kingswear Station. I followed the train's progress for a mile until the puffing clouds of white steam disappeared in the trees and dark green vegetation above Noss Creek.

I sat with Lacey on my lap, surveying the river as I stroked his soft fur and scanned the river for other boat traffic. Glancing between the pilot book and the view ahead, I mentally ticked off landmarks as we headed for the visitors' moorings on the Dartmouth side, opposite Coronation Park.

With plenty of space available, I had an easy job bringing Jessica alongside. A few minutes later, I'd made off the mooring lines and killed the engine.

"We've done it, Lacey. A brand new town to explore…"

Before I could lift Lacey off the boat, he ducked under the guard wire and jumped down, squatting on the pontoon for the longest wee in dog history.

"Ahhhh. That is so much better. Did you say walkies, Harry?"

Mindful of other yachtsmen, I retrieved a bucket from Jessica's cockpit locker and sluiced seawater over the area where Lacey had just been. Our pontoon wasn't connected to the shore by a walkway, so I let Lacey wander away from Jessica, allowing me to slowly rotate through three hundred and sixty degrees, absorbing our surroundings in the Dart valley.

"Hello little one. Where have you sailed in from?" said a friendly voice.

I glanced towards the end of the pontoon, where a grey-haired sailor in his early sixties made a fuss of Lacey. He almost folded his body in half, his tail practically swatting his own face as he showed his appreciation for being stroked so enthusiastically. I wandered over to be sociable.

"Long passage?" asked the sailor.

"Weymouth. We left early this morning."

"Took advantage of the wind shift, eh? Smart move. It's lively for the rest of the week."

I nodded and surveyed the pretty wooden sloop behind him.

"Is she yours?" I asked, admiring the rich wood grain and shiny varnish.

"For my sins. Lovely to look at, but demanding of my time and costly to maintain. Not unlike my wife," he added, a twinkle in his eye.

"But well worth the effort, I'm sure," I replied, liking him immediately.

"Without a doubt. The dog sail with you all the way?"

I nodded, watching Lacey roll over onto his back, kicking his legs as he stretched and made whimpering gurgling noises.

Belly rub, mister… belly rub for the adorable doggy.

Such a floozy!

"Hardy little dog, aren't you?" said the sailor, obliging by tickling Lacey's tummy.

The sailor stood up and began walking back to his boat.

"You've had a long sail, I'll leave you to relax. If you need anything, give us a knock. Name's Bert," he said, waving as he climbed aboard his yacht.

"Thanks, will do. I'm Harry," I replied, returning his friendly smile.

*

I left the kayak tied up on the dinghy pontoon

and carried Lacey up the stone steps, putting him down on the pavement to walk across the road towards the large playing field.

Lacey strained on the lead, tail wagging, tongue lolling from his mouth.

"We'd better be a bit more careful here, with the booze. Small town, local people talk. So no getting me into trouble, okay…"

I crouched down and unclipped the lead.

"Trouble, me? You taken a look in the mirror recently? Let me goooo…."

Lacey heaved, yanking my fingers out from under his collar, running across the field as fast as the plaster cast allowed, its awkwardness gyrating through his body as he barked at the seagulls, which squawked and scattered.

"Come on you feathered freaks!"

I ambled on behind, breathing in the smell and atmosphere of a new port, the sound of Lacey's barking muffled from the far side of the field.

Seventeen

I tied Lacey's lead to a convenient shackle outside the mini-supermarket and left him basking in the sunshine while I went inside to forage for our dinner. It wasn't long before I heard his insistent barking.

"Don't leave me this way... I can't survive without your luuurrrvvve…"

That pesky dog…

I left my half-full basket inside and poked my head around the door.

"What's up monster? I'll be out in a minute," I said to him in a soothing voice.

"What's taking you so long? You hunter-gatherers aren't very efficient. Did evolution pass you by?"

"I won't be long, Lacey. Carry on sunbathing."

A few minutes later he started barking again. I dashed around the aisles as fast as possible and arrived at the checkout queue just as he stopped yapping. Through the glass shop window, I could see a girl stooped down on the pavement stroking Lacey.

"What happened to his paw, mummy?"

"A policeman stepped on it," I said, exiting the shop. Lacey saw me and leapt up, wagging his tail and whining at me.

"Nice try Captain. What you got for me?"

"Ahh. That's terrible. Nasty policeman," said the girl.

I eased Lacey's nose out of the shopping bag and smiled at the girl's mother who stood nearby, pressing buttons on her mobile phone.

"So what was all that noise about, Lacey? I wasn't gone long," I said, trying to sound stern and concerned at the same time.

"Come on Mo, dinnertime," said the woman.

The girl stroked Lacey one last time and accepted her mother's outstretched hand.

"Bye doggy," said the girl, as she walked away.

My eyes lingered for a few seconds on the mother's shapely figure.

"She's got a nice arse, Harry."

The mother flicked her hair then stole a quick look over her shoulder at me, or maybe Lacey. I dropped my eyes to fuss over the dog, but I noticed her blush as she looked away.

"She looked fairly normal, what do you think?" I whispered to Lacey as I untied his lead, raising my eyebrows at his irritable grumbling.

"Sado-masochist, definitely. But you go for it, Harry. Great entertainment for me."

Did Lacey just pull a what-planet-are-you-on face?

We walked off in the opposite direction to the mother's shapely legs, Lacey taking his time to sniff all the lamp posts along the way.

*

I woke with a start, the mobile phone ring

deafening in the confines of the cabin. Lacey grumbled as I reached for the light switch and eased myself out of the sleeping bag.

I ambled through into the main cabin and switched on the chart table light, bathing my hands in a red glow. I snatched the vibrating phone off the chart table and glared at the time: 04:11.

Great.

I hesitated, not recognising the number, wondering if I should I let it go to voicemail.

"Hello?"

"Harry, its Keith," whispered a gravelly voice, making him almost unrecognisable.

"Are you okay?" I whispered back, aware of the other boats moored up in close proximity.

"Yeah, it's been a bit chaotic, you know. How's that dog doing?"

"Okay. We've reached an understanding. He's quite a character."

Keith chuckled softly. "He certainly is. So you're doing exactly what he wants, when he wants to do it?"

"Mostly, yes."

"That's pet ownership, bro. Did you have a good time in Weymouth? You left a bit sharpish."

"Um yeah… interesting nightlife, not really my cup of tea."

"Yeah, I heard there was some clowning around. Nice photo."

I frowned, my brain taking a few seconds to compute.

"You've seen pictures?"

"One or two. Those handcuffs looked tight."

"Why didn't you…"

"Listen, I left in a hurry. Didn't get a chance to ask how you are."

"I'm alright. Good days and bad. Mostly good."

"Okay. Stick to your plan and take it easy. On another matter, Gertie says she's sorry. Not the usual hollow, off the cuff bullshit. *Really sorry.* You understand?"

I took a long, deep, unsteady breath.

"Okay, but how do you…"

"All that *stuff* happened a long time ago. There's no shame or embarrassment, it is what it is. You're on the right course now. Don't stray from it, promise me."

"I'll try, but…"

"Try not, do must!" he said, mimicking an angry Yoda voice.

"You crazy fool."

"Better believe it, bro. Oh, watch out for Alice, she's pretty pissed off. Enjoy the fun times ahead."

"Keith, where are you…"

His voice hung around in my head, hazy outlines of words dispersing with the phone's continuous dial tone, leaving me with many unanswered questions.

*

I slept in late the next morning, woken prematurely by a strange hot, wet sensation around my toes.

"Ugh, that's disgusting Lacey!"

I pulled my feet away from Lacey's tongue and blocked his normal crawl up inside the sleeping bag routine. But he diverted, squeezed out of the hole at the bottom and bounded over my crunched-up body, heading for my face. I wrestled him away in a wake-up-and-feed-me play fight, then hauled myself out of bed to put the kettle on.

Warmth peeked through the washboards, prompting me to slide the main hatch open, revealing bright sunshine and a blue sky.

At last, a proper summer.

A vague recollection drew me to the chart table, where my eyes rested on a post-it-note and the single handwritten word: 'Alice.'

I repeated the name in my head.

One of Gertie's friends?

Or Keith's?

How did Keith know so much about what I've been up to?

I pondered these questions as I stirred scrambled eggs in a pan on the stove.

"The vet!" I shouted, making Lacey jump up and bark at me.

"Where? She's not poking around down there again, or she'll get the old squeeze and squirt routine…!"

"Shhh, Lacey. It's okay. I've just remembered, that's all."

"Bloody hell Harry, why'd you punish me like that? Jeez… can't an old dog get some kip without the pet-police spazzing out?"

I knelt down to try and comfort the agitated dog.

"The vet's going to visit us, that's all... is it Lacey dinner time?"

That calmed him down. He immediately sat on the floor, eyes fixated on me, licking his lips.

I finished cooking the eggs, removed the bacon from the oven and split the food between my plate and his bowl.

"That'll keep you quiet for a while," I said, placing his breakfast on the floor next to a bowl of water.

"Yum, yum, my favourite. Outta my way, hungry dog coming through!"

Eighteen

There's something different about my surroundings, I pondered. What is it?

I stretched out, luxuriating in the soft linen that smelt fresh and clean, not musty like the boat.

That's odd, there's no bundle of soft fur beside my feet.

I blinked my eyes open, the familiar post-alcohol woozy sensation saturating my senses.

There's a white painted ceiling above me.

I turned to face right, my eyes aching in the sunshine flooding through the thin curtains. Cream painted walls each side of the window, neutral colour furnishings. Neat, tidy and functional. Occasional touches of colour like the floral duvet. Overall, a warm and inviting room. I turned my head to my left. Long curly auburn hair lay between the duvet and a pillow.

Not again, Harry…

I carefully lifted up the duvet just enough so I could peer down below and confirm what I already suspected.

Yup, you're naked.

I twitched my toes.

No dog.

I gingerly lifted the duvet a little higher. Her hair spilled over pale freckled shoulders. I studied the curvy naked body of my bedmate and allowed my gaze to wander down to the smooth curvature of her bottom.

What to do…?

As carefully as possible, I eased out of the bed and laid the duvet back behind me. Glancing around the room, I spotted my clothes hanging on the back of a chair. I slipped them on, then crept to the door and carefully opened it.

The same neutral painted walls welcomed me into the hallway, a night light enhancing the soft tone, becoming redundant now as sunlight bathed the perimeter of a blind. Of the three landing doors, two hung partially open. I found the bathroom first, quickly taking care of the need for a wee. That done, I eased the second door open and peered into a child's bedroom. I began to retreat, but spotted a pair of chocolate-brown ears twitch on the pillow beside the child's head.

Lacey opened a lazy eye. He yawned, then pulled himself out from under the duvet and dragged his long body across the bed as he stretched.

"Come on Lacey," I whispered.

Lacey plonked down onto the floor, shook himself and sauntered over to me, his head down, tail wagging enthusiastically.

"Nice pull Harry, I like it here."

"Where's your lead?"

"Not my department."

I instinctively checked my pockets, but it wasn't there.

"I'm going back to bed. Bring me a cuppa tea and bacon sarnie in an hour…"

"Lacey," I hissed, reaching into the room to grab his tail as he turned and walked back towards the bed.

I scooped a hand under Lacey's belly and lifted him up, ignoring his grumbling objections as I retreated, pulling the door gently shut.

"Spoilsport."

I stood in the hallway with Lacey in my arms, listening to the quiet house and trying to order my thoughts into some sort of logical sequence.

What's your plan now, Harry? Do you really want an awkward 'morning after' conversation?

Trying to regulate my heavy breathing, I slunk down the stairs, cringing when they creaked. We paused in the entrance lobby long enough for me to catch a reflection of myself in the mirror. I stared at my dishevelled hair, bleary eyes and sallow skin. And yet, did I detect a mischievous smile twitching on my lips?

You're a tart, Harry Straight, I silently mouthed at my reflection.

I glanced down, drawn to a framed photograph on a table. The attractive mother cuddled her daughter on a beach. I recognised them from the supermarket the previous day.

She's an attractive lady, I thought. Why are you running away…? I opened the front door and carried Lacey into the warmth of bright sunshine.

…because you have to.

Nineteen

I hurried away from the house, heading downhill. Lacey wriggled in my arms.

Damn, what did I do with his lead?

Improvisation seemed the only logical solution, so I used my belt, undoing Lacey's collar and refastening it through the buckle. I scrunched up the slack jeans material around my waist in one hand and grasped the makeshift lead with the other.

We found some grass on the verge, allowing Lacey to take care of his morning toilet routine, leaving me to search my memories and try to piece together how I'd ended up in a strange woman's house.

"Coffee is what I need, Lacey. And a big fried breakfast."

*

It soon became apparent that we'd ended up on the Kingswear side of the River Dart, which meant either I'd paddled the kayak over last night or had taken the small floating bridge car ferry. I felt pretty sure I'd started the evening on the Dartmouth side of the river, so it seemed a fair bet that I'd come across on the ferry.

How on earth did I get into all these odd situations?

The answer to my question began whining and pawing my leg. At this time in the morning, with a walk already taken care of, it could only mean one thing.

"Feed me. Feed me. Feed me…"

I squatted down next to Lacey, cringing as my joints clicked with a dull ache.

"Okay little one, I'm peckish too. My tummy feels like we may have skipped dinner, so I'll get you some food soon, okay?"

*

The ferry had already begun operating, so Lacey and I tagged on behind the three cars making the short journey across the river back to Dartmouth.

I caught a wink from the deckhand. I attempted a smile, then looked away over the sparkling river. A lovely old pilot cutter motored past us, heading out of the harbour. Despite the warmth of the early morning, the crew wore full wet weather gear and lifejackets, no doubt anticipating a blustery sail. I waved as they passed behind the ferry, rewarded with a cheerful acknowledgement from the helmsman.

The floating bridge ferry shuddered and scraped to a halt on the Dartmouth slipway. The ramp lowered with a metallic rattle, allowing the cars to trundle off the ferry. I followed them up the slope, taking care not to slip on the seaweed left by the falling tide.

I found a quirky breakfast café less than one hundred yards from the ferry, tucked under a row of arches. Lacey and I settled into a table outside in their dog friendly courtyard. I ordered a strong black coffee and full English breakfast, adding an extra sausage and slice of bacon for Lacey, already pawing me and licking his lips in anticipation.

After an excellent breakfast, I ordered a takeaway coffee and wandered along the quay with Lacey, enjoying watching the harbour wake up and come to life. I stopped at a bench above the water taxi jetty and sat down to bask in the sunshine.

I peered through the coffee steam at Kingswear, trying to retrace my steps and pick out the house where I'd spent the night.

"It's gorgeous, don't you think?"

Lacey looked up at me, his bottom jaw dropping into a light pant. I draped my arm around him, casting my eye across the water to the boats moored up mid-stream.

"So many hopes and dreams floating out there, eh boy…"

*

Lacey and I ambled along the quay, enabling me to scan the pontoons below for my kayak. We passed the small drying inner harbour where open day boats lay on the mud, waiting for the next high tide.

The tide's ebb and flow could be compared to

life's ups and downs, I reflected, wondering how much we're all affected by the moon's phases. We're all seventy per cent water, after all.

Wow, Harry, that's pretty deep for this early in the morning…

I stopped walking and turned back to face downstream towards the harbour entrance, where sunshine now bathed the Dartmouth side, burning off the last patches of mist lingering over the castle.

What is it… hovering at the edge of my subconscious?

The sensation of her touch, on my skin. That look in her eyes: a mixture of concern and sympathy. Or perhaps, *compassion.* Her fingertips had hovered a few millimetres from touching my tummy, trying to understand.

"What happened?" she'd asked, her soft voice barely audible.

But no words came, they stuck in my throat, too painful to speak aloud. I'd shaken my head, wanting to explain, but failed. So she'd simply held me, our naked bodies pressed together yet remaining platonic.

I felt bile rising in my throat. The nausea drew my thoughts away from her bedroom, back to a cynically tainted reality. I didn't make it to the nearest rubbish bin in time and had to crouch down close to the harbour wall as I scrunched my eyes shut and threw up.

When I opened my eyes, I saw Lacey perched precariously over the quay, licking the remnants of my breakfast off the stone wall. I gagged, almost sick again.

"Ugh, Lacey! Have you no dignity?"

I pulled on his lead, practically dragging him away from the edge.

"Are you okay?" said a wheezing voice.

I fished a tissue out of my pocket and wiped my mouth, then glanced up at the elderly gentleman propped up by his walking stick. I nodded and absently let go of Lacey's makeshift lead to sit down on the nearest bench, resting my elbows on my knees, taking deep sporadic breaths. When I looked up my heart missed a beat; Lacey had gone.

"He's here, I've got him," said the gentleman, holding the belt lead in one hand, stroking Lacey with the other.

"Thank you," I said in a croaky voice.

He smiled and shuffled over to the bench to sit down next to me. Lacey jumped up and climbed onto his lap then turned towards me, flicked his paws up onto my shoulder and poked his wet nose into my face.

"Thanks Lacey. Sicky kisses, lovely."

I scooped him off the elderly gentleman's lap.

"Sorry about that, he's forgotten his manners."

"Don't fret, he's okay. I had several, over the years. The last one was such a character... he ruined me."

I nodded, glancing down at Lacey, now sat on my lap surveying the river.

"He's my first... and last," I said.

"They do that, get under your skin."

I felt his frail hand rest gently on my shoulder.

"Are you okay?"

"Hard to say, truthfully."

He turned away, looked out over the harbour. We sat there in companionable silence for a few minutes.

"My wife, she used to love this place. It's always alive with activity, whatever the season. It's the simplest things sometimes that are the most rewarding."

He turned to face me.

"She used to say: if you've got your health, you're rich."

I held his gaze for a moment, then looked away and took a slow deep breath.

"True enough," I said quietly.

"How are you feeling?" he asked.

"Better, thank you."

He stood slowly, using his stick to balance on, a trace of pain flickering across his face.

"That's my morning exercise. Time to read the paper and enjoy a cup of tea. Take care of your furry friend."

"I will. Thanks again."

He nodded, held eye contact for a moment, then began to hobble away, pausing to half-turn.

"Every day is a bonus," he said, nodding a goodbye.

I watched him lean on the stick in time with his shuffling steps. I didn't look away from him until he'd crossed the road and turned the corner.

*

Left in quiet contemplation, I allowed my

thoughts to drift to Jessica. What were the conditions like the last time she'd been here in Dartmouth, nigh on forty years ago? It was an obvious stop-off point when transiting the coast between Falmouth and Poole, so without checking the logbook I felt confident my father would have pulled in here.

I reached into my pocket, withdrew my phone and scrolled through my contacts until I found the right number.

"Sandy Shores Nursing Home, can I help you?"

"That sounds like Anna. It's Harry Straight."

"Hello Mister Straight, are you keeping well?"

"I am. How is he?"

"Not such a good day today, difficult for him to connect. It's the slow decline we talked about, I'm afraid. How's your progress?"

"I'm in Dartmouth for a few days waiting out the weather. Still on target for his birthday."

"Good. I'm sure your visit will help."

I thanked Anna and hung up, toying with the phone.

"Difficult to know, Lacey, but I have to try, right?"

*

Lacey and I enjoyed a relaxed paddle back to Jessica, the kayak bobbing over the wake from river tour boats and passing yachts. The water rippled around us, sparkling, promising more adventures.

Back on board Jessica, I settled down on the cabin's port settee berth and attempted to stave off my hangover with a large glass of water. I picked up the logbook, curious as to what my father had made of Dartmouth all those years ago. I flicked through the pages until I found the correct entry.

2nd day of June, Nineteen Seventy-Seven
Lined up on the day mark, east of the entrance. Left Checkstone buoy to port. Sails down, motored into the deep fjord entrance and protective valley sides. Anchored off Kingswear Station to resupply. Hard weather closing in. Moving upstream to Dittisham imminently to ride it out. Another disrupted night's sleep. Keith never cried like the new baby. Mother reasons it's teething. I disagree. It's becoming apparent that he's a difficult and demanding infant. Sleeping solution for Captain and crew required as matter of urgency. Tough love is what that boy needs.

A shudder twitched up my spine, causing me to jolt upright from my comfortable reading position, startling Lacey who scrabbled off my lap and moved to a more stable perch.

"Oy, mister! Let sleeping dogs snooze away their hangover, comprende?"

I stroked Lacey to calm his grumbling and replaced the logbook in the boat library.

That generation, so hardened.

I felt the boat heel over as a gust shook the mast and whistled through the rigging wires.

"I think we'll head upstream, Lacey, it'll be more comfortable. We're a bit exposed here. And according to the pilot book, there's a smashing pub nearby. What do you think, you getting thirsty?"

Twenty

I pulled the collar of my sailing jacket up, shielding my neck from the cool breeze. Overhead, the clear blue sky from the morning had clouded over, harbouring patches of dark grey.

"I think we'll make it before the rain comes, Lacey. Lots of nasty weather later…"

Lacey stretched out beneath the cockpit coaming behind me, sheltering from the wind.

"What about my tan, Harry?"

I pulled the throttle back to half power, grasped the tiller and smiled at Lacey's doggy grumbling sounds. He looked happy enough, occasionally opening an eye when I spoke to him, or to consider the relevance of a change in engine tone.

I eased the throttle into neutral and watched the upper chain ferry trundle across the river in front of us. It passed by with a mix of whirling electronic beeping, clanking chain and diesel engine throb, accompanied by silent pulsating strobe lights that cut through the increasing gloom.

With the ferry safely behind us, we motored past Old Mill Creek and the marina at Lower Noss point, the water flattening off as the river narrowed, protected now from the blustery south-westerly. The gradual left hand curve in the river slowly revealed the red topped Anchor Stone marker pole, standing as a warning, mid-stream. The rocks below the marker had been largely hidden under the rising tide, but still lurked, waiting for an unsuspecting sailor. I adjusted course to leave the Anchor Stone well to our left and lined up Jessica's bow on a spare blue visitor's mooring buoy.

"See that boathouse to our right, Lacey? That used to belong to Agatha Christie. It's part of the Greenway estate, where she spent her summers writing."

I glanced behind me at Lacey's half-open eye. He blinked at me, then rolled onto his side. By now we'd drawn parallel to Greenway Quay, where a vintage coach waited to collect National Trust visitors from visiting Agatha's house.

Ahead and to our left, the pretty village of Dittisham offered welcoming lights, cosy beacons to guide us through the gathering storm clouds which drew daylight to a premature, dreary close.

I throttled back to neutral, letting Jessica coast, aware of the Harbour Master launch approaching from my left. A jolly woman in her fifties with 'Shannon' on her name badge pulled alongside.

"We're going to get busy, with the weather closing in. So pick up a free visitor's buoy by all means, but be prepared to have other vessels rafted alongside. I'll be back to collect your mooring fees in the morning."

I thanked Shannon and took a moment to scan around the spare moorings to try and pick the most sheltered spot.

"Ooh, you're a sweetheart, aren't you…?"

Lacey poked his head above the cockpit coaming then pushed up and shook himself. He trotted over to Shannon and ducked his head under the guard wire to accept some affectionate stroking. It still amazed me, the effect Lacey had on the opposite sex.

I waved my thanks to Shannon as she headed off towards another arriving yacht and steered towards a buoy near the Dittisham shore, around a hundred metres from the village pontoon.

"Time to batten down the hatches, Lacey…"

*

Safely tied up to the mooring buoy, I made off all the halyards to stop them rattling on the mast and retreated into the cabin before the first spots of rain gathered intensity. After dinner I planned a short paddle ashore for a couple of pints of real ale, after which a snug berth for the night to ride out the storm beckoned.

Lovely.

*

Instinctively, I checked my mobile phone before we left the boat. It wasn't showing any signal, so I left it on the chart table.

With a combination lock on Jessica's main hatch, I didn't even have to carry a key. This thought reminded me of something a friend once said to me. He'd suggested that the complexity of someone's life, and therefore their stress level, could be determined by how many keys they possessed. None now, in my case.

"How's that for two fingers up at society, Lacey?"

But Lacey ignored me, as he usually did, so I busied myself sorting out the kayak for our trip ashore.

If you want stimulating conversation, I thought, best go to the pub…

I checked myself, a cold sweat threatening to flush through my pores as a flashback of Gertie in her clown outfit assaulted my thoughts. I shuddered and lowered the kayak over the side of the boat, just managing to grab Lacey before he leapt on board.

"Whoa, easy boy, no rush."

"Speak for yourself, Captain. It's beer time!"

*

The wind helped push us towards the village pontoon, making for an easy paddle despite the restriction of my bulky sailing jacket.

"Hold on Lacey," I said, leaning forwards and crunching my legs up to support him against my chest as another strong gust wailed through the moored yachts, making their rigging sing, buffeting the lightweight kayak.

We nudged through the other dinghies tethered to the pontoon and I tied the kayak with a decent length of rope. The light from the large pub window drew us to land, the condensation hinting at a warm welcome inside. Rain began to splatter down, making the rickety wood pontoon slippery underfoot. I slowed down, keeping a careful eye on Lacey as he disappeared onto the small section of beach.

I pulled my hood tighter as the rain lashed down in squally gusts, forcing me to stoop lower on the pontoon, raindrops pummelling my waterproofs.

Poor Lacey, he'd be soaked.

Armed with a plastic bag, I followed Lacey onto the narrow strip of beach to clear up after him, keen to hurry onwards to the welcoming bustle of the pub.

Lacey shivered, soggy and bedraggled in my arms. I hunched over in an effort to shield him from the worst of the weather as I opened the door to The Ferry Boat Inn. I immediately experienced an intoxicating concoction of sensations: the feeling of warmth, sound of conversations, whiff of spilt beer, smell of hot food and wet musty clothing.

Despite the amount of people inside, I managed to find a small corner table and hung my wet weather gear off the back of the chair, close enough to the open fire to feel its warmth.

"Foul night to be on a boat," said the world-weary chap at the table next to me as he sucked on an empty pipe.

"It's really coming in now," I agreed, peering through the cluster of legs to see where Lacey had got to.

"The dog's alright love, he's sat by the fire drying off. What can I get you?" said a barmaid.

The perfect welcome.

*

Despite being a small village pub that ordinarily might be a bit indifferent to non-residents, everyone seemed really friendly. Maybe the regular visiting yacht crews contributed to the relaxed atmosphere.

I checked in with Lacey, happy to see him stretched out on the hearth. He opened a lazy eye and flicked his tail when I tickled behind his ears. But he didn't seem interested in the water bowl I placed by his side.

"A proper seadog, that one: dutiful on board ship, but happier on land. And by the looks, prefers a drop of hops."

I glanced over at a rutted and weather-worn bearded face with ruddy cheeks and clear blue-grey eyes.

"I'm trying to get him to cut down," I replied, stroking Lacey's warm damp fur.

The fire flickered as the front door opened, buffeting the pub with a blast of chilly moist wind, signalling the arrival of another saturated boat crew. Lacey licked my hand and lay back down, stretching his paws towards the dancing flames as he closed his eyes and sighed happily.

*

Unusually, I found myself nursing the same pint for a long time, happy to sit quietly in the corner, alone with my thoughts. Perhaps Lacey's contentment to flop in front of the fire and not pester me for a slurp of my beer set the tone for the evening.

The taste of the alcohol carried me back over the last twenty-four hours. Vague, fuzzy images flickered past like the remnants of a surreal dream, well on their way to vaporising once I'd remembered enough, with no rewind button. If I didn't stay focussed, the missing segments of my recollections and the sensations that accompanied them would be lost forever in my subconscious, tantalisingly and frustratingly unreachable. So I picked up a pen, opened the logbook and began to write.

The same woman. The one from the supermarket with the young girl, her daughter I think. That look we'd exchanged, no more than a few seconds and yet… a connection. Her eyes had reached into me…
Catching the bus to Slapton Sands with Lacey, excited about a long walk in the sunshine. A long tranquil ten mile amble along the coast path back to Dartmouth. Stopping for sandwiches on a cliff with spectacular views out to sea, the calm before the impending storm.

The last mile, trudging past Dartmouth Castle. Hot from our epic walk, stopping at the small beach at Warfleet Cove so I could let Lacey paddle in the cool water. Removing my socks and shoes, scooping Lacey up, gently lowering him into the water, chuckling at his mid-air doggy paddle. My laughter at his theatrics, echoed in a higher pitch shriek further up the beach. Turning to see the same little girl running to the edge of the water, her bucket and spade cast aside. Lacey doggy-paddling in the water, nose up like a periscope. His body rotation, tail swishing side to side like an erratic rudder. Paws scrabbling at the sloping sand. Hauling himself out of the water. Shaking himself off, scampering across the beach to snatch the shaft of the spade off the shingle, barking as he ran. Specks of sand on his nose. Lacey holding the spade above his head, brandishing it like a hard-won trophy. The little girl shouting and screeching in delight at Lacey's bravado antics.

My conversation with her mum, starting with an apology for Lacey's naughtiness. Watching together as the little girl chased Lacey, trying to get her spade back.

The mum introduced herself as Mary and her daughter, Imogen, or 'Mo' for short. I did my best to rescue Mo's spade, but Lacey pranced and dodged, enjoying the

game and refusing to surrender.
Eventually Lacey dropped the spade on the sand by my feet, his tongue lolling at the side of his mouth as he dug a hole, flicking sand up through his hind legs. Mo's approaching dinnertime prompting the awkward moment of their departure. How to 'leave' things, made easier by Lacey, almost as if by telepathy taking his cue to start pawing me to feed him. Walking back together, engrossed in conversation about her life in Kingswear and mine living on a small sailing boat. Losing time.

My offer to buy her a drink later that evening, if she found herself on the Dartmouth side of the river. Or perhaps some other time, if too short notice for a babysitter. Parting at the floating bridge ferry near the harbour mouth, going our separate ways with a smile and formal handshake.

Later at the pub, its name escaping me, only its green window framed façade vivid in my mind. Another boisterous evening with Lacey, thirsty after his long walk, attracting random conversations with strangers. Until Mary gingerly opened the pub door and her eyes found mine.

Easy conversations over a drink or two about nothing in particular, the tone light and engaging… Slipping her hand in mine as Lacey and I walked her to the last ferry of the night to Kingswear. Waiting at the ramp as the tugboat pushed the floating bridge ferry towards us.

Decision time…

Preparing to say goodbye, my surprise and agreement when she offered Lacey and I coffee and a comfy couch for the night.

Squeezing my hand when I asked, 'Are you sure?' stroking my cheek, kissing me lightly on the lips. The hint of her delicate perfume intoxicating, my lips tingling as we parted.

A rug and bowl of water for Lacey, laid out on the kitchen floor. The barely touched coffee cup reclaimed from my hand. Leading me upstairs to her bedroom. My awkwardness as I stood there, needing to tell her, unsure how I could do so delicately. Her apprehensive expression when I'd explained about my tummy. Her gasp as I removed my tee-shirt. My familiar lurch in self-confidence at how repulsive my body looked.

I jolted in my seat, the sensation of falling forwards saved by the shock of Lacey's paws on my lap as he scrambled up to lick my face.

Spluttering, twisting away from him, I became aware of people peering at me from behind their drinks, trying to mask their inquisitiveness. I dropped my eyes, wiped away Lacey's slobber.

Why are you reacting like this? You've hardly had anything to drink…

I glanced up as a hand placed a full pint of ale on the table next to my empty glass.

"Maybe this will help, maybe not. But you look like you could do with it."

I looked up into the weather-worn bearded face of the old sailor.

"Thank you, that's very kind..." I said absently, still trying to get to grips with the reality of the moment, the reclaimed sensations of last night slipping away.

He reached out to stroke Lacey who strained against my hands to sniff out the fresh pint of beer.

I watched the old sailor shuffle past me, his wife following as they picked their way through the pub, heading for the door. Around me the volume of normal conversations seemed to ramp up a notch and curious eyes moved on. I placed a shaky hand on the cool glass and took a long drink, then I stood and headed for the bar to ask for a bowl.

Twenty One

I found myself in the unusual position of leaving before closing time. I watched Lacey's paws patter in puddles, sniffing out his perfect wee spot as I realised I had absolutely no intention of returning to the cosy pub to finish my drink.

It struck me as an odd decision, but in a good way. Progress, perhaps…

I turned my collar up against the gusting wind, glad the rain had abated for the time being.

"We'll head back downstream tomorrow. Maybe we'll go and find Mary, what do you think?" I said to Lacey, ignoring the fact that even if he could understand me, he wouldn't have heard me above the howling wind.

I turned away from the beach and stepped up onto the pontoon, now partly resting on the sand due to the low tide. Lacey scampered after me, his paws skidding on the slippery walkway.

Paddling the kayak back to the boat proved to be a hard slog against the gusting headwind, which kept buffeting the kayak off course, forcing me to work hard. I focussed on Jessica's anchor light to guide me, yet couldn't be certain we were on the correct course as there appeared to be two other boats rafted up alongside her.

I kept paddling hard, finally arriving twenty minutes later, breathless and aching.

The other boats had moored up on Jessica's port side, both around thirty-five feet long, dwarfing Jessica's modest length.

"I'm getting too old for all this, Lacey," I said, casting my eye over the other yachts, one of which looked like a training boat judging by the website address on the mainsail cover.

I scooped Lacey up under Jessica's guard wires and heaved the kayak aboard, lashing it securely on deck. Having checked the fenders between Jessica and the training boat, we settled down inside Jessica's snug cabin and prepared for a relatively early night.

I switched out the light and eased my cold feet down to the bottom of the sleeping bag where Lacey waited to warm them up. Despite the wind droning through the three sets of rigging and Jessica's mast shaking with every gust, I quickly drifted off to sleep.

*

Lacey's growl woke me, my toes sensing his body tense beneath the sanctuary of the sleeping bag. I forced my eyes open, my ears tuning in to the steady drone of an outboard engine, working hard against the tide.

The engine tone eased off, making the distant voices seem louder.

"Other way… other… oops," said a voice outside the boat.

Jessica shuddered, the bump exaggerated, echoing like a drum inside the cabin.

Lacey squeezed out of the access hole at the bottom of the sleeping bag and stood to attention, barking. I heard stifled giggling and more intermittent engine revs from outside.

"Shh… it's okay Lacey, they're just going back to their boat…"

"Let's be havin' ya. Come on, you soggy seaweed sailors!"

I tried to gather Lacey into my arms to calm him down, but he wriggled away, jumped off the bed and pawed the door.

"It's okay, Lacey."

I reached down between the vee berths and scooped him up. He sat on my lap, growling, his head twitching, eyes darting around the cabin. The outboard engine noise died away, leaving hushed voices and creaking mooring lines on the boat next to us. Jessica dipped as the crew climbed aboard their yacht. Footsteps padded across the other boat's deck and a companionway hatch squeaked open.

The voices died away and Jessica stopped rocking. Only the howling wind remained, moaning sporadically through the rigging wires, a soulful drone in the stormy night.

Lacey's tense muscles begin to relax, but he continued to listen.

"At ease, soldier. Sentry duty's over," I said, unzipping the sleeping bag and lifting the corner to allow him to crawl back in.

Lacey settled by my feet with a grumble.

I sank down onto the foam mattress, relaxing into a slumber as I listened to the wind blowing hard outside.

Knock, knock, knock.

"Hello... um, *Jessica*. Sorry to disturb you..." said an apologetic voice.

Lacey scurried out of the sleeping bag, bounded up to the space beside my head and yapped, imitating a rock concert drum roll, inches from my ear.

I winced, clutched my palms to my head and reluctantly prised myself out of the sleeping bag. I stumbled through the main cabin, nearly tripping over Lacey who bounced around my feet, barking relentlessly.

I slid the hatch open and poked my head up into the blustery night.

"Hi, really sorry to disturb you, but do you have any sugar please?" said the girl.

I recognised her from the pub. Late teens or early twenties, difficult to be precise due to the hood pulled down over her ears and high-collar sailing jacket.

"Sugar?" I replied, deadpan.

"Yes. For coffee."

I felt Lacey bang into my leg as he leapt onto the companionway steps and tried to haul himself into the cockpit.

"Just a sec..." I said, reaching down to gather Lacey in my arms and lift him up onto the deck.

"See, nothing to be afraid of."

"Ahh, what a cute dog..."

The girl ducked her head down into the training boat.

"Sam, you've got to see this puppy," she said in a muffled voice.

Lacey scrabbled in my arms, desperate to go and say hello, but I held on, reluctant to let him out on the slippery deck without his lifejacket. I grasped his collar and climbed out into the cockpit so he could sniff the girl's outstretched hand. An older girl, probably in her late twenties, joined the first up on the training yacht's deck, both of them doting on Lacey.

"I'll get you some sugar if you'll hold onto the dog?"

"Of course, what's his name?" asked the older girl.

"He's called Lacey."

I passed Lacey between the boats into the girl's outstretched arms.

"Hey, Harry. What's this, pass the pooch? I ain't that sorta guy…"

"Ahh, he's scared of the water… we're Samantha and Tilly. Sam for short."

"Harry," I said.

I left the girls making a fuss of Lacey and disappeared into Jessica's cabin to find the sugar. By the time I reappeared, the first girl, Tilly, sat in the cockpit cradling Lacey while Samantha tickled his belly.

That dog, I chuckled, he pulled every time…

"Here, is that enough?"

I handed a zip lock bag containing several tablespoons of sugar over the guard rails.

"Lovely, thank you. I don't suppose you'd like to join us all… for coffee?" said Samantha.

"Oh, um… that's a nice offer but…"

"Don't say no, Harry. We're holding Lacey here as a hostage!"

"And we could use your help… the boys are feeling a bit outnumbered."

The girls giggled as Lacey grumbled in Tilly's arms.

"Harry, why the hesitation, fella? Have I taught you nothing?"

"See, Lacey's saying you should come. The heating's on and it's nice and warm, down below…"

I pondered the invitation, finally shrugging. "Okay."

"Attaboy Harry. Woo-hoo!"

*

I descended into the warmth of the training boat and turned to face the open plan layout, which had a chart table on the left and a large galley to my right, where a lady in her late forties poured hot water into coffee cups. Ahead of me, a double leaf table stood between two opposing C-shaped seating areas, where several other inquisitive faces greeted my arrival.

"Hi, I'm Harry," I said, sweeping my eyes around the group.

The lady in the galley offered her hand.

"I'm Trudy."

We shook hands, giving me a precious few seconds to try and work out what I'd just walked into. There appeared to be an underlying awkwardness in the cabin, but that may just have been my impromptu arrival.

"Hey Harry, how old is Lacey?" asked Tilly.

"Older than he looks, but he lies about his age."

The younger of the two men sat around the table half-stood to shake my hand, his knees pinned awkwardly under the table.

"I'm Ben. Nice to meet you," he said.

"Rob," said his male colleague, sat between Tilly and another girl in her early twenties.

The remaining two girls introduced themselves as Natasha and Laura.

"Shuffle up everyone. Harry, please sit here," said Trudy as she distributed steaming cups of coffee around the table.

"Jessica is a pretty little boat. Do you sail her single-handed?" asked Tilly.

"Unless you count Lacey, yes. But he's more of a social secretary than a proper crewmate."

That raised a few smiles. I squeezed behind the table and sat down next to Samantha, then glanced around the cabin. Spacious and modern compared to Jessica, but not as homely.

Trudy shuffled in opposite me and leaned over to lift the lid on a centre section of the table, from which she pulled out a bottle of rum.

"Liqueur coffee anyone?"

Cheery and enthusiastic reactions encouraged Trudy to top up the coffee cups with generous measures of rum. Outside, the wind picked up, pushing the boat over ten degrees. The mast shuddered, rigging screeched and bucketfuls of rain pummelled the deck. Hands grabbed sliding cups as the table tilted.

"Whoa… it's picking up again."

The conversation paused as we all exchanged nervous glances.

You're the newcomer here, I told myself. Try to help nudge the conversation along…

"Where are you guys all heading?" I said to the group.

"Ben and I are en-route from Plymouth to the Isle of Wight. I'm meeting my wife and kids there for a week's sailing around the Solent," said Rob.

"Then I'm heading home on the train. We got to Dittisham just after the girls," said Ben.

I nodded and sipped my coffee, wincing at its potency.

"We're on a week's training course," said Trudy. "If this weather blows through as planned, we'll sail to Salcombe tomorrow, then head east again to Weymouth and back home to Lymington. We bumped into the boys earlier this evening by fighting them off this mooring…"

"It's called chivalry, letting you go first…" said Rob.

"Yeah, right. We beat you fair and square and only agreed to share so we didn't have to pump up our dinghy," Tilly added.

"Whoa, easy there shipmates. The Harbour Master instructed you to allow us alongside and you wenches were too lazy to blow up your own bloody dinghy!" said Ben.

"No, no, nooo," said Tilly, banging her cup theatrically on the table. "The boys here are lightweights and needed a bit of ballast so their dinghy wouldn't be blown all over the place. We came to their rescue and offered our services."

I found my head ping-ponging between their good-natured comments, relaxing into their company.

"Rubbish! You bought your passage ashore in our dinghy with a round of drinks…" said Rob.

"Yeah, pity they didn't realise it was a one way ticket…" Ben chimed in.

Tilly turned to me. "Which is how we all ended up here," she said. "The cheeky bastards insisted we renegotiate the return trip in exchange for a cup of coffee and a shot of rum."

"Easy there, less of the cheeky… we just saw a business opportunity…"

"Business opportunity, my arse!"

"You're lucky girls, we could have made you scrub the deck."

"Hence the sugar," I said, my head fuzzy at having to keep up with their banter.

"Exactly. Here we all are," said Trudy, exchanging eye contact with Rob.

A hush descended.

"So, Harry. Have you ever been to a swingers party?" said Tilly, poker faced.

I felt everyone's eyes on me, watching my reaction. Next to Tilly, Samantha stifled a drunken snigger. Tilly used her elbow to nudge her, maintaining a neutral expression.

"No. Have you?" I replied.

"What do you think this is, *sugar?*"

"I'm not sure I'm ready to swap Lacey with any of you," I replied, glancing around the table.

"Good answer, Harry. Very… diplomatic."

"Do you always throw social hand grenades at strangers?" I replied.

"Of course. It's a character test," said Tilly.

"Yours or mine?"

"Ah, good point. Actually, I'm intrigued when I see boats rafted up alongside each other like this."

"In what way?" said Rob.

"It must go on, right? I mean, boat people get bored, just like everyone else."

Tilly leaned forwards and scanned the other faces around the table, then lowered her voice.

"What if… dodgy stuff does go on? Maybe there's a secret code."

"A sign saying: throw your boat keys in here?" giggled Samantha.

"Nah, too obvious. Something like… the alphabet flag pennants that are hoisted up either side of the mast. What if they flew those flags in a sequence, one above the other to signal 'it's party time'…"

"So they spell 'S', 'E', 'X'… bit obvious," said Ben.

"What about… 'S', 'B', 'S'…" said Tilly.

"Which stands for: *sailor boys shagging?*" said Trudy, prompting giggles around the table.

"I think the Royal Marines *Special Boat Service* already has the monopoly on those initials," said Rob.

Tilly shook her head, pushed her hands across the table and half-stood, raising her palms to the group.

"Special Boat Services, *plural*. And plural, ladies and gentlemen, equals pleasure."

Tilly sat back and downed the rest of her rum coffee.

"Ugh, that's cold."

"Rum top up, anyone?" suggested Ben, wielding the spirits bottle.

Several others offered their cups.

"Hey guys, this is a great idea! Imagine setting up a party boat and charging a membership fee. I reckon there'll be a technical loophole, some old maritime law for a house of ill repute on the water, to keep one step ahead of the authorities..."

"But how would they know anyway, if it's on a boat?"

"Exactly! It's brilliant. I could fund my way through university with something like that," said Tilly.

"Funding your education through prostitution. A tad risky and morally dubious, don't you think?" said Trudy.

"Organising, not participating," said Tilly. "Although... that could be fun too..."

"And potentially lucrative," said Rob.

The conversation petered out. Some of us used the uncomfortable pause to sip our extra ration of rum and hide our eyes from the group.

"Has anyone actually been to a swingers party?" asked Laura.

I shook my head. Natasha did the same, as did Samantha and Ben.

"I've not really swung, but I once participated in a threesome," said Tilly.

"What was the mix, male or female?" asked Ben.

"My boyfriend and his mate."

"You lucky hoe!" shouted Samantha, heading up the whoops and table banging.

"Were you up for it, or did he have to persuade you?" squealed Samantha.

"He didn't need to encourage me, I'll try anything once."

"So how was it?"

Everyone stared at Tilly. She shrugged, nonchalantly.

"Started off okay, you know, one each end… but oddly my boyfriend seemed more interested in his mate, if you know what I'm saying. So I left them to it."

A silence descended once again.

"I went along to a club once, but only to watch. It was a dare, with a girl from work. We wondered what it would be like, you know, picking up a stranger. We didn't tell our partners."

We all turned to gawp at Natasha.

"I found it all a bit surreal. Watching near-naked swingers having polite conversations with strangers before they coupled up and got down to it," she said.

As I listened to Natasha, I found my thoughts drifting back to Mary, recalling how I'd luxuriated in the warmth of her body next to mine, the fresh smell of the bed linen.

Someone topped up the cups from a fresh bottle of rum, but I barely noticed.

"I used to go to a swingers club with my ex-husband."

I glanced over at Trudy, aware of all the attention around the table now focussed on her.

"It was called wife swapping back then. We had a few fun-buddy couples that we hooked up with, from time to time."

"Bloody hell, Trudy. You dark horse!" screeched Tilly.

"What was it like?" said Samantha.

"A lot of fun, in the early days. I could tell you some stories… but after a while the emotions took over. It all ended badly."

"Yeah, I get it. The risk of losing your relationship. But was the sex any good?"

"It wasn't good, it was spectacular! I've never had so many orgasms."

More whoops and table banging followed.

"So how do we organise this?" said Tilly, over the commotion.

The background chatter dropped away to a fidgety silence.

"Organise what, exactly?" said Samantha.

"The nautical equivalent. Five girls. Three boys. One lifetime experience… for most of us," Tilly added, winking at Trudy and raising her eyebrows at Rob.

"Who's in?"

Twenty Two

"You humans have some strange customs…"

Lacey's grumbling yawn triggered a ripple of amusement. I flicked my eyes at each sheepish face in turn. Some glanced around the cabin, trying to read everyone else's reaction, while others dropped their gaze, unable to make eye contact.

"Okay, I'm game," said Trudy, raising her hand.

"Me too," said Natasha.

I watched Ben raise his hand, then Rob and Samantha.

"Laura?" asked Tilly.

"I'm not sure. This is a bit… random."

"It's just a bit of fun, that's all," said Samantha, reaching out to gently lift Laura's hand up.

Tilly turned to face me.

"Harry?"

"Um… I'm not sure this is my sort of thing… I mean you're all lovely people and all, but…"

"Come on Harry, we need you to even up the numbers," said Trudy.

"Yeah, you're not going to be able to go back to your own boat knowing this is going on," someone else chipped in.

I shifted in my seat.

"Okay, I'm in."

We all lowered our hands, an air of uncertainty and excitement electrifying the atmosphere.

"So how do we, you know… divide everyone up?" stammered Laura.

"Good point. We're an uneven split," said Natasha.

"I have an idea," said Trudy, shuffling out of her seat to make her way to the chart table.

"These are training school business cards. Us girls will draw something boat-related on the back of a card and make a second copy, which we'll keep. We'll shuffle the rest and the boys pick the one they like. On the top left corner, write either an 'M','F' or a question mark to indicate whether you'd like a male or female partner. The question mark is for those who don't mind. The boys match their cards with the relevant girl. Once that's sorted, each pair will draw for which boat and what cabin. After an hour, it's free time for everyone to wander between areas at will. Okay?"

I watched Trudy fidget the business cards between her fingers as I thought through her methodology. Something told me she'd done this before…

An apprehensive but agreeable murmur met Trudy's suggestion. She handed out the business cards and rummaged in the chart table for enough pens to distribute amongst the girls.

"This does mean that two girls will end up together," said Samantha.

"That's inevitable. But they have the choice to

sit and chat in their designated cabin, or…
experiment."

I noticed Samantha flush and drop her eyes
to concentrate on her drawing, using her hand to
shield her illustration.

Lacey shook himself on Samantha's lap, then
worked his way around the table by stepping on
everyone's thighs, seemingly inspecting their
artwork as he headed towards me.

"Nice drawings, ladies…"

I ducked away from Lacey's nose in my face
and let him settle on my lap.

Once the girls had all finished sketching,
Trudy gathered the cards together and shuffled
them.

"We're ready. Harry, will you cut them
please?"

Trudy held out her palm. All eyes focussed on
the cards.

I lifted two business cards off the top. Trudy
pushed these to the bottom of the pack and
offered the cards to Rob to choose one. He
passed the rest to Ben, then me.

"Okay gentlemen. Show us what you've
got…"

*

I sat on the bed in the training boat's spacious
and comfortable stern cabin, my heart pulsating.
The cabin door squeaked open and Laura
stepped in. She looked even more nervous than
me. I attempted a reassuring smile.

"Hi… " she said.

"Hi."

She leaned back against the door, one hand resting on the handle.

"This is really bizarre… I never expected this when I signed up for a competent crew course."

I chuckled.

"Yes, I'd like to see where this is in the syllabus."

She nodded. Silence engulfed the cabin.

Lacey's collar rattled on the fibreglass partition as he pulled his long body up towards the standing headroom end of the bed, trailing his back legs on the cushion.

"Oh Lacey, you made me jump," said Laura, clutching her chest.

"You okay with dogs? I could put him back on my boat, but he'd probably bark…"

"No, he's fine. But I'm not sure I'm drunk enough for… *this.*"

I nodded, reached down to stroke Lacey, who leant against my side, resting his right paw on my thigh.

"I know what you mean…"

A tingling feeling made my palms itch, as if peering at the ground from a high building.

"Harry, get with the programme! It's jiggy-jiggy time!"

Lacey craned his neck to look up at me. Laura and I stayed silent, avoiding eye contact.

"So how does this work? Should we undress, or fool around for a bit first?" said Laura.

Images of what might be going on in the other cabins flashed through my mind, heightening my interest levels *down below,* and yet, I hesitated.

"I met someone, recently… I may well regret not doing anything here, because you're an attractive girl, but… I don't think I can. It doesn't feel spontaneous, or mutual. So we could just talk, if you like…"

"That would be great."

I watched relief brighten Laura's face. She sank down on the edge of the bed, tension and apprehension draining away.

"Besides, you like Ben," I added.

She stared at me.

"Am I that obvious?"

"I noticed the way you looked at him."

She nodded.

"That's me, heart on my sleeve."

"Who did he end up with?"

"Natasha."

"Right. Did any of you know each other, before the sailing course?"

"Samantha and I are friends. The others I met at the start of the week."

She dropped her eyes, hands fidgeting.

"Maybe nothing will happen. They're probably just talking…" I said.

"Are you kidding? He's gorgeous!"

Her expression changed when she realised what she had inadvertently implied.

"I'm sorry Harry, I didn't mean that you're not a nice guy, it's just…"

"Lacey's cute, but not enough to leap over an attractive bloke your own age? Relax, I don't fancy you either."

I smiled and sat back against the bulkhead, draping an arm around Lacey.

"Thank you Harry, you're a good guy."

Lacey yawned, loud and wide, then hobbled to the edge of the bed and jumped down.

"Bored, bored, bored."

He pawed the door and whined to be let out.

*

I lifted Lacey up through the companionway and settled him down on the cockpit floor. He sniffed around, then settled for a wee. I hunted around in the outside lockers and found a bucket tied to a rope, which I used to sluice seawater over the deck.

"Gotta love these training boats, so well kitted-out," I whispered to Lacey.

He hovered beside the hatch, trying to lick Laura's face as she lifted him down into the cabin. Patches of clear sky peeked through the cloud, revealing stars and glimpses of moonlight.

"Harry…?" Laura whispered. "You staying up there?"

"For a few minutes."

I turned to face forwards, towards the flashing red Anchor Stone marker. To my right, I could see the dim lighting from a converted boat house, tucked into the trees. It looked like a fabulous property.

A rustle of movement from the cabin prompted me to step back and allow Laura space to join me in the cockpit.

"Wow, the stars are amazing," she whispered, craning her neck skywards.

"No light pollution here."

We stood there looking up at the sky for a while.

"Lacey okay down there?" I asked.

"Uh-huh. He's snuggled up in the cabin."

I smiled, a thought occurring to me: Home is where my dog says it is...

"Tell me about her, Harry."

I dropped my eyes from scanning the stars and considered her expression.

"Who?"

"The new lady. The one who saved my honour."

"Which one?" I said, before I could stop myself.

"There's more than one?"

"I'm not really sure... it's complicated."

"Is she married?"

"I don't think so."

"Are you?"

"I was, a couple of years ago."

"What happened?"

I dropped my eyes to the inky water.

"Everything and nothing. I don't want to burden you with my story..."

"We've got the time and it'll distract us from the sex sounds."

I chuckled, lifted my gaze to her fresh-faced optimism, seemingly unblemished by life.

"True enough. I might as well tell someone else, other than..."

I glanced at her, then began to shake my head.

"No, it's not fair. My story is... tricky..."

She placed a hand gently on my forearm and held my distracted gaze.

"You look like you need to… it's something major, isn't it?"

I looked away.

"I'm… sorting a few things out, before… before…"

She squeezed my arm, her eyes encouraging yet patient. I took several long pauses as I gulped in more air. Then with a heavy heart, I took one last deep calming breath and told her everything, warts and all.

Twenty Three

"I don't know what to say Harry, other than I'm sorry…"

"It's just life, isn't it?"

"What will you do… after?"

"There's stuff to organise, I suppose."

"What about…"

A screech from the depths of the boat pulled us back to reality. I ducked my head through the hatch into the cabin, just in time to see Lacey being shoved out of the bow cabin by a pair of slender hands. The door swung open enough to reveal a snapshot of the fun being had inside.

Tilly straightened up from crouching down on the floor, almost naked save for her bra and knickers. Above her, Natasha sat on the edge of the vee berth, arms wrapped around her bare breasts, mortified. Just before the cabin door slammed shut behind Lacey, a pair of lacy knickers slipped off Natasha's ankles onto the floor.

Oops.

Lacey turned back towards the door and tapped his paw on it.

Bang!

An unseen hand whacked the door, making Lacey jump back, then bark.

"Bugger off, dog!" shouted a muffled voice. *"We're all adults, what's the problem?!"*

Lacey stood still, listening for a second. Then he turned away from the door and wagged his tail at me.

"They didn't look like they were making polite conversation, Harry."

"Excuse me for a moment," I said to Laura, descending in to the cabin.

I waggled my finger at Lacey.

"You're such a naughty dog! We're guests here, remember."

Lacey sat down and yawned.

"This is where the action's at, boyo. So what are you doing playing boo-hoo sob stories with Little Miss Perfect?"

"What's going on down there?" said Laura, poking her head down into the cabin.

"Um, I think it's called… curiosity.*"*

"Who had that cabin?" asked Laura.

I picked Lacey up and carried him back outside into the cockpit.

"That would be the girls…"

"Tilly and Natasha?"

I nodded, watching her wide-eyed gasp.

"Special Boat Services*…* as only girls can," I said, raising a mischievous eyebrow.

"Bloody hell. Breakfast is going to be interesting."

I nodded, aware of Lacey's rhythmic shivering in my arms.

"I'm going to shove off back to my own boat, leave your crew to, um… enjoy each other… That leaves you with the stern cabin to yourself. Okay?"

She nodded, an infectious smile playing on her lips.

"Yeah… sure. Thank you Harry. And I'm sorry about…"

"Enough now. Save the sympathy for your crew."

I left her there and carefully carried Lacey over the gap between the boats. When I turned round, Laura had already disappeared below deck.

*

I slept in late the next morning, waking with a pleasantly clear head and more impressively, a clear conscience. I felt sure the same couldn't be said for my fellow sailors…

Lacey crawled out from the open bottom of my sleeping bag, dragged his body across the opposite berth and shook himself awake.

"Morning Lacey. You caused some mischief last night, naughty boy."

He leapt across the void between our berths and attempted his usual face-washing routine – mine, not his.

Once I'd wrestled him off, I lay there contemplating making a fresh cafetiere of coffee. The muffled and unmistakable rumble of a diesel engine clattering into life roused me from my deliberations.

"Shall we see who's leaving?"

I lifted Lacey up into the cockpit and poked my head out to see Rob and Ben casting off with

Samantha, who sat in the cockpit of their boat. I waved, but she avoided eye contact. I watched their boat motor away, amused by the lack of acknowledgement from any of them.

"That must have been an interesting evening, eh boy…" I whispered.

I turned away from the departing boat and nodded at Trudy, who stepped up into the training boat cockpit holding a steaming cup of tea, closely followed by Laura. They both watched Rob's boat leave, the scene played out in surreal silence.

Only when Rob's boat passed to the left of the Anchor Stone did Ben turn to face us and raise his hand to wave goodbye. Rob stood rigid on the helm, his back to us. I watched their bow wave ripple across the water, flat now with barely a breath of wind. Such a contrast from a few hours earlier.

"There goes a man with a guilty conscience," said Trudy.

I watched her follow the track of Rob's boat, her eyes unreadable beneath a pair of sunglasses. She turned to face me.

"Morning Harry. Did you sleep well?"

"I did, thank you Trudy. Did you… sleep?"

I couldn't help a mischievous grin.

"Oh, you know. A little, here and there."

She returned my smile.

"We're making breakfast in a bit, if you fancy joining us?" said Laura. "We seem to have a spare place at the table."

"Lovely, thank you. Do I have time to run Lacey ashore for a walk first?"

"Of course," she replied.

*

Lacey and I hiked up the steep road from The Ferry Boat Inn towards the church, rewarded at the top of the hill by a gorgeous view across the river. To my right, I could see Jessica and the training boat swinging lazily on their mooring not far from the Anchor Stone. Ahead on the opposite shore to Dittisham, Greenway Quay bustled with day trippers. To my left, a larger expanse of water shimmered in the sunshine across to Galmpton, where the river turned sharply left, its perimeter dotted with a hundred small boat moorings.

By now, the sun had climbed high overhead. I made a mental note to explore further upstream towards Totnes, reputed to be even prettier. Then we set off back down the hill for breakfast.

*

The sound of stainless steel cutlery tapping on plastic plates and Lacey's intermittent 'feed me' whine punctuated the silence. I glanced around the table, bathed in an awkward atmosphere and sense of emptiness without the three co-conspirators.

I cleared my throat.

"Nobody actually died, did they?"

Trudy caught my eye and winked at me.

"I mean, that was Samantha I saw jumping

ship? Or was it a hologram, to throw us off the scent? Maybe she's at the bottom of the river, an anchor chain weighing her down…"

Laura glanced up, flicked her eyes at Tilly. Natasha blushed, hiding her face behind a cup of coffee.

"Judging by the enthusiastic noises coming from her cabin, she's very much alive…" said Tilly, giggling and looking first at me, then Laura.

"Well, I had a fun evening. I thought the conversation over coffee was very thought provoking and enlightening," I said.

Natasha stole a glance at Tilly.

"Tilly and Natasha, if you'd be kind enough to wash up please. Laura, you're navigating today. Plan a passage to Salcombe, departing at eleven hundred hours," said Trudy, standing and clearing away the plates.

"That's my cue. Thank you girls, it's been… an education, meeting you all. I wish you fair winds and good luck with the new venture," I said, picking Lacey up off the floor as I made my way to the companionway steps.

"New venture?" asked Trudy.

I smiled at their inquisitive faces.

"Special Boat Services. I'll look out for the signal flags…"

I could almost see drunken recollections flash across their faces. I stepped up into the cockpit, leaving my social hand grenade rolling around at their feet, the pin teetering.

I'd barely stepped across onto Jessica when I heard my name being called.

I turned to see a red and yellow Dartmouth Harbour water taxi heading towards me. I squinted in the sunshine, trying to make out the figure stood beside the driver, waving at me.

"Harry!"

The unmistakable voice of Alice, the vet, drifted across the water.

Twenty Four

I felt Lacey flinch in my arms as the water taxi slowed. I put him down on the cockpit seat and watched the boat draw alongside.

"Hi Harry. Surprised to see me?"

"Um… yeah. I thought you were still annoyed with me, after the drunken texts…"

"Oh that. Forget it. Bad timing. Hello Lacey, is Harry looking after you?"

Lacey twitched his tail and whimpered. He transferred his body weight to hold up his plaster cast.

"You gonna sort this out, Doc? I wanna run free, you know."

The vet inspected Lacey's cast.

"No more phone numbers, Harry? You're losing your touch."

"Must be my age."

She arched her eyebrow and surveyed Jessica.

"Permission to come aboard, Captain?"

"Of course, please do."

Alice paid the water taxi driver, climbed up onto the gunnel and swung her leg over the guard wires.

"Thanks Allan, pass on my best to Jill," she said as Allan dipped his head and released the mooring line from Jessica and motored away.

"She's a pretty boat, Harry. Small, but perfectly formed. Not unlike this cute boy…"

Alice picked Lacey up, holding him so they could eyeball each other.

"You still don't trust me, do you little one? Understandable, given our last meeting."

"Too right, Doc. Bad things happen to good doggies in that place."

Alice replaced Lacey on the deck.

"Friends of yours?" she said, indicating towards the training boat.

"Sort of acquaintances."

"Ooh, cryptic. Ships that pass in the night?"

"More along the lines of ships that unwittingly observe others passing in the night…"

I wondered if Alice had any clue what I was hinting at, because her composure gave nothing away. She glanced over her shoulder. I followed her gaze to Trudy, in the cockpit of the training boat. Trudy smiled at us and started the engine, quickly joined on deck by Natasha, Tilly and Laura, all of whom wore sailing waterproofs and lifejackets.

"Okay Laura, you have command. Please instruct your crew," said Trudy in an assertive voice.

"Tilly, would you mind casting off please?" said Laura, taking up position behind the steering wheel.

She turned to face me.

"Goodbye Harry. I hope everything works out… "

Laura smiled and looked away to focus on Tilly pulling the mooring rope.

"Clear," said Tilly.

Laura turned the wheel, pushed the throttle lever and steered the training boat away from Jessica. I watched the gap between the boats open up, a textbook departure.

"Have fun, above and below deck…" I called out, watching the boat turn in a neat circle towards the Anchor Stone.

"You must have had a lively evening… given the conditions."

I switched my gaze from the training boat to Alice and nodded.

"Never a dull moment on the water. How did you find me?"

"I remembered the boat name from the police visit. A friend of the family works for the Harbour Master, they keep records."

"I see. You visiting your parents?"

"Yes. I thought I'd take the opportunity to check Lacey's cast, see if it can come off."

"All part of the service? Or do you still not trust me to look after him?"

"Maybe a bit of both. I texted you, to say I'd pop over."

"I didn't get it. No signal upstream."

"Not to worry. Do you have a kettle on board this fine little ship?"

"Sure, grab a seat."

I stepped down into the cabin, leaving Alice to cuddle up next to Lacey in the cockpit.

"Lovely. You make the tea, I'll buy you lunch. You look like you need feeding up and I know the best place for really fresh crab sandwiches. Have you had any recently?"

I shielded my eyes from the sun glinting through the hatch and stared at her po-faced expression. Unable to think of a suitable response, I retreated to the galley.

"Not recently, no. Milk and sugar?"

*

Jessica's engine gurgled into life, churning seawater through the cooling system, splashing it out with hazy exhaust smoke.

We cast off the mooring buoy and steered downstream, motoring past the industrial backdrop to Noss Marina towards the upper chain ferry, beyond which the pretty pastel-colour terraced houses of Dartmouth and Kingswear nestled in the valley sides, now bathed in glorious sunshine.

Alice sat back in the cockpit next to Lacey, soaking up the sun's warmth.

I glanced at her. Yet another curve ball, I noted, then attempted to forget about another problem – what about Mary...?

"I can see the appeal of this life, Harry."

"It's simple, that's what I really enjoy about the boat."

She turned away to look at the endless rows of moored yachts.

"It's real, I think," she murmured.

We motored on at a leisurely pace, letting the beauty of Dartmouth sink into our pores and refresh our souls.

*

I dangled my feet over the edge of the quay, finishing off the penultimate bite of my crab sandwich. On the pontoon to our left, tourist passenger ferries loaded up for a river tour. To my right, the steep valley sides protected the entrance to the harbour, the angle of approach shielding open sea from view, giving the impression of cocooned safety.

"So, Harry, what's been going on? I bet you and Lacey have been having a wild time."

"It's been quiet actually, without any armed police."

Alice rolled her eyes and licked her fingers as she polished off the rest of the sandwich.

"Keith is a colourful character. Rose has some interesting stories about him."

That's my brother… they do say pets are an extension of their owners," I said, offering the last piece of sandwich to Lacey.

"How has he been?" Alice asked, nodding at Lacey.

"Mostly sober."

Alice glared at me.

"Harry! You can't let Lacey drink. It's not good for him."

"He's been better… we both have."

She held eye contact with me.

"I'm serious."

I turned to Lacey.

"You're off the sauce, effective immediately."

"So you say, Sinbad."

"That's better. I reckon his cast can come off. Have you got time to pop into my parents' house? I've got my medical bag there."

"Sure."

I handed Lacey's lead to Alice and collected the sandwich wrappers and coffee cups, depositing them in the nearest rubbish bin.

"It's this way," she said, leading Lacey away from the quay.

I caught up, unable to help stealing a glance at Alice's slender figure before I scolded myself: Harry, get real. You're becoming a womaniser...

*

I cringed and turned away from the high-pitched dentist's-drill squeal. Lacey tensed in my hands and tried to wriggle away, but I held him firmly so Alice could cut through the cast.

"There, all done."

Lacey struggled again, so I lowered him onto the floor to test out his new leg. He limped for a few steps, then settled down into a steady trot around the kitchen, sniffing as he went.

"He doesn't appear to be in any pain," said Alice.

"He looks okay," I agreed. "Thank you."

Alice smiled and turned away to wash her hands.

"I have a soft spot for Lacey. Although his new owner is a difficult one to work out..."

I watched Alice dry her hands on a towel. She turned around to face me just as her mum breezed into the kitchen.

"That's men for you, dear. Your father still confuses me. Hello, you must be Harry, the criminal's brother."

"Guilty as charged, ma'am."

I shook the mum's hand.

"'Ello 'ello my beauty…"

Lacey trotted over to the door as a golden Labrador entered the kitchen, its long tail swooshing enthusiastically. I watched the two dogs circling and sniffing each other's bottoms, wondering what on earth went through their minds…

"That's Holly," said Alice.

"Ah-hah. Does the other half get visitation rights?" I asked.

"Not a chance," said Alice, turning to face her mum. "How was the Nordic walking?"

"It's like shadow boxing to a hip hop beat in time with lots of buttock clenching," her mum replied. "Most uncomfortable and repetitive at first, but a reasonable workout. Not unlike sex."

Twenty Five

"Wooooohooooo! Freeeeeddddoooommmmmm!"

"It's a joy to see him running again. I didn't realise he was so fast," I said, watching Lacey sprint across the playing field, barking at the seagulls, followed at a slower pace by Holly the Labrador.

"He looks good. What's going to happen to him, long term?" asked Alice.

"I've not thought that far ahead. I don't know what Keith's situation is... or if the police have got anything to charge him with. Maybe he'll be able to take Lacey back soon."

"How would you feel about that? You and Lacey appear to have bonded nicely."

"I guess time will tell. There are a few variables on the horizon..."

"Such as?"

I turned away from her.

"No one knows what's around the next corner," I said softly.

"True enough."

We walked on, watching Lacey and Holly scatter resting seagulls at the far end of the field.

"What sort of person are you, Harry?" said Alice after a while.

"With regards to Lacey? You just said he's looking good..."

"Relax, you're off the hook there. He's being well looked after," she said.

"Unless you're a seagull... or a policeman."

She didn't laugh, or change her intense expression.

"Are you an unreliable rogue, like your brother?"

"Haven't you already formed a professional opinion?"

She stopped walking, pulled hair out of her eyes and turned to face me.

"You're quirky and interesting, Harry. I didn't come all this way just to see my folks, or remove Lacey's cast... a local vet could have done that."

"Oh. I didn't think we'd got on that well..."

"We didn't. But given the unusual circumstances, I've decided to give you a second chance."

"I see."

Alice smiled warmly, her cool professional aloofness dispersing. She looked relaxed, happy and... sexy.

Uh oh. Fight, flight, or...

"Harry...!"

I could hear Lacey's barking getting closer.

Alice leaned in, her lips parting the smallest amount.

"Look out Harry, incoming...!"

Freeze.

"Warp speed. Hyper drive, full throttle. We need 'em all. Go, go, GO!"

"Oommph!"

I crumpled backwards, millimetres away from

Alice's incoming kiss. I doubled up on the ground, groaning from the impact of Lacey leaping up and head-butting me at full pelt in the groin. I might as well have been rugby-tackled in the goolies by an eighteen-stone prop forward.

I rolled around on the ground in agony, vaguely aware of Lacey prancing around my head, yapping.

"I had no choice, Harry. I had to go for the monkey nuts!"

I gasped for breath, tears filling my eyes, the pain excruciating.

"What happened?" said Alice, leaning over me.

I lay there, in a foetal position, snatching puffs of breath and clutching my pride in my hands.

"Below the belt, Lacey… not funny…" I wheezed through gritted teeth.

"Can't you see who nearly caught you snogging Doctor Death?!"

Alice helped me to roll up into a sitting position.

"Dog… playing game... caught me, delicate area…" I gasped.

Alice giggled. She shot Lacey a *faux* scornful glare.

"You must have deserved it. What have you been up to?"

I shook my head, eased up to a crouch, catching my breath.

Damn you dog!

Lacey jumped up on his hind legs, his front paws landing on my thighs, toppling me over.

Something, a sixth sense perhaps, or the familiarity of her movement, made me glance off to my right as I began to hunch upright. Just in time to catch a side profile of Mary's head, shoulders and torso as she walked past on the other side of the playing field hedge.

I looked away from Mary and stared at Lacey, nuzzling around Alice's legs, his tongue-lolling, panting and unblinking eye contact unsettling me.

"Saved your life, bro!"

If I didn't know better, I'd have sworn the bloody dog was laughing at me.

I stayed crouched down until Mary had walked a safe distance away, then slowly stood up.

"Don't be angry with him, Harry. He just wants to play."

"Playtime's over," I said firmly.

I clipped the lead onto Lacey's collar and turned away from Mary.

As we walked towards the town, I sensed Alice edging closer to me, in danger of slipping her arm around mine.

"Were you born here in Dartmouth?" I asked.

"Kingswear, on the other side of the river."

"Is there much rivalry between the two towns? I mean, isn't that a big thing for your folks… relocating like that? Years ago they'd probably have been lynched for mutiny."

A troubled expression creased Alice's brow. We walked on for a bit in silence before she spoke.

"That's very perceptive of you, Harry."

"Really? I'm not known for being on the ball."

"There was a falling out, with another family. My parents moved to show support for me."

"Oh. Why?"

I glanced at her, sensing her pain. Too late to backtrack now.

"A neighbour's daughter, supposedly a friend of mine... she got involved with my fiancé one Christmas. We only visited for a few days, but that was the start of their affair. It was a horrible, messy business."

"So your parents moved across the river because of that?"

She nodded.

"Lots of spiteful things were said, it wasn't pleasant for my folks, living there. So they moved. It was difficult, but they saw it as a matter of principle."

"I'm sorry."

She shrugged, wiped her eyes.

"It's difficult for me, coming back here. Dartmouth is a small town, everyone knows everyone. The only saving grace is the water. It's enough of a barrier to make visiting bearable."

"When did this happen?"

"A few years ago. Silly really, to let it upset me still."

"Have you seen her since?"

I watched Alice nod, a faraway look in her eye.

"Occasionally, from opposite sides of the street. We're pretty good at avoiding each other."

*

It didn't seem appropriate for me to make my excuses at the earliest opportunity and run for the hills, so I decided to hang around until I could leave Alice feeling a bit happier. I offered to buy her a drink as thanks for removing Lacey's cast. Under the circumstances, it seemed like the right thing to do.

We settled into a snug table in the Dartmouth Arms, a traditional pub with lots of dark wood and a low ceiling, overlooking Bayards Cove and the harbour entrance.

"So where's next, Harry?"

"Sailing destination? Probably the River Yealm, then Fowey and a final hop down to Falmouth."

"What happens then?"

"I find out if I'm brave enough to go and visit my father and try to break through his dementia and bombastic nature, if there's anything left of it. And then, if I get that far… finally try and make my peace."

"I don't envy you that."

"No. Not something I'm looking forward to."

"Why do it at all? If there's been so much animosity, isn't it better to let it lie?"

I took a mouthful of beer and swallowed it quickly without savouring the taste.

"There's probably not much time left, so I need to try."

I drained the rest of my pint in three gulps and moved my leg away from Lacey's insistent pawing.

"Oy, stingy pants. Where's mine?"

"Another?" I asked, already on my feet.

"Why not."

I placed the empty glasses on the bar, ordered the next round and glanced over my shoulder at the table, watching Alice lift Lacey onto her lap.

This should have been a simple trip without complications, I reminded myself. How did I get into these sticky situations?

"Hello stranger."

My heart rate trebled in an instant. I turned towards the voice.

"Hi... Mary. What a lovely surprise."

The barman placed two glasses in front of me and took my ten pound note off the bar where it had dropped from my fingers.

"Two drinks. Entertaining?"

"Um, yeah, a friend," I stammered.

"Oh. Where's Lacey?"

"She over there..." I pointed.

Lacey sniffed the air and swivelled round on Alice's lap to face us.

"Uh oh, Harry. You're in the doggy doo-doo now..."

Alice followed Lacey's gaze towards me and Mary. I felt Mary move closer, slip her arm through mine, pulling me close to her.

Lacey dropped to the floor as Alice stood up. Anger flashed in her eyes, nostrils flared, her neck crimson.

Cue music: The Good, the Bad and the Ugly...

The next few minutes unravelled in painfully slow motion. Background pub chatter ebbed away as drinkers edged back and squashed together to reveal clear floor space between us.

I tried to step away from Mary, but she held me tight to her side. Alice walked towards us, her tractor beam stare locked onto Mary.

The arm slipped out of mine. Mary's hand pushed me to one side. I watched her fists clench as Alice advanced, her eyes filled with loathing.

"Cheap sleaze!" yelled Alice, lunging at Mary.

Mary swung her fist, missing only because Alice had closed the gap. Alice's fingers tightened around Mary's throat.

"Bitch!"

The momentum knocked them off balance, two screeching, punching tomcats brawling in the middle of the pub.

"Liar!"

Drinkers moved back as the women rolled at their feet, grabbing hair and ripping clothing. Alice knelt astride Mary's writhing torso, pinning her down as she slapped her in the face, her arms thrashing like a relentless windmill.

Whack, whack, whack!

"Thieving, dirty, slapper!"

Mary thumped a knee into Alice's back, then clenched her hand around Alice's hair, wrenching her off to one side.

"Aaarrrgghhhh… slut!"

"Good on ya Alice, she had it coming!" someone shouted.

They rolled over again, scattering the pub patrons who reformed a new ring around the biting, scratching, screaming girls. Lacey skipped around them, woofing.

"Ooh, nice left hook Doctor Death! Scratch-a-roo, mighty Mary!"

I forced myself to yank my treacle-like feet off the floor and hurled myself between them, trying to block Mary from smashing her fists into Alice's stomach and face.

"Leave 'em be, this is better than the boxing!" yelled a spotty teenager.

Alice wrenched me aside and launched herself at Mary, white clenched knuckles flying. I stepped sideways, blocking the onslaught and dragged Alice away, grateful to see two large chaps hold Mary back.

"Get your own man!" Alice shrieked.

"All's fair in lust, you whore!" screamed Mary.

I hauled Alice's sweating pulsating body outside the pub, wrapping my arms around her chest, grabbing at her flailing wrists, using all my strength to contain her anger.

"Let me go Harry, you slimy two-timing bastard!"

I hoped the cool air outside the pub would have a calming effect on the baying mob after the furnace-like interior, but to my horror the two other fight referees bundled Mary outside, followed by most of the pub's drinkers, who formed a semi-circle in the street.

"Let 'em at it!" cried an old boy leaning on his walking stick.

"I've got twenty on the vet!" shouted a wide-eyed lad in his twenties.

"Come on you gutter wench!" screeched Mary, struggling to break free from the men holding her, blood from a cut lip dripping off her chin onto her torn blouse.

"You're a cheap rotten-fish-face-slapper!" Alice screamed, thrashing against my arms.

I tightened my grip around Alice, her lithe body heaving with deep hoarse breaths, her ripped shirt hanging open over her black lacy bra, angry red scratch marks scoring her neck and cleavage.

"Calm down, please…" I stammered, glancing at Mary, who spat blood onto the pavement.

"This is your fault Harry, you did this!" Mary shrieked between gasps for breath, her eyes full of rage.

"I didn't know… how could I know?" I shouted back, doing my best to drag Alice away.

"Let me go! That bitch stole my man!" yelled Alice.

"Who's it going to be, Harry?" screamed Mary, struggling to wrench free from her captors.

I stared wide-eyed at Mary, the adrenalin pumping through my veins as I struggled to contain Alice.

"Make your choice!"

My heart thumped inside my empty chest, a bass drum that echoed behind my prickly eyes. Faces in the crowd jeered and taunted, baying for blood.

Shit!

I flicked my eyes at Mary, searching for the truth in her wild eyes.

Sensing Alice's tension seeping away, I released her from my arms, a vague sensation of loss nagging at me.

"I didn't want all this. I'm sorry, to both of you. I just want to finish my journey, it's all I have right now…"

My words sounded hollow and detached. I turned away, searching for Lacey. I found him sniffing around the pub wall.

I whistled, summoning the dog, quickly closing the distance between us.

"Harry Straight, you're a sodding coward!" shouted one of the women, but I didn't pause to decipher which one. I'd already picked up Lacey and had begun hurrying away as fast as my wobbly legs would allow.

Twenty Six

I slid the hatch closed above my head and sank down onto the nearest saloon berth, my whole body shaking. I hung my head over my knees, took deep gulps of stale air. Lacey jumped up next to me, whining as he propped his front paws on my shoulder, nuzzling his wet nose into my ear.

"Want my advice, Harry? Go for Mary. Her daughter gives me lots of titbits and their house is warm with a nice sunny garden. Also, the neighbour has a cat, so that's my entertainment sorted."

*

I took Lacey for a walk early the next morning. Afterwards I found myself sat down on a bench overlooking the passenger ferry pontoon with a takeaway coffee.

"What a palaver, eh Lacey. I've never had two women fighting over me. What's a guy to do?"

I turned at the sound of squeaking car brakes. The front doors opened and two figures got out.

"Harry Straight, the dirty dog of Dartmouth and the infamous testicle-munching mongrel.

You should still be in Weymouth," said DI Randall as he plonked himself down next to me.

I held Lacey tighter, a guttural growl vibrating in his throat.

"It's the pigs!"

DC Best stood on the other side of me, a few feet from the bench.

"I had to sail with fair winds, Inspector. Otherwise I could have been stranded there for a week."

"What's the matter, unfriendly locals?"

DI Randall watched me cough on my coffee. He pulled out his wallet, held out a ten pound note for DC Best.

"White coffee, two sugars. And something sweet, a pastry perhaps. Have one yourself."

"Yes sir."

I watched DC Best take the note.

"Where'd you get yours?" she asked.

I pointed towards the ferry. "Right up there, first left."

She nodded her thanks and walked away.

"It would have been better if you'd let us know you'd moved on," said the Inspector.

I shrugged, wondering how friendly the conversation would be.

"Did the Harbour Master log my boat?"

"That would have been a logical way to find you, had you not used your mobile phone. Bit early for Keith to ring. Most antisocial."

"That's my brother… no sense of timing."

DI Randall shuffled his body round to face me and stretched his gloved hand across the bench behind my shoulders.

"Where is he?"

I stared out across the harbour.

"Given the fact that you must have bugged my phone, you probably know more about his location than I do. Didn't you trace it?"

"Inconclusive. Odds on he won't use the same pay-as-you-go phone again. Which leaves us asking you the same old question."

"Sorry Detective, I can't help you."

"Ah, breakfast. Excellent."

I watched DC Best hand the coffee and paper bakery bag to DI Randall, then sit down on the bench with Lacey sandwiched between us. Lacey sat up straight, his eyes darting between the two detectives, licking his lips and whimpering.

"Save some for the cute doggy. Pleeeeaaasssse…"

"Tell me about your boat."

"Why?"

"I'd rather have a pleasant non-work related conversation while I'm eating my breakfast."

"So this isn't police business anymore?"

"Not for the next ten minutes. This is a pretty place, beats our normal greasy spoon. Wouldn't you agree, Best?"

"Yes sir, very picturesque."

I alternated my gaze between the detectives, mimicking Lacey.

"Where are you heading?" he asked, spraying sugary pastry from his mouth.

"Falmouth, ultimately."

"Very nice, Falmouth. I had an aunt who lived there."

I glanced at Lacey. A long glob of drool dangled from his mouth.

"You didn't get anything from Keith's phone call, he's too careful. And you didn't come all this way for the local bakery. So what else is going on?"

"You should be flattered we want to spend time with you."

I held eye contact with the Inspector.

"Not that a womaniser or pub brawler is someone I particularly care for," he added.

"Whoa, hang on Inspector. I was breaking up a fight, not starting one…"

"That isn't the way we heard it from our Dartmouth colleagues. It seems the parents of one of the victims are on the board of the local Neighbourhood Watch."

"Victims? You can't be serious…"

"You've upset the locals, Mister Straight. It's becoming a habit. If I were you I'd make myself scarce. I'd hate to see you lynched… how would we track your brother down then?"

DI Randall stood up, tipped his head at his colleague.

"Stay in touch. We'll be keeping an eye on you."

He dusted pastry flakes off his tie and looked down at me for a few seconds, then he turned and walked towards his car. DC Best fell in walking beside him.

Great. An early morning run-in with the law. What a perfect start to my day.

*

My alarm woke me early the next morning. I forced myself to get up, light the stove and make fresh coffee. I pulled back the curtain and peered out of the small Perspex window. Street lights pierced the darkness, illuminating a thin layer of low-lying mist.

"Stealth mission this morning, Lacey."

I paddled across the inky water, the kayak pushing fresh ripples against the calm river. Lacey shivered in my lap, his steady pulse of energy lasting the duration of each stroke.

I watched Lacey rustle through the dewy grass, sniffing, stopping sporadically to mark his territory. I kept glancing around the deserted field, but I didn't see another soul.

We hurried back to the kayak. I paddled faster on the return journey, bobbing over the small chop, splashing water over the bow.

Lacey sat in the cockpit and watched me deflate the kayak, my fingers working fast.

"Thirty minutes until the tide turns, Lacey. We'd better hustle."

Lacey hardly reacted when I turned the engine over and it settled into its familiar steady tempo. He followed me around the deck in his lifejacket as I tended the mooring lines, his tail twitching.

"Safe trip, skipper," called out a voice behind me.

I glanced up, nodded an acknowledgement to the owner of the old wooden sloop.

"Hang onto your furry friend. Wind over tide later."

"Will do, thanks," I said, pulling on the stern line, springing Jessica's bow off the pontoon.

We motored away, my stomach tingling with a mix of apprehension and excitement. I eased the tiller over and steered towards the main channel, leaving two classic gentlemen's motor yachts in our wake as we passed the fuel barge and aimed for the harbour entrance. A line of street lights flicked off, drawing my eyes to the Dartmouth side of the river, where a lone figure stood on the quay above the pleasure boat moorings.

Alice…?

She turned to face me, arms folded, expression fixed. She didn't call out, or wave. I raised my hand and adjusted course towards her, then turned away to reach down and ease back on the throttle lever. But when I looked up, she'd already turned her back and had begun to walk away.

I opened my mouth, but no words came.

"What can I say that would change anything?" I muttered to Lacey.

We motored on, leaving a hotch-potch of conflicting emotions.

I steered behind the floating bridge ferry, chugging across the river from Kingswear. The ferry carried two cars and one foot passenger.

Mary.

She'd pulled her coat tight around her waist, hair fluttering in the breeze across her bruised, blotchy face. She glanced over at me, swept her hair out of her eyes and tucked it behind her ear. Beside me, Lacey began to whimper.

"Harry, what you doing? Snug house and cuddly family, that way, bro!"

I raised my hand, same peace offering, similar response. We held eye contact for a few seconds, then she turned away from me towards the landing ramp on the Dartmouth side.

Once again I allowed Jessica to motor on past. We headed out into the gentle swell beyond the harbour entrance, my white knuckles gripping the tiller, daring myself to turn back.

*

We cleared the hazardous rocks surrounding the entrance, allowing me to set the sails and switch off the engine. With the auto-helm steering, I took a few minutes to study the chart. By my calculations we had eight to ten hours sailing to the River Yealm, for six of which we'd have the tide with us, helping to push us along at a decent speed. After that, the tide would turn and the easterly wind would oppose it and we'd be battling wind against tide, just as the wooden-boat skipper had predicted.

"Could get a bit bumpy later, Lacey. We'll need to be careful," I said, finally allowing my thoughts to drift away from my navigation calculations as I pondered my non-sailing concerns.

Two women fighting for my attention. How the hell had that happened?

*

"I'm not sure about this rock and roll motion, Harry."

I reached out to stroke the dog, sat staring anxiously over the side of the boat.

"It's alright Lacey, it's just getting a bit lumpy."

I watched Lacey try and reposition, his paws slipping on the polished gel coat.

"That's easy for you, human, in your fancy sailing shoes. Paws don't grip… Octopuses however, they'd have made good boat pets."

Lacey braced himself between me and the stern cockpit coaming, rocking with the boat's motion, his eyes closed.

The sails occasionally flapped and cracked like a whip as we climbed the top of a wave and lost the wind, making the rigging shudder. Lacey opened his eyes and whined at me.

"You sure about this, Captain?"

"We'll be okay…" I reassured him, but he held my gaze, reflecting my self-doubt.

I flicked my eyes over the rigging as the sails flogged again, warning me that Jessica's rudder had momentarily lost its grip, causing us to round up to the wind. I yanked on the mainsheet rope, eased the sail out and pulled the rudder over, trying to catch the wind and build our speed to carry us safely over the next crest.

In the few seconds pause, I grabbed Lacey's lifejacket handle and unceremoniously lifted him down into the cabin, rushing back to the helm, just in time to yank the tiller back on course.

Jessica's bow plunged down into the trough. I felt the boat surge as we sped up towards the next wave, the bow dipping, gushing a plume of white water over the deck, the wind gust hurling the spray at me. I shook cold water off my head, wiped salt from my eyes and made adjustments on the tiller to prepare for the next crest.

Lacey's head appeared at the open companionway, his paws dangling over the lip.

"Stay there Lacey, good boy."

But he wouldn't listen and hauled himself up into the cockpit, trying to jump up beside me onto the slippery, pitching seat.

"Don't leave me, Captain!"

"Lacey, no. It's not safe for you up here..."

I felt my stomach lurch as the boat dropped down into another deep trough. I fought the tiller to try and maintain speed and steerage as we climbed the frothing wave. But the bow lifted high, momentarily stalling the boat before it slammed down, making Jessica shudder, threatening to rip her mast supports from the deck.

Cold seawater seeped down my back. I shuddered and clenched my teeth. Lacey braced himself against me and shook his head, his ears flapping, scattering water. I unzipped my jacket and scooped him inside to try and keep him warm and dry.

"Good job I've trimmed down, eh Lacey, there's room for two of us now."

His shivering began to ease as my body heat leeched into him.

"There, that's better..."

Some passage plan, Harry! You stupid fool...

I felt Jessica's speed pick up as another gust buffeted us.

"Hold on Lacey!"

I tried to adjust course and release the mainsheet simultaneously, yanking down on the rope to free off the sail and depower the boat, a split-second too late…

The wall of green and white frothing seawater hit us side on, just as a stronger howling gust of wind knocked the mast over, rotating Jessica through the wind, flipping Lacey and I over the port side into the angry sea…

Twenty Seven

I scream and scream and scream. Blood vessels at straining point, facial muscles contorting with pain as a thousand red hot needles stab deep inside my stomach, burning soft pliable flesh, forcing me into a foetal position. Salt water fills my mouth and lungs as I cry, my arms useless to keep me afloat as I sink below the surface. Sunlight disappears overhead as a dark blue-green gloom closes over. My world gets darker and darker…

*

Wake up and THINK!
Stop panicking, Harry.
Pull cord…
Pull… the… cord… NOW!
The sound of a muted explosion, then a rush upwards, the lifejacket firm and buoyant around my neck and chest, yanking me towards the surface.

*

I retch, coughing putrid seawater, mercifully able to scream in agony

once more. Someone is holding me, keeping me in the cool water.
The friendly face is reassuring, despite barely able to stay afloat. A familiar, calming gaze that never leaves me…

*

"Arrrgggghhh!"

I coughed seawater, gasping for fresh air as I broke through the surface, bobbing over the angry swell. I frantically rotated my head, searching for the boat… there, lying on its side. Being blown away from me…

"Lacey?" I yelled, spluttering as another wave lifted me up over its crest.

I kicked my feet, hurriedly turning in the water, searching for him. The flash of red lifejacket caught my eye, swimming towards me, accompanied by his muffled yelping.

"What'd you do that for? I've already had a wash this month!"

Lacey stuck his nose in my face, his tongue licking my cheek.

"Good boy! This way…"

I pushed his doggy-paddling body in front of me and swam for the boat, adrenalin flooding my system. The weight of Jessica's keels should have heaved her upright, but the mainsheet rope had snagged around the rudder, tensioning the mainsail every time Jessica tried to right herself. I frantically grabbed the rope, knowing I didn't have much time before the cabin flooded and she went under.

I hooked the taut mainsheet rope under my foot, grabbed hold of the guard wire and hauled myself up, transferring all of my weight onto the rope.

"Come on Jessica!" I yelled.

I felt the rope give a little. The sail began to flog as Jessica started to rise up, then faltered as we bobbed over the next crest and the rope tightened again.

"Again, Harry!" I shouted.

I lifted my body up and heaved down on the rope with all my strength.

"Arrrgggghhhh!"

Twang!

Whooooosssshhhh!

The force of the rope yanking free from the rudder catapulted my foot away from the boat, throwing me back into the water.

Disorientated, I paddled around in time to see Jessica's rigging shudder as she righted herself into the wind, her sails flogging wildly.

"Yeah!"

I swam back to the boat, snatched at the stern boarding ladder and clung on.

"Lacey!"

I heard barking to my right.

"You're really beginning to piss me off now, Captain!"

I hauled Lacey back on board and stepped over the guard wires into the relative safety of Jessica's cockpit.

We sat there for a moment, ankle deep in water while I surveyed the damage.

Twelve inches of seawater sloshed around below deck. Serious, but salvageable if the bilge pump did its job. I kissed Lacey, lowered him down onto the cabin starboard berth and closed up the companionway hatch. Then I quickly checked our proximity to the shore.

Two miles of open water. No immediate danger of being pummelled on the rocks. Okay...

I turned my attention back to the boat, aware of Lacey's barking.

"Oy, maggot brain, I ain't sharing no watery grave with Davey Jones!"

"It's okay Lacey, you're safe down there," I called out in my most reassuring voice.

I began pumping the manual bilge handle, hunching low to avoid the boom, thrashing around above my head.

I wondered if the engine would start.

I shuffled across to the control panel and twisted the key. The engine turned over, but wouldn't fire.

Bugger!

"Okay, no problem, try again later. Get her sailing, Harry, move this boat..." I stuttered, my teeth chattering.

I hauled in the slack mainsheet rope until the boom stood forty-five degrees from the centreline, then set the same amount of genoa. With the tiller gripped in both hands, I pulled it hard towards me, willing Jessica to turn.

I glanced down at my feet, relieved to see the water in the cockpit draining away.

The sails stiffened as they filled and Jessica gradually began to make way, wallowing over the swell with the weight of the extra water down below.

With one hand on the tiller, I got to work on the bilge pump handle again, maintaining a steady rhythm.

"Options and priorities, Harry... think!" I yelled. I glanced at my watch, searching my memory for the passage notes I'd prepared.

Another two hours of tide at full strength opposing the wind. It'll be worse if I turn back and run for Dartmouth. No immediate safe harbour. Conditions will calm down when the tide turns. The wind is due to ease later too...

Lacey's barking roused me from my deliberations. I stopped cranking the bilge pump handle and slid the hatch open.

"It's okay, Lacey."

"I'm paddling down here, Captain. Water's supposed to be on the outside!"

I scanned the cabin sole, noticing less water sloshing around Lacey's paws.

"Stay there Lacey, good boy."

I slid the hatch closed and wracked my brain for the best course of action. I didn't fancy the River Yealm's narrow entrance, tacking into an easterly headwind with no engine. Two more hours to Plymouth, by then the tide would have turned, calming the swell. There would be plenty of sea room and more activity on the water if I ran into more problems...

Plymouth it is.

Twenty Eight

My arms ached from my efforts on the bilge pump, despite swapping sides every thirty strokes. I eased the hatch open, pleased to see the shiny fibreglass floor, minus any water sloshing around.

No sign of Lacey, but I suspected he'd huddled up in a corner, there wasn't anywhere else for him to go. I could feel much more response through the tiller now without the extra weight of water below deck.

Happy days.

The outline of Rame Head, black and foreboding, grew steadily larger, helped by our increasing boat speed and the shallower rolling swell, dropping off now the tide had turned. The wind had eased off too, now blowing steadily rather than the unpredictable squally gusts, making for a pleasant sail.

I cast my eye over the instruments, then checked the sail trim and location of other boats.

No immediate danger, I can risk it.

I engaged the autopilot and opened the hatch to climb down into the cabin. A soggy mess of books, charts and wet clothes greeted me.

"Lacey?" I called, shining a torch into the pilot berth behind the chart table.

Lacey's shiny eyes stared back at me. He stretched and dragged his long body towards me, making his normal grumbling noises.

"Are we there yet? I need a wee… then food. Lots of food… and beer. For the fear."

*

It's amazing the difference a few hours can make. We'd left the Great Mewstone and Wembury Bay behind some time ago and now approached Plymouth Sound on the tail end of Mother Nature's tantrum. Jessica's bow pushed easily through the gentle glassy swell, now ranging no more than half a metre.

Lacey cuddled up next to me in the cockpit, wrapped in two towels to keep him warm. I sipped hot, sweet tea, savouring its comforting warmth, swilling the last few mouthfuls around in the mug. I raised the cup, about to drain it, then stopped myself and held it under Lacey's nose, watching him lap it up.

All I needed now was for the engine to start…
I closed my eyes and turned the key.
Please, *Big Man…*
Dum… dum… dum… verroom!
"That's more like it!"

With the autopilot taking the strain, I furled the genoa in, lowered the mainsail and settled back in the cockpit with Lacey.

"We're on our final approach now, boy. Through The Narrows, next stop the marina near Devonport and the nearest pub…"

*

No amount of hot water could stop me shaking.

I stood in the cubicle under the cascading shower holding Lacey against my chest.

We nearly lost the boat out there... how bloody stupid of me.

My chest ached from the immersion in the cold water, causing me to wince every time I took a deep breath.

Not good, Harry.

I couldn't hold Lacey any longer, I had to put him down. He stepped out of the cubicle and shook off the excess water. My short sharp breaths jabbed my chest in painful gasps. I reached behind my back, fumbled for the mixer tap and turned the water off. Sinking down against the cold tiled wall, I hugged my knees to contain my trembling and scrunched my eyes shut to fend off a tidal wave of emotion.

I felt his soft furry head nudge my leg. Finally still, I lifted my chin from my knees, my breathing calmer, yet still irregular and panicky, like trying to extract oxygen at altitude. Lacey's dark eyes stared at me. He whimpered softly, his tail twitching.

"Wake up, human. Lacey dinnertime."

He sprung up on his hind legs, pressed his front paws into my shoulder and pushed his nose under my chin, encouraging me to lift my head up.

"I don't think I can go on, Lacey."

He sank back onto the floor, then eased his nose under my arm, persistently nudging it.

I relaxed, allowing him to climb up under my elbow onto my lap.

His front paws hooked over my shoulders, his head resting to one side of my chin. He didn't try to lick my face anymore, he just lay there quietly against my chest, cuddling into me.

We sat there together for a long time. No movement, just our regular breathing merging into synchronicity.

"Okay, I'm ready," I said at last, nuzzling my face into Lacey's damp fur, kissing his head.

I gently eased Lacey off me, then with some considerable effort, I stood up and stepped out of the cubicle. The towel felt extra soft on my prune-like skin, the process of drying myself carried out in a daze. I got dressed, then wrapped the towel around Lacey and dried him as best as I could.

"Lacey dinnertime?" I mumbled, my voice faint, a distant echo rattling around in my empty head.

Lacey yapped at me and licked his lips, forcing me to attempt a smile.

"Steak dinner for your furry friend? Standard trauma survival food. You're buying, Harry."

*

I pushed the plate of unfinished food away. My stomach still felt like a cold wet sponge, wrung tightly in a clenched fist. Lacey didn't suffer from any such problems, judging by his paw tapping on my shin. I gazed down into his hypnotic eyes and retrieved his bowl from the floor, scraping the remains of my meal into it.

I watched him scoff the food for a few seconds, long enough for me to follow the direction of the bowl being pushed across the pub floor.

Drips of condensation trickled down the outside of the full pint of beer stood on the table in front of me, collecting in a pool on the beermat. Beside the glass sat an untouched double brandy. I alternated my gaze between the two drinks, imagining the taste of each in my mouth. Cool, refreshing and uplifting… warm, fuzzy and comforting.

Which one first?

Either, or perhaps… *neither...*

"Are you okay, love?"

I lifted my head and looked over at the barmaid stood beside my table.

"Sorry, miles away."

"Are you alright?"

"Um… bit too early to say."

"You've been deliberating for some time. I can take these away if… if it helps."

I flicked my eyes down to the table. I found myself nodding, without understanding why.

"Would you mind? I don't think I should drink right now."

"I understand. My partner, he struggles too… it will get easier."

I nodded my thanks and watched her collect both glasses.

You need to finish this journey, Harry, I told myself. If you don't go back to the boat now, you never will…

I screwed my eyes tightly shut, clenched my shaking hands together, then forced my eyes open and summoned all my strength to stand up.

Twenty Nine

I stood on the pontoon staring at Jessica. Lacey sat beside me, waiting patiently. I dropped my eyes to meet his.

"What do you think?"

Lacey held my gaze, unblinking. I tore my eyes away from the quirky little dog and looked back at the boat.

"You know, Jessica… I haven't thanked you. For hanging in there and looking after us. I suppose I ought to thank your builder too."

I reached out and laid my hand on the deck.

"What's it going to be, Harry? The longer you stand here…" I said, my voice sounding unconvincing.

I stooped down and lifted Lacey up, guiding him under the guard wires. Then I hauled myself aboard.

*

I knew that if I didn't keep myself busy I might never sail the boat away from Plymouth, so I began cleaning up the cabin. Anything that could be salvaged, I lay out on deck to dry. Books that had turned to pulp, I threw out.
I rinsed down and disinfected the galley surfaces, cleaning my way down to the floor. I

aired my sleeping bag and pillows on deck and made a trip to the marina laundrette.

I found my waterlogged mobile phone but couldn't get it to work, despite removing the battery and sim card to dry out.

"No great loss, Lacey. Who's going to call me anyway?" I said, bagging the phone components.

When I'd retrieved everything I could, Lacey and I sat up on the foredeck on one of the cabin cushions. It felt different, relaxing on this part of the boat, being remote from the accountability of the cockpit. I found it strangely comforting.

With the evening sun still warm, I lay back and stared up at the sky, an overwhelming tiredness enveloping me. I propped a damp pillow under my head and draped my hand over Lacey's back. He rolled over, pressing his warm body into my side. My aching muscles began to relax, the tension ebbing away as I sank into a deep, dreamless sleep.

*

I woke once in the night to a kaleidoscope of stars high above me. Puzzled, I lifted my head and glanced around, the moonlit water shimmering beyond the guard wires.

I reached down to my side, felt the velvety softness of Lacey's ears. He twitched awake at my touch, nuzzling his head into my hand.

"We should probably go down below, Lacey," I murmured, but I felt too comfortable and exhausted to move. Despite my need to sleep, something struck me as odd: Why didn't I feel cold...?

I rolled the blanket's texture between my thumb and first finger. The soft wool didn't feel familiar. It smelt fresh too, of lavender.

"Someone is looking after us," I muttered, smiling as I allowed myself to drift back to sleep, as a billion stars looked on.

*

The blanket conundrum continued to puzzle me the next morning.

I folded it neatly and placed it on a plastic bag on the pontoon, to protect it from the morning dew.

"We should probably leave a thank you note, Lacey," I said aloud.

Lacey looked up from cleaning his paws, cocked his ears and tipped his head inquisitively to one side. I searched the boat, but lack of dry writing paper proved to be a problem.

But you've got something better, haven't you Harry, I realised.

The engine started without a problem. I slipped the mooring lines and steered Jessica away from the pontoon, turning to glance back at the blanket folded neatly on the pontoon, weighed down by a partially-drunk bottle of brandy salvaged from the galley. I wouldn't be needing it anymore.

*

This time I'd taken a lot more care over the passage plan, double-checking the weather forecast and factoring in the likely sea conditions.

We motored across Plymouth Sound and picked up the start of the channel ebb, the south-easterly breeze blowing at a steady twelve knots, making for a relatively flat sea. Perfect sailing conditions. Safely past Rame Head, we turned right, the wind direction allowing me to set the sails.

I marvelled at the power of Mother Nature as the clattering diesel donkey died and the wind pushed Jessica along with barely a whisper, trailing a gentle wake behind us.

"One more stop Lacey, nearly there."

*

I whiled away the hours in the cockpit, reading Jessica's boat logbook with the auto-helm whirling as it made course adjustments. Occasionally I'd lift my head from the handwriting to keep a lookout and glance over at the barren, rugged coastline.

"It's called 'The Jurassic Coast' for good reason, eh Lacey?"

Depending on the light, the black jagged rocks could look threatening or picturesque.

Clear bright skies illuminated bold spiky shards and craggy peaks. Cloudy conditions, however, brought a sinister and imposing profile to the coastline.

With a steady motion under Jessica's keel, I turned my attention back to the logbook. Until now I'd skipped through some of the factual excerpts, as my mood and interest level dictated, until only the last group of entries remained.

> *19th Day of August, Nineteen Seventy-Seven*
> *Depart Weymouth Bay 11:00 hours. South-westerly. Force 3, perfect conditions. Baby Harry in the doghouse for early morning tantrum. Captain Anthony overrules mother – she's too soft with the boy. Keith reprimanded for carving his initials in the bow cabin woodwork. Six strokes of the cane across his backside for defacing my boat.*
> *ETA Poole, 19:00 hours. Fish dinner on the quay, drinks with the Moreys to look forward to.*

I lifted my head from the text, checked our course and looked out for other boats. Then I dropped my eyes back to my father's elegant swooping handwriting.

> *Poole Harbour entrance made at 19:06 hours. Slack water. Entered under sail, held all the way to the docks. Dinner and merriment awaits.*

That concluded the day's entry. I turned the page, knowing there had to be more. But the tone of the next entry, dated three days later, surprised me.

> *I wish we'd never had kids. The anguish they put you through isn't worth the…*

Thwack!

I stared at the logbook, pressed firmly shut in my clasped hands.

Lacey lifted his head from sunbathing. He stared at me, unblinking.

"Some people of that generation… did they have no compassion?"

Lacey pushed himself up and stretched, then climbed up onto my lap and shuffled round so he could see the coastline. I tickled behind his ears, allowed my thoughts to drift back, all those years ago.

So many hospital visits… more frequent in the early days. I couldn't remember much from that far back. Only the day itself had stayed with me. Agony retains a lot of imagery.

Thirty

We made our final approach to Fowey on a slack tide with barely a breath of wind, the combination of which had settled the sea state to a flat calm.

The engine pushed us along at half power towards St Catherine's Point Lighthouse, a few degrees below a north-west heading. White buildings perched on the left side of the entrance, some in neat rows, others scattered ad hoc. I held our course until the blind side of the entrance opened up, making sure I steered well clear of the rocks before I began edging up towards Ready Money Cove, taking care to avoid the semi-submerged rocks off Neptune Point.

"I love days like this, Lacey. There's something magical about arriving somewhere new."

Lacey sat beside me and sniffed the air, his eyes half-closed.

"I can smell the beer already…"

Beyond the imposing entrance, Fowey consisted of a wide basin with countless boat moorings dotted across the water.

"Safe haven, Lacey."

I'd read in the pilot book about a walk-ashore visitors' pontoon farther upstream at Mixtow Pill, so we held our course past the quay and RNLI station. I shook off a shudder at the sight of the lifeboat, remembering how close we'd come to requiring their services.

We left the industry of China Clay Quay to port and turned into Mixtow Pill, finding a spare mooring alongside the visitors' pontoon.

"Walkies, Lacey?"

"You betcha! Did you say there's a pub on the way?"

*

I toyed with my orange and soda, unable to get my father's written words out of my head.

'I wish we'd never had kids', he'd written.

The logbook lay unopened on the pub table. I'd subconsciously brought it with me, despite vowing that I'd read about as much as I wanted to. And yet, here it was.

"What do you reckon, Lacey?"

I glanced down at him, but found no answers in his unblinking gaze.

With a deep sigh, I picked up the logbook and flicked through the pages to find my father's last set of entries.

I wish we'd never had kids. The anguish they put you through isn't worth the endless hours of nurture and unconditional emotional investment.

I can barely bring myself to record the events of Wednesday last. We'd arrived on Poole Quay from Weymouth in good spirits after an uneventful passage, childish tantrums aside. Elizabeth and I dressed smartly for the dinner date with the Moreys. Keith and baby Harry had been fed and put to bed. But baby wouldn't settle. I spoke sharply to Elizabeth, concerned we'd be late.

"You go ahead, I'll get him off to sleep and join you in a few minutes," she'd said. How I wish I'd waited. But I was impatient and didn't want to be late, it's rude.

So off I went. True to her word, Elizabeth joined me twenty minutes later.

Halfway through the second bottle of wine with our friends, we heard the screams.

We rushed back to the boat to find utter chaos. Keith was barely treading water beside the boat with baby. My fury exploded with a foul mouth rant at Keith for being so bloody idiotic. What the hell was he thinking, swimming with an infant? He'd drown the child and probably himself too. Baby screamed constantly. Not just a cry for food or a nappy change, this was a blood-curdling agonising wail.

I realised this was no childish prank, something serious had happened.

So I raced across the boat and offered my outstretched hands, pulling baby out of Keith's hands. But Keith yelled at me: "No! Harry's burnt!"

I froze, cradling the screaming child in my hands, suddenly aware how hot he was. I eased the top of the Babygro away from

Harry's neck, sickened to see a pulpy
mess of skin on his tummy.
"Harry needs to be in the water…" Keith
shouted. I fought the urge to throw up,
tasting acid bile at the back of my throat.
"Keep his tummy below the water!" I
screamed, virtually throwing the baby
back into Keith's arms.
"Call an ambulance!" I shouted up to the
concerned faces on the quay, before I
jumped into the water next to Keith. I
pulled Harry away from Keith, clutching
the screaming mite, all the time yelling for
an ambulance, leaving Keith to drift away
beside me.

My hands trembled as I turned the page.

23rd day of August, Nineteen Seventy-
Seven
Baby Harry is clinging to life after the first of
many operations that will be required until
he stops growing. More skin grafts will
follow, they tell us. Words cannot express
the constant sickness I feel, deep inside.
A hot water bottle, wrapped in a towel so it
didn't burn his skin, had been placed next
to him. They told us it had most likely been
overfilled, which caused it to explode. Who
has so little common sense? Elizabeth and
me, that's who. Idiots.
STUPID. BLOODY. IDIOTS.
The doctors said the water immersion

saved his life. A bath of cold water is the prescribed first aid treatment, but there's nothing of that size on the boat. So Keith did the next best thing and leapt into the harbour with Harry in his arms, holding his head above water, despite not being a strong swimmer…
Why did I leave Elizabeth to deal with baby Harry on her own? If I were a God-fearing man I would pray for forgiveness. Instead, I cry and drink.
Then I drink and cry some more. I don't know what else to do.

In a trance, I turned the page over, then fanned through the rest of the book. Only one entry of a few lines remained.

12th day of September, Nineteen Seventy-Seven
It is with a heavy heart that I watch Jessica being lifted out of the water and set down in the boatyard. I'll pack her up for long term storage, I don't know when I'll be back. My son is still in hospital, clinging to life. My wife and I are drinking to excess. I must stay strong for Harry, so I will put on a brave face and battle onwards. But inside I feel like Jessica as she is laid up and left – empty and without happiness or hope. I am lost at sea, at the mercy of God's will.

I stared at the empty lines beneath the handwriting, my white knuckles gripping the sides of the logbook. I screwed my eyes shut, forcing back a tidal wave of confused emotions, my stomach so tightly clenched I couldn't breathe.

"This is quite possibly the cutest doggy I've ever met."

I blinked, snatched a few short breaths and forced myself to step out of the darkness, away from an emotional abyss.

I flicked my moist eyes up at a woman in her mid-forties, stood cradling Lacey in her arms. I closed the logbook, held it between my trembling hands and forced myself to meet her gaze.

"This one has a mischievous side. He was begging for a share of my dinner."

I nodded.

"He does that. Saves me a fortune in dog food," I said in a parched, gravelly voice.

"What's his name?"

"Lacey."

"That's a pretty name for a gorgeous dog. I hope you don't mind me picking him up, he's just so… fluffy."

"His fur gets frizzy after it rains and he dries out."

I heard the strained tone of my own voice. It didn't sound like me. Another one of those surreal *outside-looking-in* moments.

"I'm Hazel. Do you mind if I sit down?"

I shrugged.

"You look like you've had a tough day," she said as she pulled up a stool.

"You can see that through my mascara?"

She smiled at me, a look of concern in her eyes.

"Your eyes are puffy. They're a dead giveaway... a woman?"

"Nope."

"A man?"

"Sort of, but not in that way."

She broke eye contact, busied herself with tickling Lacey's tummy.

"I can leave you to it, if this is bad timing..."

I took a deep unsteady breath, exhaling all of my defensive energy.

"Sometimes I dwell on the past... it's not healthy. I'm Harry."

I offered my hand. We shook in a business-like manner.

"Want to talk about it?" she said.

"No, thanks."

Lacey fidgeted in Hazel's arms, twisting his body and grumbling as he climbed out of her embrace and settled on her lap, facing me.

"I like this one, Harry. Comfy bazoobies."

"He's a little character. I bet he gets you lots of attention... with the ladies," said Hazel.

I held her gaze.

"The ladies do seem to like him," I replied carefully.

"And do they like you too, Harry?"

"Sometimes," I said, a cautious edge creeping into my voice.

Hazel's eyes twinkled with mischief, which had the odd effect of thawing the icicles prickling my gut.

"That must be nice..."

Where are you going with this, Hazel…? I pondered.

"It can be, from time to time," I replied after a long pause.

Her face lit up with a playful smile.

"Which is good for both parties…"

I reached for my glass. The taste of orange and soda made me wince, triggering a series of flashbacks reminding me why I had a non-alcoholic drink:

Falling into the sea.
The boat nearly sinking.
Clutching Lacey in the shower.

"You okay? You've gone a bit pale."

I blinked at her, retrieving my focus from the middle of the far wall.

"Sorry… rough day," I said.

"Can I get you something stronger to drink? It might help."

I shook my head slowly.

"A few days ago it might have… but not anymore."

"I'm sorry if I've intruded… would you prefer to be on your own?"

I sat back, breathing easier now my stomach had warmed up.

"Not especially… it's nice to have some company. Do you live locally?" I said, pushing the logbook a few inches farther away from me.

"I do."

I watched her pick up a beermat and twirl it between her fingers.

"Do you mind if I'm direct, Harry?"

"Sounds ominous…"

"Mmm. Politeness and unnecessary small talk… tends to slows things down."

I frowned, surprised at a twitch of arousal, down below.

"How so?"

She placed the beermat on the table, clasped her hands together and levelled her eyes on mine.

"It's like this, Harry: I have a need, for… intimacy," she said in a low voice.

I swallowed, my dry throat in danger of croaking my reply.

"Oh. That's… intriguing…"

"Isn't it."

She began fiddling with the beer mat again.

"So for the right… *consideration*, would you be interested?"

I stared at her, then flicked my eyes around the pub, almost as if searching for a hidden camera. I leant forwards, lowered my voice.

"I've never paid for that sort of thing… with a… you know… *lady of the night.*"

She giggled and flicked her hair, then leant forwards and whispered.

"I think you've got your wires crossed, Harry… I'd be paying you."

Thirty One

My jaw hung open for several seconds.

"You're kidding."

She shook her head.

"Hear me out."

I sat back, folded my arms.

"I split up with my husband three years ago. He was a lying, cheating, manipulative bastard. And he destroyed my self-esteem, which has left me bitter and mistrustful of men. Despite this, I still miss the lack of physical contact… but I'm deeply suspicious of new partners. I have trust issues. So I've devised a coping mechanism, to protect myself from emotional involvement. I control my physical encounters with men by carefully selecting them and paying for their services."

"So it becomes a business transaction?"

"Exactly. As the client, I'm in charge."

"Which allows you to protect yourself behind an emotional force field."

She dropped her eyes to Lacey. "See, I knew your daddy was the type to understand."

"It seems a little… detached."

"It doesn't have to be. It's just a set of rules we both sign up to."

"I see."

I sipped my orange soda, amused to see Lacey straining his neck to sniff the air, whining.

"We're on the wagon Lacey, remember."

"So you say, Romeo. I'm thirsty!"

I reached out to stroke Lacey, then glanced up at Hazel.

"It sounds a bit domineering… not really my sort of thing."

She smiled, radiating warmth.

"This isn't motivated by control, Harry. It's about being more respectful, of my needs and yours."

"So no red room of pain?"

She laughed, blushing.

"Far from it. I have fairly conventional, bordering on conservative, tastes. I've no desire to inflict or receive pain. The opposite in fact."

"Right… but isn't this a bit, you know, cold and clinical?"

"I hope not. The money exchange allows me to establish an emotional distance, but I'd be paying for a quality service, so to speak. I like slow and sensual mostly, passionate sometimes. You'd have to fully participate and enjoy the experience for us both to feel involved and satisfied."

Is she for real? I thought, a dull ache growing behind my eyes.

"Do you have a price list or something? I mean, money isn't a motivating factor particularly, I think I understand your reasons. But I'd need to know what you have in mind…"

"I don't have a list as such… it's more an order of play…"

"Hey, you don't work for the circus do you? He doesn't do clowns…"

Hazel giggled at Lacey's whining.

"Is he okay?"

"He wants beer."

Hazel shot me a confused look.

"Long story. Neither of us is used to being in a pub while sober."

"It seems like you have your own issues to work through, Harry."

I held her gaze, conceded with a shrug. "Am I going to have to sign a contract?"

"In a way. We shake hands on a verbal agreement."

"Okay… I'm listening."

She nodded, her cheeks glowing.

"There's a stage by stage progression. I have somewhere for us to go. My friend, sitting over there, waits outside the door. Any problems, she rings the police."

Hazel pointed to an adjacent table. I turned to look over my shoulder at a woman in her late thirties sat on her own. The woman winked at me and raised her glass of wine. I turned back to face Hazel.

"I pay for each stage of our encounter, starting with ten pounds for gentle kissing. Next, for twenty pounds, we kiss again for several minutes, during which time I take your shirt off and you slowly unbutton my blouse. You don't unclip or remove my bra, that's off limits.

Taking your time and using your fingertips, you caress my back, neck and tummy. Think: *sensuous,* all the time.

If I like the way it's going, I remove my shoes and skirt. Thirty pounds changes hands. For this, you continue to kiss me gently, while slowly brushing your fingers over my tummy, down towards my special place. Once there, your fingers will work their magic for several minutes. If all that goes well and I'm feeling enthusiastic, forty pounds requires you to remove your trousers and pants. You stand there, hands by your side, eyes closed while I touch you, *down there.* At this stage I may decide to use my mouth, but I may not. For fifty pounds you put on a condom and I ask you to make love to me, gently, while kissing me tenderly. I may not necessarily orgasm during our lovemaking, but this won't detract from my enjoyment. If, however, I do climax, I pay a fifty pounds bonus. I like to cuddle up afterwards, so you need to lie there and hold me for fifteen minutes. Then, you stay in bed while I get up. You watch me dress. I kiss you goodbye, on the cheek this time and I leave you with potentially two hundred pounds in cash. You wait for twenty minutes before you leave the room and we never see each other again."

I stared at Hazel, all sorts of crazy thoughts whizzing through my stone-cold-sober brain:

1. Bloody hell, I'm getting turned on!
2. Is she serious?
3. She's a con artist, she'll rob me.
4. So what.
5. It's something new, exciting and different.
6. I can't. What about my stomach…
7. More to the point, what about Mary?
8. And Alice.

9. But you haven't had sex with either of them. So technically you're not betraying anyone.
10. And you could do with having some fun…

I tried to swallow, had to take a swig of my drink to lubricate my throat.

"If we do this, there's something you should know. About my… *physique.*"

"Okay, go on."

"I have scars, from a nasty burn on my tummy. Since you'd be paying, you should know it's not very attractive. In fact, it's…"

"We all have our scars, Harry. Some on display… others buried deep."

The trace of an ambiguous emotion flickered behind her eyes, but I couldn't place it.

"Are you sure? It's actually quite unpleasant…"

"It won't bother me," she said firmly. "Is there anything else I should know?"

"Like what?"

"Anything relevant to the transaction we're discussing."

I shook my head.

She took a slow deep breath.

"Okay. So, Harry… what do you think?"

*

I handed Lacey's lead to Hazel's friend who took up a sentry post outside the bedroom door. I reached down to stroke him.

"I'll be back soon, little one."

"Make sure you don't short change the lady. Bonus beer tokens are at stake!"

I turned to Hazel's friend. "You will look after him?"

"Of course, love, we'll be right here. You treat Hazel with respect, alright?"

I nodded and followed Hazel through the bedroom door, music from the pub downstairs just audible.

Hazel shut the door behind me and leant back against it. I glanced around the simply furnished room. A solid pine bed stood against the right hand wall. Directly ahead, an old lattice-leaded light dormer window jutted out from the eaves of the roof, looking out over the harbour. Straw-colour painted walls gave the room a light and airy feel, despite the low wood beam ceiling.

"Is this your normal room?" I asked.

"I'm an occasional guest rather than a regular visitor. The landlady is a friend, she understands."

I sat down on the edge of the bed.

"Feels comfy."

A nervous and expectant smile creased her lips. She approached me, indicating with her hand that I should stand.

"Stage one… ready?"

She passed me a ten pound note. I held it in my hand, fiddling with the texture in my fingers.

"It's okay Harry, really. It doesn't make you a bad person for accepting money, nor me for paying."

"The implications of this are… strange."

"It's to make me feel comfortable."

I nodded and pocketed the note, waiting for her to move closer.

"Remember, the word is sensuous..."

We kissed, gently at first, our lips barely touching, then I responded, but let her take the lead. Gradually as we kissed, she parted her lips, slipping her tongue tentatively into my mouth. She tasted of white wine and mint chewing gum.

"Mmm, that's nice," she murmured, slowly pulling back. "Stage two coming up..."

She withdrew a thin fold of notes from her purse, peeled off a twenty and placed it in my palm.

"...okay?"

I nodded and pushed the note into my pocket. I watched her unbuttoning my shirt, easing it off my shoulders, revealing the tee-shirt underneath.

"Remember, I have..."

"Shh... it's okay. I understand."

She held my gaze, then gently lifted my tee-shirt up over my head. She emitted the tiniest gasp, her brow creasing as she stared at my tummy. The burn scar started an inch below my left nipple and finished just above my groin, covering most of my stomach. My shiny skin rippled with uneven joins and patchwork-quilt stitching scars. The burn looked like miniature tree root tentacles, held taut, permanently blended into my tummy. Almost as if someone had heated up a plastic plate, or an old vinyl record, then at the point of dissipating into a runny, melted blob, they'd thrown it at my stomach where it formed a glossy textured *splat*.

My scar made people wince and look away, the pain it had caused me vivid in the viewer's mind.

"Does it hurt, to touch?" she whispered, her voice breaking.

"No. There's hardly any feeling there."

I watched her trace the outline of the ugly ripples of my disfigurement with her fingertips.

Tears began to trickle down Hazel's cheeks. Her body trembled, but she said nothing. Her shaking fingers carefully examined every part of my scar. She looked up at me, took a slow uneven breath and lifted my hands to the top button of her blouse. I tried to gently wipe her tears away, but she shook her head and guided my fingers back to her chest.

I carefully undid the remaining buttons, allowing her to shrug the blouse off her shoulders. She leaned in close, we kissed, her lips salty with the taste of her tears.

My fingers stroked her back, tracing the outline of invisible patterns on her velvet soft skin. I felt wetness on my cheeks, caused by fresh tears falling from her sad eyes.

"I know you'll understand," she whispered, as she reached behind her back to unclasp her bra and shrug the straps off her shoulders.

She stepped back, allowing the bra to fall off her arms onto the floor. I dropped my eyes from hers, down towards her chest, my heart missing a beat at her own scar: a neat pattern of stitches along the bottom edge of where her right breast should have been. I flicked my eyes up to meet hers, a lump in my throat, tears welling in my eyes, unable to say anything. She held my gaze, traced her fingers down over my arms, collecting my hands where they hung limp by my side.

"Please, don't stop touching me…" she whispered.

I nodded, my fingers trembling as I placed one palm on her healthy breast, the other over her scar. Ever so gently, I brushed my fingertips over her skin, touching and caressing as my own tears fell freely.

*

We lay there, locked together, our breathing slowing. Her chest lifted and relaxed into my shoulder, head nuzzled into the round gap under my chin. Her hair smelt of lemon, soft and cool against my skin. She stroked my shoulder, the rhythm slowing in time with her breathing, calming now.

"Thank you Harry. That was gorgeous…" she mumbled.

I lay there absorbing her body's warmth. My eyelids flickered, becoming heavy. So relaxed and at peace, that I couldn't fight against the euphoric tiredness any longer and I drifted into a deep slumber.

Thirty Two

The sensation of something vaguely familiar landed on the bed, sinking the duvet as it scampered up beside me, drawing me away from my lovemaking-induced coma. My nose twitched at the distinctive doggy smell.

I woke with a splutter, a hot wet tongue and cold nose nuzzled into my face.

"Ugh, Lacey!"

I rolled over and tried to escape, but he climbed over my writhing body, persistently following my face, his wagging tail flicking the duvet.

"That took longer than normal, horny Harry!"

I wrestled Lacey into my arms, but he wriggled away and buried his head under the duvet, tunnelling his way down to my feet.

"He was scratching the door and whining to come in. He really loves you, Harry. You're very lucky."

I turned towards her voice. Hazel stood by the window, her back to me, looking out over the harbour and Fowey town streetlights.

"I'm quite fond of the loveable rogue."

Hazel turned to face me, her face glowing pink, a distant floaty look in her eyes.

"You've been good for me, Harry. What we've just shared… was everything I hoped it would be. I'm still tingling. Thank you."

She reached over the bed and kissed me on the lips, holding me in her embrace for a few seconds.

I propped myself up on my elbows as she pulled back. I watched her walk slowly around the bed towards the door. She reached out for the handle, then paused and glanced over her shoulder at me.

"I've left the balance of your money on the table, bonus included. You've been so lovely… under different circumstances, if I were ready… well, who knows…"

She smiled with a mix of warmth and melancholy.

"You're a beautiful person, Hazel… and under different circumstances…" I replied quietly, holding her gaze.

She almost hesitated, but something inside must have urged her on, because she opened the door and gently pulled it shut behind her. She didn't look back.

*

I lay there, staring at the ceiling.

"What do you think the protocol is, Lacey? Do we stay here until the morning, or sneak out now to avoid any knowing looks from the staff?"

I rolled out of bed and pulled the duvet with me, revealing Lacey, stretched out. He opened one eye, his tail twitching in short strokes.

"I'd say order room service, Harry… but you've just eaten…"

I tipped my head at the door.

"Come on lazybones. Best not outstay our welcome."

"Now? But it's cold and dark outside."

I dressed, watching Lacey hunch up on his front legs and drag his body across the bed. He shook himself, then settled back into the duvet, rotating around and collapsing down in a ball, cocooning himself.

"No sleeping, Lacey. We're heading back to the boat," I said, clipping his lead onto his collar.

"But I'm soooooo snug…"

I tugged on the lead, smirking at his disgruntled 'harrumph' sigh.

We nearly made it out the front door without seeing another soul.

"Have a pleasant evening sir," said a cheerful voice.

I flinched and turned towards the pub landlady who'd served me earlier that evening.

"Oh, right… thank you."

I opened the door and scurried away, childlike in my eagerness to escape a telling off, or worse, a knowing wink.

We trudged up the lane towards the footpath that would take us across the field and back to the boat. My torch picked out the stile over the stone wall, allowing us to leave the road and stroll through the wet grass. As I approached the brow of a small hill I slowed, glanced up at the sky, then stopped walking.

Someone else with a scar, I thought.

A strange sense of peace overcame me as I realised I wasn't alone with my disfigurement…

I snatched at a rogue tumbling breath, blinking rapidly as I hyperventilated. I stood there and stared at the sky. Someone else, far braver than me, had faced up to the world with a physical deformity… adapting and overcoming… coping admirably.

I gasped a sniffling breath, tried to force the emotion back in, but couldn't and, I realised, shouldn't. Instead I just stood there and surveyed the sky, letting my tears fall, killing time by picking out different star clusters and shapes. Without any light pollution to mask the effect, the stars shone brighter than I'd ever seen them. Rotating through a complete circle, I marvelled at the beauty of the night sky.

"What if we don't get there in time, Lacey… what then? I don't think we should wait for his birthday."

Lacey stopped sniffing the grass and cocked his head at me. I used my sleeve to wipe the moisture away from my eyes, then I glanced down at him.

"I'm ready now."

*

My morning cup of tea curled steam up to the boat's low roofline, collecting and billowing, lingering before dispersing.

'Under different circumstances…' she'd said. So where did that leave me with Mary and Alice?

I checked myself as a cloud of reality sunk in. What did it matter now…?

I forced the sick feeling deep inside and gritted my teeth. Onwards, Harry, I decided. You're not in the box yet…

I tipped the remainder of my tea into the sink and glanced around the cabin.

"We're taking you home, Jessica."

*

The familiar diesel rumble rattled the locker catches against metal clasps, their resonance prompting me to stop and take a moment to savour my achievement.

Nearly forty years left rotting in a boatyard… eighteen months hard work to get here. Now only one sail away from home…

"Ready Lacey? No sleeping on watch, okay."

Lacey stretched out in the cockpit and shut his eyes.

"Wake me when we get there, Captain."

I cast off the ropes and steered Jessica into the main channel, leaving the ceramic factory behind. Condensation twinkled on the deck under the glare of early morning light as the sun rose gracefully over the harbour moorings. Heading westwards, sailing into the setting sun… how fitting.

"Pretty magical, eh Lacey?"

I looked down at him, laid out in his favourite position behind the rudder stock. Oh for the simplicity of a dog's life.

I sighed, inhaling deeply, savouring the last of the morning chill as I held the damp breeze in my lungs.

The air tasted fresh and pure and smelt of the sea, enticing and adventurous.

*

The magic of the morning extended across the entire day, with conditions remaining constant, allowing me to relax and wallow in nature's purest addiction: just living in the beautiful moment.

By the time Falmouth Bay presented itself, we'd been happily chugging away at half-speed on flat water for three and a half hours. I felt so relaxed that the sudden tightness in my stomach as we rounded St Anthony's Head surprised me.

This wasn't a gradual transition from carefree to anxious, instead a blow from an ice-cold sledgehammer whacked me in the gut, its chill suffocating. I scanned the clear blue sky, expecting a dark cloud to be blocking the sun, then fought back an acidic taste at the back of my mouth. I pushed the sensation down into my hollow stomach.

It'll get worse Harry, until you see him, I told myself.

I pulled back on the throttle, allowing the boat to glide in neutral.

Do I really want to do this?

But I knew I couldn't back out now. With this thought, a locked door sprung open, years of conflicting emotions tumbling into conscious thoughts, bringing implications for reneging on promises to myself never to revisit the past.

You made this decision, eighteen months ago, I reminded myself. When the doctor delivered his sad news. That day when time suddenly became so precious.

The engine picked up speed as my trembling hand pushed the throttle lever forwards. I adjusted course to enter the main channel and steered towards the West Narrows and the inner harbour.

Stomach cramps stabbed painfully deep inside, putrid bile again rising up my throat, forcing me to lean over the guard wires as I threw up, my gut wrenching as if being pummelled rhythmically by an angry boxer's clenched fists.

I spat the remains of my breakfast into the sea and rinsed my mouth with bottled water.

"This could be tougher than I thought," I said to Lacey, who sat looking at me with a bewildered expression.

"Move over bulimic human, you need a doggy hug."

I sat down to stop Lacey pawing my leg and let him climb up onto my lap. His soft warm fur felt comforting against my tightly knotted stomach.

Why are you putting yourself through this, Harry…? I asked myself over and over again.

Thirty Three

"It's kaput, sir. See the water damage indicator."

I shrugged at the salesgirl.

"I'd best have a new one then, please."

I watched her load the new phone with my sim card. She replaced the battery and cover and waited for it to switch on.

"Your old contact numbers have all been transferred. I'll just set the time and date for you…"

A beeping tone and vibrating alert interrupted her.

"There you go, new messages. It's a similar model to your old phone, so you access everything in the same way, okay?"

I thanked her and left the shop.

"Oy, dimwit. Forgotten something?"

I turned at Lacey's barking and walked back to untie his lead from the lamp post.

"Sorry boy, here I am."

The phone began to ring. I glanced down at the screen, noting the voicemail service number.

Lacey tugged on his lead, eager to get going. I held the phone to my ear, my limbs frozen as I listened to a familiar voice, her message left earlier that morning.

"Hello Mister Straight. This is Anna, from Sandy Shores Nursing Home. Can you give me a call as soon as possible please? It's regarding your father."

I stood at the foot of the bed, my heart racing, palms sweating. The frail figure lay under a blanket, an oxygen tube clipped to his nose. Once-strong limbs lay useless beneath the bedding. His withered and spindly hands clutched the pillow. He looked like a fragile bag of bones.

"His body is slowly shutting down. It could be a few hours or several days. But in cases with these symptoms, it's just a matter of time," said Anna.

I'd not moved for several minutes, or had any constructive thoughts. I just stood there, staring at him as he slept, a weird floating sensation weakening my limbs.

"Would you like a chair?" asked Anna.

I shook my head, forced a swallow to try and dampen my dry mouth. My legs began to shake. That familiar hospital detergent smell, carried on wafts of the overactive heating system, made the stale air lifeless and claustrophobic. I needed to get out.

I passed through the double doors into the main corridor and heard Lacey's distant barking, hoarse from overuse. He must have been going at it since I'd left him.

I filtered past the smokers sat in wheelchairs outside the main entrance doors and found Lacey standing on all fours, howling.

"Where have you been?! This place is bad news, Harry..."

"Sorry Lacey. Let's go for a walk."

"Too right! It smells like black death out here."

I knelt down to comfort him, stroking his back.

"Come on boy, I need a drink."

I untied his lead, shaking my head at his excited prancing doggy-dance.

"A proper drink? Whoopee! Welcome back bro... mine's a Guinness!"

*

I knew I shouldn't. I'd been doing so well, had begun to view things differently. But seeing my father, my *Dad*, like that...

Not for fun, or to forget, I needed a drink just to feel something. Anything.

"Journey's end," I said to Lacey, raising my glass to him.

I tipped a splash of Guinness into his bowl and took a long swig from my pint.

Boy, that tasted good.

My eyes panned around The Chain Locker pub, recalling – from many nights boozing there in my teens – that it would soon fill with afternoon drinkers, building to a rowdy enthusiastic crowd by the evening.

"Many a shipmate lost in here, Lacey."

But he didn't respond, too busy chasing every drop of liquid from his bowl.

"What's this Harry, one man and his grog?"

I turned to see a barmaid clearing an

adjacent table of empty glasses. She looked to be in her late thirties, medium build, hair cut in a neat bob framing her attractive freckled face and wide, friendly smile. Something familiar teased my memories.

"Are you that drunk that you can't remember your first girlfriend?"

"Jenny?"

"You betcha. What's the doggy called?"

"Lacey."

"He's gorgeous. What brings you back?"

"Family stuff."

"Your Dad?"

I nodded, draining the rest of my pint. Jenny crouched down to stroke Lacey.

"Is he still a tyrant?"

"Not so much these days. He's in a nursing home… not expected to come out."

"I'm sorry to hear that."

"Don't be. I've not seen him in years."

Jenny stood up. She considered me with a thoughtful expression.

"Let me get you a drink. Same again?"

I glanced down, refocussing on the empty glass grasped in my hand and the redundant froth patterns forming inside.

A devil on one shoulder. Angel on the other…

I nodded reluctantly and handed her the glass.

"Thanks."

I looked down at Lacey, pawing my leg.

"Drink for the doggy, mister."

"I know, Lacey. It's a slippery slope. I'll have to plead extenuating circumstances."

"What's with the big words, sailor? I'm thirsty too!"

"There you go."

Jenny placed a fresh pint on the table and chuckled at Lacey's grumbling noises.

"I'm on my break. Mind if I join you?"

"Please, be my guest."

She pulled up a chair and sat down.

"Cheers."

I lifted my beer, touched it against her glass of coke.

"It's been twenty-three years, I worked it out," she said.

"Blimey. Did you marry?"

"Nearly ten years ago. Two kids and a cat called Gerald. You?"

"I was married, for almost eighteen years. We divorced recently."

"What went wrong?"

"Me, I think. My scar was… too much for her. She went off with someone else."

"Sorry again."

"Don't be. With hindsight, it never felt right. But I wasn't brave enough to admit that to myself."

"Talking of things that were never meant to be… I need to apologise for the way things were left."

"I've not got the energy to hold onto any anger. Time moves on…"

"Even so, it wasn't my finest hour."

"Was he worth it?"

"You were always the better man. I wish I'd

been stronger, more mature about your…
physique…"

She glanced down at her watch, finished her drink and stood up.

"No rest for the wicked. It's nice to see you again, Harry. Sorry you're here under such sad circumstances."

I nodded and dropped my eyes, toying with my glass, not really thinking of anything in particular. I just let the surreal 'being here' sensation wash over me.

As much for something to do, I reached into my pocket for my new mobile phone and tabbed through my messages. I deleted the voicemail notification, then selected a text message from Mary. I didn't realise she had my number. Yet another memory blank at the hands of the demon drink.

> Harry how could you? I thought we had something special. Mary

I studied the text, trying to regress and immerse myself in the time we'd shared. But even shutting my eyes couldn't transport me back.

The timing isn't right, Harry, I reminded myself. How could it be, today of all days?

I opened my eyes, tabbed through to the next message, from Alice.

> Not pretty, I know. But you have to understand what that woman did to me. Be careful Harry and look after Lacey. DD

The phone felt heavy in my hands, some sort of responsibility weighing it down. I glanced at my other hand, gripping the pint glass.

This is a pretty messed-up set of scales, I thought, even by your standards, Harry.

*

I tried to get drunk, I really did. Maybe the shock of seeing my once-strong, thick-set father shrivelled up in the hospital bed, or too much emotion-fuelled adrenalin, blocked the effect. Perhaps just being back here, two decades later, prevented me from enjoying the detachment that the booze should have provided.

Whatever the reason, I got bored of being unable to lose myself in the bottom of a glass. At around nine, with my stomach craving food and barely able to stay awake, I walked Lacey to the supermarket to stock up with supplies.

But we didn't make it that far.

"This way, Harry."

Lacey tugged on the lead, trying to take me into the car park on my left.

"Lacey, the supermarket is this way. Don't you want any dinner?"

"Dinner, yes. Cold crappy dog food, no. Especially when there's my favourite, right over here…"

"No Lacey, this way…"

I tugged on the lead again, but he hunched down low and braced himself, growling.

"It's THIS WAY, Humpty-Dumpty-human!"

I really wasn't in the mood for Lacey's stubbornness. I prepared to scoop him up into my arms, but then I caught an intoxicating waft of fried onions, chilli sauce and cooked meat, and my stomach rumbled. Sensible home-cooked food or an unhealthy yet heavenly kebab? Lacey pulled on the lead again, shifting my momentum in his direction. He glanced over his shoulder and barked at me, tugging relentlessly against the lead's tension.

"Come on Harry, meat feast, this way!"

"Go on then… it's not like I'm really that concerned about my waistline anymore…"

So off we trotted, towards the sizzling, smoking and sweet-smelling kebab and burger van.

"What'll it be?"

"Large donner please," I said to the cheerful pedlar-of-coronary-doom.

"Chilli sauce and salad?"

I glanced down at Lacey, sat by my feet, staring up at me and whining as he licked drool away from his slobbering chops.

"The works, please," I replied, flicking my eyes up into the van, hunger cramps prickling deep inside my stomach. Lacey's bark drew my eyes back to the ground, where he pranced excitedly, his tail wagging.

"Good man! Load it on, I'm bloomin' Hank Marvin!"

*

Despite struggling to *feel* drunk the night before,

boy oh boy did I have the hangover from hell to prove my efforts. My brain felt like the last pickled onion rolling around in a gallon of vinegar. Whenever I moved, the onion banged into the side of the jar, jolting a searing pain behind my eyes as if I'd been whacked in the head with a cricket bat. I lay there in the bow cabin in the early hours of the morning, wallowing in a world of hurt.

I pushed up onto my elbows, vaguely aware of the first shards of sunlight stretching across the cabin.

Big mistake.

My world began to spin.

I barely made it out of my sleeping bag and staggered into the heads before I threw up. My violent and sustained vomiting scorched my throat and left me knelt in a crumpled heap on the floor, hugging the toilet bowl. But that wasn't the end of it, oh no. A gurgling deep inside my stomach forced me to heave myself up onto the toilet seat and endure a torrent of diarrhoea.

I cleaned up and stumbled out of the heads, drawn to the main cabin by a strained, hollow retching sound. Lacey's long thin body convulsed as he threw up. He took a few wobbly sideways steps and vomited again, creating a second bright yellow frothy patch on the floor.

My stomach clenched, forcing me to turn away and take several deep breaths, fighting the urge to be sick again myself.

I knelt down next to Lacey and gently stroked his taut, hunched-up shoulders. He coughed the last of the bile onto the floor, slouched down and hung his head.

"You want some water, Lacey?" I asked, removing a tissue from my pocket to wipe his mouth.

I pulled his rabbit water bowl nearer, but Lacey turned his head away, his dull listless eyes staring at the floor.

"Maybe the kebab wasn't such a great idea… Come on, let's put you back to bed."

His tail twitched as I gently lifted him up. He seemed lighter than I remembered. He felt frail.

I eased him into the sleeping bag and tucked the sides under his chin.

"You'd think we'd learn, eh?"

I stroked Lacey's head, watching him fight to keep his eyes open. He looked exhausted.

Lacey edged his nose away from the water bowl as I tried to offer it again.

"You must try to drink, little fella."

But he grumbled and shifted further away from me.

Not a chance, mister. I feel like dog crap.

I sat down on the bunk opposite, wondering what to do. My stomach twinged again, encouraging me to hastily revisit the heads. I flicked an imaginary coin in my head and decided being sick seemed more likely. But as I would find out over the next few hours, the sickness and diarrhoea kept coming in alternate and debilitating waves.

*

We must have slept for several hours, on and off, our slumber interrupted by intermittent toilet visits. We cuddled up under the sleeping bag during the dry spells, making a sorry pair. By mid-afternoon we'd managed to lay quietly for three hours without being ill, so I thought I could chance popping out for a brief visit to the nursing home. I left Lacey and headed off to the shower block. When I got back to the boat, Lacey had barely shifted position. Hopefully he'd got over the worst of it and would sleep it off.

I checked my watch and set the alarm on my phone to remind me to check in on Lacey in an hour. I really didn't want to leave the boat, but I needed to visit my Dad, conscious of the nurse's stark prognosis.

Despite my recent shower, I felt the back of my shirt stick to my hot sweaty skin. I wiped my feverish brow, wincing at the unpleasant effect of my body overheating. But it couldn't be helped, I needed to get to the hospital. I paused to consider whether I should wait a few more hours. But I doubted that any infection I might be carrying would make much difference to Dad at this late stage…

"If you're not better when I get back, I'll ring the vet. You be a good boy and get some rest," I said as I kissed Lacey on the head and reluctantly withdrew. I left his water bowl easily accessible on the adjacent berth. He barely opened his eyes to acknowledge me.

Thirty Four

I stared at the crumpled figure in the bed and still I felt nothing.

I'd been in a hospital before, many times. I'd sat staring at all the tubes, monitors and nurses fussing around my mum. I'd been on the inside too, looking out. Too young to remember the first few times properly, but later as my body grew, so the visits to specialist plastic surgeons increased. Operations to relieve the taut skin, replacing old skin grafts with new, allowing my tummy scar to stretch with me.

Painful.

Necessary.

Avoidable.

I could still remember the looks exchanged between the nurses whenever my parents had visited me. By my early teens, they no longer came together. Too much blame and bitterness orbited between them. Easy to see by then, harder to overturn or repair. All too soon the roles reversed. I became the hospital visitor when the guilt became too much for Mum to face any part of the day sober, the drink claiming her life tragically early.

Why didn't you intervene, Dad? You could have taken her to a clinic, got her proper treatment. You could have brought her back…

I almost laughed at the cruel irony of history attempting to repeat itself.

"He's comfortable, Mister Straight," said a nurse, ducking her head into the room to check Dad's vital signs and glance at the chart. "We'll call you if there's any change."

I nodded, unable to process what she'd said.

"Has he been awake at all?"

"Occasionally, for a few minutes."

"Did he say anything?"

"It's mumbling, mostly. I can't recall he's said anything specific or been particularly lucid."

I sighed, rubbing my knees, trying to encourage some feeling back into my aching limbs.

"I'm going to stretch my legs. Can I come back later? I'm not sure when the visiting hours are…"

"Of course, anytime. The normal rules don't apply at this late stage…" she said, her voice trailing off.

I glanced up at her, caught the sympathy in her expression. A wave of nausea enveloped me, transporting me back twenty-five years or more, to a time when I'd laid in a hospital bed myself. I'd glared at my father and had seen a similar expression on a different nurse's face when he'd told me my mother had died.

*

I managed to walk past several pubs, despite the temptation to step inside for a much-needed drink. I thrust my hands in my pockets and hurried through the stale smell of cask-drawn liquid happiness as fast as I could, heading back to the boat.

I slid the hatch open, expecting to see Lacey's wagging tail.

Nothing.

"Lacey," I called, hurriedly removing the washboards and climbing down into the cabin.

Lacey lay on top of the sleeping bag, shivering. Beside him, more bright yellow vomit.

He tried to open his eyes when I scooped him up, but his eyelids fluttered half-open then slowly closed. I carried him into the main cabin and wrapped my fleece around him to stop the shivering.

I felt my hand shake as I reached for my mobile phone.

"Harry, this is a pleasant surprise. Can I call you back? I'm with a patient..." said Alice through the phone's speaker.

"Lacey's not well. He's being sick regularly, won't eat or drink and can't stop shivering. I've been ill too, I think it could be food poisoning," I interrupted.

The vet's tone changed instantly from cautious cheerfulness to rational professionalism.

"Okay. What did he last eat and when was that?"

"Half of my kebab, late last night. Stupid of me, I'm normally pretty healthy, aside from..."

"Get him to a vet, immediately."

"Seriously?"

"Absolutely serious. Take him straight away. Ring me when you know more."

"Okay, thanks."

I hung up, my hand shaking as I cradled Lacey on my lap.

"Harry, you stupid bloody fool!"

*

I sat in the waiting room, my body hunched over, elbows on my knees, hands clasped behind my head. The tightness in my throat and risk of losing my composure forced me to take slow, careful breaths. My hands scrunched clumps of hair, pulling it until my scalp hurt.

"Mister Straight?"

I looked up, pushed unsteadily to my feet. The vet, a kindly man in his fifties, stood in front of me wearing a serious expression.

"We've put Lacey on a drip to get some fluids back into his system and have taken blood samples. The initial results indicate toxins in his system. If the test values don't improve in the next twenty-four hours, then it's bad news. Really bad news."

I nodded vaguely and tried to respond, but I couldn't.

"You did the right thing bringing him in. We'll keep him in the medical room overnight. The duty veterinary nurse will ring you if there's any change. Please come back in the morning and we'll run some more tests. Okay?"

I nodded, but couldn't make eye contact with the vet or the other pet owners in the small reception. I kept my eyes on the floor and shuffled towards the door, struggling to put one foot in front of the other.

The bright sunshine outside the surgery did nothing to lift the cloud of doom hanging over me. After the day I'd had, there was only one place I could possibly end up. I turned away from the harbour and headed up the hill.

Thirty Five

It felt good to walk, despite the effort it took. I skirted around Pendennis Castle on the coastal path that wound its way around the point, until St Anthony's Head lighthouse lay directly ahead on the opposite side of the harbour entrance.

To my right, the English Channel stretched out past Manacle Point towards the horizon, tiny ripples far below offering a perfect day on the water. To my left, Falmouth's vast harbour meandered amongst spits of land and pretty bays. In the distance, Turnaware Point marked the entrance to the Truro River and some of the most sheltered anchorages on the south coast.

Such a spectacular view, the perfect place for a memorial bench. The original seat had lasted fifteen years, so I'm told. The recent replacement bore the same plaque that I remembered from all those years ago:

In loving memory of Elizabeth Straight
(1951 – 1989)
Wife to Anthony, mother to Keith and Harry.

I used my sleeve to buff up the brass plate and sat down, grateful to rest my legs. Exposed to the light breeze, I began to cool down, before the sensation of sunshine soaking through my skin triggered more feverish hot flushes.

"I'm sorry it's been so long, Mum. I've thought about you so much over the years… just couldn't bring myself to come back while *he* was still alive… I had it all planned out, what to do after seeing him. But it's all so messed up, even more than it was. I thought I'd feel a sense of achievement, getting the boat here… to make my peace with the past. But I feel so… *lost.*"

*

It must have been the stress of the last few days catching up that caused me to doze off. That and feeling warm for the first time since the boat had capsized, ironic really given the kebab incident. I slouched on the bench, hands wrapped around my tummy, chin resting on my chest.

Occasionally I'd drift forwards, the sensation of falling waking me abruptly. Then I'd reposition and succumb to a fitful and feverish sleep once more. Random images drifted through my subconscious, distant and fuzzy:

Lacey being carried away by the male vet.
My father, clinging to life in his hospital bed.
Jessica's recent launch day in Poole…

"I've always loved this place."
That voice… distant, yet familiar.
My body tipped forwards again, falling into a dreamlike eternity…
"We used to come here for picnics. You'd have been too young to remember."

I instinctively jerked my head back and woke with a start.

That glorious view… the lighthouse, sea and harbour. Years since I'd last sat on my own up here… and yet, I didn't feel *alone…*

I turned to my right to stare at the man sat beside me, his features partially hidden behind a baseball cap and sunglasses.

"Keith?"

My brother glanced left and right along the path, then turned to smile cautiously at me, the warmth of his voice pulling me away from the slow procession of memories flitting through my mind, bringing me back to an odd reality.

"How you doing, bro?"

"Hey Keith," I mumbled, my voice sounding weak and hollow. "What are you doing here?"

"Keeping a low profile. You seen the old man yet?" he said.

"Yesterday and again this morning. He's not so good."

"I know. Don't be too hard on him."

"I'm here, aren't I?"

"Yes, but…"

Keith turned away from me and looked out to sea. I studied his expression.

"What happened back then… got muddled, tainted your view of him," he said.

"In what way?"

Keith shook his head, a sad expression clouding his features.

"You made this trip to draw a line under the past…"

"I did."

"So are you able to do that?"

"You're talking about… *closure?*"

"Yes. It won't be long."

"I know," I said quietly, following his gaze out to sea.

We sat there for a while in companionable silence. When he eventually spoke, his tone sounded soft and strangely sincere.

"I'm proud of you, Harry. And so is Dad, even if he was never very good at showing it."

"You were always his favourite."

"Perhaps. But when I told him some home truths a few years ago, he soon changed his mind…"

I studied Keith's profile, my forehead creasing into a frown.

"It's funny. You've been on this amazing journey, thinking it's you who needed to make amends for the past, find your inner peace, so you could move on... But I've been waiting a long time for you to be ready… for me to apologise properly."

"Apologise for what?"

Keith glanced at me, then turned away and gazed out to sea. When he spoke, his normally confident, unbreakable voice wavered.

"Remember, I wasn't very old back then, I didn't understand what could happen… I didn't know the hot water bottle would explode. I'd seen Mum prepare her own, a few days every month.

She used to tell me it helped her sleep. When you wouldn't stop crying, that night on Poole Quay, I thought it would help you too.

Maybe I overfilled it, or the water was too hot, or perhaps I over-tightened the cap. I don't know…"

Keith turned to face me. He removed his sunglasses. Tears threatened to fall from his misty eyes.

"I don't understand… Mum was wracked with guilt… Dad never forgave her," I said.

Keith nodded. He clasped his hands in his lap.

"I know. She took the blame to protect us from his temper."

"But you jumped into the harbour, saved me…"

I watched tears trickle down Keith's cheeks. His voice faltered.

"When the hot water bottle exploded… it plunged me into hell. You were screaming. A blood-curdling, torturous cry for help. I grabbed you out of the bed, held you in my arms, your skin burning. I had so little time to think… I jumped into the harbour and held your head above the water for as long as I could…"

"You? But… I don't understand… I thought…"

"Mum knew that if Dad found out I'd been responsible for your burns, he'd most likely blame you for crying in the first place. So she kept quiet and accepted his wrath for everyone's sake but her own.

I guess that's why she drank so heavily… Mum took the secret to her grave. So this is my apology, Harry. I'm truly sorry.

It was an accident borne out of my lack of

common sense and inexperience, but also parental impatience and ultimately a lack of proper care. It should never have happened. But Dad bullied Mum to go and meet their friends, which left me to try and comfort you, stop you crying. All these years later, I finally found a way to try and redress some of the balance, so I could make my apology into something tangible and meaningful…" Keith's voice dropped to a whisper. "…before it was too late."

I stared at him for a long time, my fuzzy brain trying to process everything.

"Lacey?"

Keith chuckled and wiped his glistening eyes.

"He's a character, isn't he?"

I nodded, in a daze.

"Is he on the boat?"

I broke eye contact, shook my head.

"No, he's… being looked after."

Keith nodded, then rubbed his eyes.

"So you set me up with the dog deliberately…?" I said.

Keith held my gaze.

"I figured he'd be good for you."

I nodded slowly, remembering some of the amusing situations Lacey had helped get me into.

"What happens now?" I asked vacantly.

"Priority number one is I try not to get caught."

"By the police or the criminals?"

Keith gave me a strange, mischievous look.

"Both. What are your plans now?"

"That's a tricky question… I've never thought this far ahead."

"That's not like you."

"No."

I took a deep shaky breath.

"Just assumed that if I got this far, made it to Falmouth in the boat, there wouldn't be much time left."

"There's always time…" Keith said quietly.

He reached into his jacket pocket and withdrew an envelope which he placed on the bench between us.

"I guess neither of us wanted to deal with this day… but I made some provisions, when I found out about your… situation."

I stared at the envelope, then looked up at Keith.

"It's a little something to help with… whatever you want to do next."

He glanced at me, then reached into another pocket and withdrew a packet of cigarettes and a lighter. I watched him shield the flame as he lit up.

"I didn't know you smoked."

"It's more of a work thing… here, take this."

He pushed the envelope closer to me.

I picked it up, lifted the unsealed flap and fanned through the wedge of fifty pound notes.

"Bloody hell! What'd you do, rob a bank?"

Keith blew smoke and maintained a poker face.

"Mugged an old dear. Not as easy as it sounds… she was a karate black belt, third dan."

I shook my head, a smile twitching on my lips.

"It's a lovely thought Keith, thank you. But I can't…"

"Call it compensation, for your injury. Take it. Money will come and go, time just… disappears. You can use the cash for anything, it's an unconditional gift. A holiday maybe, sexual favours perhaps… or a flight somewhere… up to you."

"Are you sure?"

"Absolutely."

"Okay. Thanks."

"What do you think you'll do?"

I stared at the sparkling sea.

"Go and see him again, hang around to see that part of the journey through. After that, there's probably somewhere I can go… near to the end. But before I get to that stage, I need to have a long think… perhaps I'll go and see a bit more of the world."

"What about a second opinion…?"

"I've already tried, at the beginning of all this. This is the hand I've been dealt, simple as that." I turned towards him. "It's just life, right?"

"But you didn't go for any treatment. What if now…"

"I did all the hard time in hospital there is, remember? Treatment would only have added a few more painful months here, an extra nauseating week there. What would be the point?"

"There must be something that can be done…"

"You already did it for me, Keith, sending

Lacey my way. And for that, I am eternally grateful."

"I just can't believe that's it… What can I say to try and change your mind…?"

I shook my head and remained silent for a while.

"Tell me something real… tell me about your plans," I said eventually.

Keith shook his head, his gaze lost at sea.

"I don't really see the point bro, given the circumstances."

"Tell me anyway."

Keith sighed heavily.

"Before that, how… you know… how long do you have?"

I shrugged.

"I'm already on borrowed time. I'm certainly feeling like my body is beginning to seize up and shut down, so I don't know… not long," I said softly.

Keith shook his head, attempted a sheepish smile as he reached into his pocket and dangled a set of car keys from his fingers.

"I had planned to offer you a temporary swap, once you made it here. Life on the ocean wave in exchange for the open road. Thought I could persuade you to lend me Jessica, so I could change her name and disappear for a while."

"It's bad luck to change a boat's name. Aren't you superstitious?"

Keith focussed on my stare.

"Not anymore."

"You think it'll work? Allow you to escape, home free?"

"It might have, if you'd been well enough… but no offence, Harry, you're not looking good. I'm going to turn myself in, do a deal so I can hang around until… you know, it's time…"

"You can't, I won't let you."

"Like you're gonna be able to stop me?" Keith chuckled and playfully squeezed my shoulder. "I've got a few things to sort out, but once that's all done I'll see you with Dad at the nursing home, okay? Hang in there little brother, I'll be back to spend some time with you. No arguments, end of discussion."

Keith stood up and began to walk away.

"Don't forget the cash," he called out over his shoulder. "The old girl wanted you to have it…"

Thirty Six

I sat at Jessica's chart table in front of my open laptop and adjusted the screen angle so my face lined up in the webcam box. That done, I took a deep breath and clicked on the record icon.

"Hi Dad, it's me, your son Harry... here I am recording a video postcard that you may see, but will probably never fully understand. It's a bit odd I know, but I hope by some miracle that it's able to filter through your illness. My original plan was to turn up on your seventieth birthday and wheel you down to the marina to see Jessica, the boat you built all those years ago. Do you remember? I hoped it would help to break through the barrier of this terrible disease. But you're not well enough. So... what do I want to say...? Partly I need to say sorry, for being out of contact all those years. But for me to say that and mean it, you'd have to apologise too and given your condition, that's probably not going to happen..."

I turned away to stifle a coughing fit, taking a moment for my breathing to settle down.

"Would you like to see your boat? Remember how you helped design her, built her, then mothballed her in a boatyard after the accident? Here she is, Dad. Restored, new life breathed into her..."

I grasped the laptop, rotated it slowly in my hands, panning around the cabin.

"Do you see the woodwork? Hour by painstaking hour, rubbed down, cleaned, varnished. Eighteen months hard graft. Let's take a look at the topsides…"

I slid the hatch open, removed the washboards and stepped out into the cockpit, clutching the laptop.

"Everything is pristine. The gel coat polished to a shine, waxed to protect and preserve. Do you see, Dad? She's almost in launch day condition. I've spent everything I have, borrowed more on a credit card to make sure I finished her. And after some adventures along the way, here we are in Falmouth, on the visitors' pontoon. This is where I planned to bring you, wheel you alongside so you could see her for yourself."

With as steady a hand as I could muster, I held the screen and rotated my body around the marina a full three hundred and sixty degrees. That done, I retreated back into the cabin and settled down at the chart table in front of the laptop.

"Do you see the achievement, Dad? These hands, they are an extension of your own. Why did you never recognise that? I'm your son! Why did you choose to forget…? And why did I wait this long to remind you, before the barrier of this awful dementia. I've seen your journal entries in the logbook. I feel your pain, think I understand now. But why didn't you tell me? We could have worked through our differences, or at least tried. Because now… it's too late."

I scrunched my eyes shut, rubbed them to encourage the tension to disperse. Several deep breaths later, I opened my eyes and attempted to regain my composure for the camera.

"But we have to get through all that... pain. I realise now that you did your best to raise me after Mum died. It can't have been easy, given the circumstances. I want... no, I *need* to move on, set the past to rest before I leave this world. So if there's a chance that just a few words of this message finds you, the real you – Anthony Straight, Harry's father – please let them be these: I never blamed anyone for the accident. I made a life out of the hand I'd been dealt. One more time: *I never blamed anyone*. You know what's funny...? I can't recall exactly why we fell out so badly. I can only remember the tidal wave of negative emotion that followed. I wish we'd had the strength and courage to talk, try to put the past behind us. We both wasted so much time... I hope that deep down you loved me as much as I loved you. Goodbye Dad. I'll see you soon..."

I stopped the webcam and saved the file, then sat there for a few minutes trying to rationalise everything. But of course I couldn't, too much whizzed around in my head, the emotion clogging my logic.

Before I could sink into a mire of negativity, I got off the boat and forced myself to keep walking.

*

The nursing home corridors had a different feel at night. Subdued lighting, less people milling about, even more soulless. The duty nurse didn't question the late hour of my visit, she just nodded at me and led me through the gloom to Dad's room.

"He's about the same," she said in a low voice.

"Has he been awake?"

"Not really. The odd mumble, a few seconds of eye flickering, then back to sleep. Pull up a chair, stay as long as you need."

"Thank you… Jo," I said, squinting at her name badge.

I sank into a chair, feverish fatigue catching up with me. I tried to fight it, but this place… so tiring.

Dad's wheezing breaths focussed my attention as I hung onto each pause, ready to wake fully should it be his last. But the unsteady rhythm continued, mirroring the painful rasp in my own chest. Eventually my discomfort eased enough to allow me to drift in and out of unsettled sleep, dodging the familiar dreams that the smell of this place conjured, tormenting my restless slumber.

*

My eyes twitched at the sound of the curtains being whisked open. Overhead lights flickered into life, their sterile glare stinging my eyes.

A tickle in my throat triggered a spate of raw

coughing as I tried to clear the elusive obstruction, wincing with the effort.

"Are you okay, love? You're not looking so well yourself," said Jo.

"I'm okay…"

She flicked her concerned eyes over me. I glanced away.

"I'm off shift in a few minutes, but I'll ask Sister to check you over."

"Please, don't trouble yourself. I'm okay, really."

I watched her make her checks, then she left me standing at the foot of Dad's bed. He'd hardly moved position, his eyes remained closed.

"Do you fancy watching a movie Dad? Or maybe just listening…"

I removed the laptop from my bag and set it up, holding the screen towards the top of the bed.

"Hi Dad, it's me, your son Harry…"

I sat there and let my recorded words drift over his regular rasping breathing.

"…partly I came to say sorry, for being out of contact all those years…"

I watched intently for any flicker of movement, a sign of recognition. Perhaps the twitch of an eyebrow or the first inklings of an expression forming. I sat and stared and missed nothing. But there wasn't anything to see.

I felt tears well in my eyes as I listened to my recorded voice, tinny and hopeful.

"What a lovely idea," said a soft voice behind me.

I turned to see Jo standing by the end of the bed.

"They do say it's important to talk, don't they… to coma patients. I'm sure this is similar."

I nodded and wiped my cheeks dry. I turned back to face Dad, just in case I missed anything.

"…I only wish we'd had the strength and courage to talk…" continued my recorded voice.

I sighed, waiting and watching until the last of my words ceased.

Still no glimmer of recognition. Such a damn shame.

"You tried, Harry. At least you tried," I whispered vacantly.

I sighed deeply, the last of my emotional energy draining from my body. I closed the laptop and slowly stood up.

"Rest easy now Dad. I'll be back in a minute… need a comfort break…"

Summoning all of my resolve, I stepped forwards and kissed him gently on the forehead.

I noted how peaceful his sleep seemed to be. I hoped he wasn't in any pain. Straightening up, I turned to leave, but the faintest sound drew me back to the hospital bed. An outward breath? A final puff of air being expelled…?

He'll breath in now, I thought, waiting…

I frowned, anticipating the regular shallow movement under the sheet of his chest rising and falling, but instead I found myself fixated by his stillness.

A sudden pain deep behind my eyes caused me to wince as twinkling dots clouded my vision.

I took a moment to regain my composure and allow the prickling starry sensation to fade, but my world began to rotate in a dizzy spiral.

I felt the laptop slip from my weak fingers and crash to the floor. Swiftly followed by a distant thud as I followed the computer's trajectory and everything went black.

Thirty Seven

"Hi love, how are you feeling?"

I squinted at the hazy outline of a nurse's face, my focus sharpening as my eyes adjusted to the light.

"What…"

"You took a tumble, probably fainted," she said.

I stared at her, trying to think back, piece together my last recollections.

"You're in hospital in Falmouth. You've been unconscious for two days. You were very dehydrated and had a strong fever. Have you been ill recently? Sickness or diarrhoea perhaps?"

"Both…" I mumbled.

"Ah-hah. What did you eat?"

"Kebab."

"Yup, that can do it. Don't worry, we'll keep you in for one more night, you should be able to go home tomorrow…"

I shook my head.

"I have… another illness. It's… not good…"

"Oh, I see. Want to tell me about it?"

"It's… cancer."

I saw the nurse frown. She leaned over the end of the bed and lifted up a clipboard to check my notes.

"We did some initial blood tests... nothing indicated anything else to be worried about..."

"It's called CCL, a form of leukaemia..." I interrupted.

"Okay love. Strange that nothing showed up on your bloods. When did you have the diagnosis and which hospital?"

"Eighteen months ago at Southampton General."

"Right. I'll get your notes. Are you currently undergoing any treatment?"

"No. I didn't want any..."

"Oh. Okay. Let me make some calls. Are you alright for a moment?"

I nodded and watched her scurry away.

This is the start of it, Harry, I thought. Time's up.

*

The nurse returned some time later with a young doctor.

"Mister Straight, I'm Doctor Thomas. I understand you're under the care of Professor Adams, a consultant at Southampton General Hospital?"

"I was, some time ago," I replied.

"Right. Good. So what we need to do is get you over there for some more tests."

I shook my head.

"No more medical stuff... I don't want to finish my days in a hospital, no offence Doc..."

"None taken. Your burn must have meant lots of visits, over the years?"

I held his gaze and nodded.

"Your reluctance is understandable. But I must insist you go back to see Professor Adams. Before we argue the reasoning behind that, I have some bad news… regarding your father."

I felt my lungs deflate, expelling oxygen, leaving me feeling hollow and heavy-limbed.

"I think I heard him go… just before I fainted," I said quietly.

The doctor nodded.

"The nurses got you stabilized first and called the ambulance, but he'd already passed away. I'm very sorry."

I acknowledged him with a vague nod and flicked my eyes away.

"We'll talk again soon, about Southampton…"

"Dog," I interrupted.

"You have a dog?" asked the doctor.

"Yes, he's…"

"…being looked after by the vet," said Keith, appearing at the doctor's side. "They gave me your mobile phone. I went through the call list, figured it out."

Doctor Thomas smiled at Keith and tipped his head at the nurse, taking their cue to withdraw.

"How's Lacey doing?" I asked.

Keith drew up a chair beside me and sat down.

"About the same as you. They'll take care of him until you're back on your feet."

I nodded and reached up to rub my sore head.

"Thanks for coming to see me. I think maybe

this is it..." I began, cut off by Keith's breezy interruption.

"Don't be soft. You've been ill, food poisoning. They told me it's unconnected to... you know, other stuff. Anyway, you like the nurses in here? I've asked them to lay on the special treatment..."

Keith winked at me and relaxed in the chair.

"Is it safe for you to be here, Keith? I wouldn't want you to endanger yourself for me..."

"Shh, later... all will be revealed," he said, lowering his voice and glancing around the ward. "The most important thing is to get you out of here and on your way to Southampton Hospital..."

I shook my head vigorously, making me wince in pain. I started to object, but Keith spoke over me.

"No arguments, no negotiation," he said firmly. "We're finishing the journey together. Before that, there's something else... did they tell you about Dad?"

"Yes..."

"Okay. I've been organising the funeral. It's all in hand. Day after tomorrow. We'll go together. Here's your mobile phone. They gave me the envelope too, I'll keep it safe until you get out. Rest up, I'll be back soon. Okay?"

*

Thinking back to Dad's funeral, it's ironic how well I'd felt. Better than in a long time. Perhaps the stay in hospital had helped, or being sober for a sustained period.

Or maybe I'd been able to let go of all that *ill feeling*... Whatever the reason, I stood by the grave huddled under an umbrella and actually felt a sense of optimism. "Time to move on, Harry," said Keith's soft voice as we turned away from the sunken coffin.

"Yes... onwards..."

I nodded and attempted to relax my facial muscles in an effort to breath out a lifetime of hurt, anger and regret as we turned our backs and walked away.

*

Keith panned around, allowing his gaze to absorb every detail of Jessica's varnished wood interior.

"She's just like I remember," he said quietly, toying with a cup of cold tea, a sadness in his eyes that I'd not seen before.

"So what happens now, with you?" I asked, my eyes fixed on his, looking for the truth in his reply.

"It's not as complicated as I might have suggested. The police, the compromising photographs... the *big organisation*... it's a distortion of the truth."

"Oh? In what way?"

"Let's just say that I've always been a bit... wayward. Partly to rebel against Dad, I suppose, but mostly because that's just who I am. A few years ago I met someone after… an incident, who encouraged me to turn my life around. Believe it or not, I almost ended up as a copper… officially, I mean. But that would have meant traceability, something my new employer was keen to avoid. So I went through a different training scheme, where the lines between official and, well… the shadows, get blurred."

Keith flicked his eyes away from me and chuckled.

"The problem with working undercover, taking on a false identity is just that: it's false. It can get found out, blown. So the latest initiative is to channel candidates into something a little more… authentic."

I searched Keith's gaze for a hint of untruth.

"You're a police informant?"

"If you like. But I'm on the payroll. I have a theoretical rank. Although, let's just say I don't keep regular office hours."

"So the two detectives are…?"

"Colleagues. They say hi, by the way. I think DC Best fancies you. I had to call in a favour or two, early on in your trip. I needed to encourage you to keep moving towards your goal. I apologise for interfering, but I wanted to see you sail away from the boatyard, have some proper adventures in the time you had left…"

"The armed police were your doing?"

Keith's mouth widened into a mischievous smile.

"That was sort of a training exercise."

"And the detectives who visited me in Weymouth and Dartmouth?"

"Like I said, I needed to keep you moving. So you could get to Falmouth. I didn't think you'd get here without a nudge or two…"

"A nudge? I capsized the boat and nearly drowned!"

"I know, but it kept you moving forwards, didn't it? What would you rather, die trying with a purpose and all your faculties and dignity intact, or stay rooted to the spot and fizzle away, dying a tragic little bit every single day with no spirit of adventure. Is that really how you'd prefer to leave this world?"

I stared at him, open mouthed. It took some time before I felt my lips twitch into a smile.

"You bugger."

"That, and much worse. Just ask Debs."

"Did she know about your… employment?"

"Yup, another of the Chief's recruits."

"Right… so you've actually been living a more honourable life than you had me – hell, everyone – believe?"

"So it would seem."

"Okay. Before my brain completely seizes up, tell me about Lacey."

Keith nodded, then he paused to take a deep breath.

"I looked after him for around three years. Dog walking is a brilliant cover for watching without drawing attention. It suited my assignment, so Debs and I fostered Lacey from an acquaintance."

"A criminal acquaintance?"

Keith shrugged, his eyes glinting.

"Someone who exists between that world and this one…"

"I see. That would explain a few things… Do you like that life? Moving around, out of contact, missing your family and friends?

"It's not ideal, but it's my penance… and compared to the alternative, sinking to the bottom, where I'd been heading… at least there's work satisfaction in being on the right side of the tracks, morally. Even if at times it means I'm sanctioned on high to exist as anything but."

I sat back against Jessica's hull, crossed my arms.

"Did the old man know?"

"No. He thought I was a waster, right up to the end."

"But you still went to visit him? I couldn't face it."

"I popped in to check on him, from time to time. But some people… there's no getting through to them."

I nodded, dropping my eyes to the floor, my gaze lingering on Lacey's rabbit water bowl.

"I think I'm ready to see him," I said.

*

Keith drew to a halt in the street outside the vet's entrance door and offered his hand.

"This is where I leave you, bro."

"You don't want to come in and say hi to the little monster?"

"Oh, I will, soon enough. Give him a belly rub from me. I've got to debrief, sort out the next assignment. I'll meet you tomorrow in Poole as planned, okay?"

"Okay," I said, reaching out to shake his hand.

I watched Keith leave, my thoughts drifting back, briefly reviewing the last six weeks.

"Funny old life…" I muttered as I leaned on the vet's door, my heart lurching in anticipation.

Thirty Eight

"Where the bloody hell have you been, Harry? You look like dog crap!"

Lacey danced around my feet, paws prancing on the cage floor, wearing an oversized plastic medical cone. His bright brown eyes stared up at me, tail swooshing back and forth, a thin curly drip tube tangling around his legs. I stepped into the cage and dropped to a crouch, making a fuss of him.

"I'm hungry! Feed me. Feed me...!"

"I'll ask the nurse to remove the drip and cone and we'll have a chat about his condition," said the vet over my shoulder.

I turned and nodded at him as I stroked Lacey.

"Back in a jiffy, little one."

*

"Come on Harry, get me outta here..."

I couldn't help but smile at Lacey trying to run against the tension of the lead on the polished surgery floor. His legs kept skidding out from under him and he had trouble steering in a straight line.

I thanked the vet and carefully picked Lacey up, cuddling him.

"Welcome back, Lacey. Is it breakfast time?"

"After the amount of meals I've missed, we're talking banquet time!"

We stopped by reception on the way out to settle up and collect Lacey's medication. I didn't even notice how much the bill was.

*

"Such a lovely day, Lacey. I'll treasure moments like these…"

I raised the takeaway coffee cup to my lips, savouring the taste. The sunshine over St Mawes bathed the town with a temporary sense of optimism, soon giving way to dull grey overcast clouds which gathered and evolved before my eyes, signalling the arrival of a new weather pattern.

I felt something cold and wet on my hand and looked down to see Lacey prodding his nose under my fingers.

"Don't be so stingy with your cuddles, mister."

I moved my arms to allow Lacey to climb up onto my lap. He wriggled to get comfy then settled, arching his head back, his eyes searching for mine.

"It's good to have you back, Lacey," I said, silently adding; if only for a short while…

I held onto the magical feeling of warmth for as long as possible, attempting to push the other dark thoughts aside.

"We'll get going soon, little one… follow the tide up towards Penryn and take Jessica home."

We sat there on Mum's memorial bench,

absorbed in the changing climate, happy for now to enjoy the simple pleasure of watching everyday lives drift on by.

*

The familiar rhythm of Jessica's engine rumbled under the cockpit sole, the vibration resonating through my feet, up my legs and into my chest cavity, amplifying the boat's beating heart.

I cast off the bow and stern lines and nudged the tiller over, edging Jessica away from the pontoon.

"What, no barking, Lacey?"

He yawned, panting in the sunshine, his lower jaw hanging loose.

"Not today hombre, just chillin'…"

In no particular hurry, I eased back on the throttle and steered Jessica on a slalom course through the maze of boat moorings. Once in the main channel, we wound our way past the village of Flushing, on the north bank. We passed pretty beaches and stone quays on our right hand side, with small quirky boatyards lined up on our left. The gentle swell decreased as we motored away from the main harbour, until the water smoothed over completely, only Jessica's bow wave breaking the glassy surface.

For some unexplainable reason I felt tempted to glance over my shoulder, into the mid-morning sun rising behind me, but I hesitated, knowing that I had to stay focussed in the moment.

We turned a sharp left opposite Sailors

Creek, bringing Falmouth Marina's east cardinal marker in line with Jessica's bow as we prepared our final approach. The high tide allowed us to coast over the drying parts of the marina with a metre-spare depth under our keel.

Perfect.

I allowed myself a satisfied grin, pleased to see that my tidal calculations tallied with the echo sounder. With shore lines and fenders already prepared, I slowed our approach and allowed Jessica to gracefully drift up to the waiting pontoon, completing a textbook coming-alongside manoeuvre.

Lacey's paws pattered on the deck, mirroring my movements on the pontoon as I scurried fore and aft, securing the mooring ropes. I wheezed with the effort of straightening up from my crouch, certain I could hear my bones creaking.

"Safe arrival, Lacey. On time and without incident."

"Not bad… for a monkey chops landlubber."

I lifted Lacey over the guard wires and set him down on the pontoon, watching him scamper up the ramp. I followed him slowly, the magic of our journey fading with every step.

*

The friendly yacht broker watched me sign the paperwork.

"She's a lovely little boat, sir. And at that price I'm sure someone will be quick to make an offer."

We shook hands, then I watched him head out of the office armed with a 'For Sale' notice. I felt my throat tighten, my eyes getting misty. I picked up my bag, already packed with a few clothes and my remaining possessions. In my other hand I held Lacey's lead, the one thing I treasured above all else.

"That's it, first mate Lacey, end of the road."

Lacey held my gaze.

"Did you remember my food bowl? Cos it's getting near second breakfast…"

I smiled at Lacey's whining and began to turn away, then hesitated. I glanced back for one last long look at Jessica. I studied her pretty lines, marvelled at the shine still gleaming from the once dull, listless gel coat. My eyes lingered, imprinting her picture in my mind.

There's an often quoted saying that the happiest two days in a sailor's life are the day he buys a boat and the day he sells it. As I stood there in the marina, gazing at Jessica with Lacey stood beside me, I realised that I couldn't disagree more.

Thirty Nine

I settled into a window seat and lifted Lacey up onto my lap. A whistle sounded outside and we began to move. I gazed though the glass, watching the platform slip away as the train gradually picked up speed.

The carriage jolting on the rails shook me in and out of my unsettled slumber, halfway between consciousness and sleep where dreams, fact and fantasy merge into a hotchpotch of uncertainty.

Nothing seemed real anymore. My resolve and enthusiasm in a purpose that had carried me onwards during the last eighteen months trickled away with the passing of every train station. Even my text message to Alice lacked conviction.

> Heading back to Poole from Falmouth with Lacey – journey's end. This is delicate, but it's time. Will you help please? I want it to be you… Harry

The journey continued relentlessly. We changed trains, stood on near-deserted platforms and tucked ourselves away in dim corners, unable to consider being sociable or optimistic anymore.

I flicked my eyes down at the phone at the sound of an incoming text message:

> Oh Harry, I'm so sorry. Of course. I'll be here. Alice. x

I fiddled with the phone, my heart racing. Lacey repositioned himself on the seat next to me, resting his head on my lap, his ears twitching as he dozed. I stroked the back of his head, causing him to half-open an eye, then fidget and settle again, emitting a grumbling sound as he stretched out.

"Relax sailor… you worry too much…"

For the hundredth time, I wished I didn't have to make this particular part of my journey.

Outside the window, countryside zipped past at high speed under a dark grey sky, nature's tears streaking across the glass.

*

Lacey tried to leg it as soon as I lowered his paws to the ground.

"No way mister, I ain't going for the big sleep… no way, amigo!"

I barely had the energy to drag Lacey's lead towards the door, let alone carry him.

"Noooo… I'm not ready!"

Alice shut the door behind us, trapping Lacey inside. I sank down onto a reception chair and hunched my arms onto my aching knees.

"Harry, are you okay? You look absolutely exhausted."

"Get me outta here!"

Alice knelt down to make a fuss of Lacey, trying to calm him down.

"Retreat! Retreat!"

I let go of Lacey's lead and watched him frantically paw the door, yelping constantly. I couldn't contain myself any longer. I hunched over, shaking uncontrollably as my tears spilled onto the floor.

Alice sat down next to me and draped her arm over my shoulder. She stayed there for a long time, letting me cry. Lacey eventually stopped barking but stood by the door whining, urging me to set him free.

"He's doing really well, Harry, all things considered. There's still a spark in his eyes... I won't put him to sleep..." said Alice in a soft voice.

I fought to calm my erratic breathing, trying to calm down enough to attempt to explain.

"I didn't bring him here for *that*..." I mumbled, wiping my eyes.

Alice's arm slipped off my shoulder.

"Okay, that's a relief. So why are you here?"

It took me a while to lift my head, straighten up and look her in the eye.

"It's not Lacey. It's... me. I can't do this anymore... it's not fair on him."

I reached for my bag and pulled out Jessica's boat logbook and passed it to Alice, my hand shaking.

"My last journal entry will explain."

"I don't understand. What are you saying...?"

"I'm asking if you'll look after Lacey for me."

Her eyes narrowed, searching mine for an answer.

"Of course, but…"

I leant down and retrieved Lacey's rabbit bowl from my bag and placed it on an adjacent seat. I saw Lacey turn to stare at me.

"Hey Captain, what's going on?"

Lacey tried to back away as I crouched down and scooped him up into my arms. I buried my head in his fur, my eyes screwed shut. He whimpered softly.

After a long cuddle, I passed Lacey into Alice's arms, doing my best to avoid his forlorn expression.

"Harry, why are you leaving me?"

"It's all in the logbook. Please let me go before you read it… I'm sorry things aren't different."

I willed my shaking legs move so I could walk away.

"Harry… are you unwell?" said Alice, blinking rapidly.

"I'm sorry it has to be this way… thank you, for everything," I stuttered, ruffling Lacey's ears one last time.

"What have I done wrong? Don't leave me…"

My weathered hand cupped Alice's face, my thumb wiping away a lone tear that trickled down her cheek. Then I picked up my bag and hobbled away, tears streaming down my face.

"Harry! Please don't leave meeee…"

Lacey's mournful howl haunted me all the way to the door and beyond.

Forty

It's funny, I never pictured you in this sort of vehicle," I said as I glanced at Keith, sat in the driver's seat of an old VW campervan.

"You don't think it suits my image?"

I glanced out of the window as we dawdled along in the motorway slow lane.

"As what? I'm not sure I can place you anywhere in society at the moment."

Keith smiled and flicked his eyes at me, for some odd reason reminding me of Lacey's mannerisms in a typical 'who me?' expression.

"What?" he said.

"Nothing, just… remembering saying goodbye to Lacey…"

"Don't give up just yet," Keith said quietly.

We drove on in silence for several minutes, just the metallic purring of the engine and road noise drone to keep us company.

"Finding out I was going to die was a crap day… it totally eclipsed getting my divorce papers," I said, a few miles later.

"Yeah, that's gotta sting," said Keith, darting a concerned look at me.

"It took me a long time to accept that I'd probably not make forty. Don't they say that's when life begins?"

We exchanged a wry smile.

"So they say…is it painful?" he said.

"It has been, in my joints."

"Is that why you drink?"

I nodded, absently.

"The alcohol isn't just for the pain, although it does help. It helps me to live in the moment, forget how little time I have left."

"Can't say I blame you. But proper treatment, that's got to be better than self-medicating…"

"A few more degrading months? No thank you."

We drove on for a while in silence before Keith spoke again.

"What about Gwen… did you tell her?"

"No. I sat down with my divorce papers in one hand and terminal diagnosis in the other and I had a long hard think. She left because she didn't love me, or couldn't accept who I was and nothing was going to change that, certainly not pity. And I understand her reasons for leaving, even if I didn't agree with them. She's not a bad person, she didn't try to twist the knife. I remember thinking it seemed malicious somehow, to burden her with my news. Better to try and part on good terms, make a clean break for both of us. Resentment lingers, it breeds bitterness and anger. So we sat down with a divorce mediator and managed to sort out the house without any major argument, settling on a two third to one third split. Where I was heading, I didn't need much. Why quibble about a bit of meaningless paper currency…?"

Keith shrugged in a 'fair enough' agreement.

"Have you been in touch, recently I mean?"

I shook my head.

"I think she still has my number, but I deleted hers from my phone. Once I had a while to reflect on the future, I realised I wanted to set her free, to build a new life. It's better this way, I feel no guilt, I'm not throwing any emotional hand grenades at her."

"Did you love her?"

I glanced over at Keith, caught the sincerity of the question in his eyes.

"I thought so. But looking back, maybe not. It wasn't the closest of relationships, although it's taken me until now to realise that. It's difficult to see any deficiencies in the early days when that's all you've known… I hoped she'd get used to my scar, accept it, but she never did. I used to make love partially clothed. Believe me, there wasn't anything exciting or intimate about that."

"So what made you decide to patch up the boat?"

"That day when I sat down with my divorce papers, the finality of everything… knowing how little time I had left. I tried to think what was missing in my life that I could fill the last few months with. I got depressed for a while, I lacked purpose in everything. Not unexpected, right? I mean, who wouldn't hit a low point… what did I have to look forwards to? But as I began to see through the gloom, I analysed my life, or what was left of it. Perhaps I wasn't looking for something material, or tangible to fill the remaining void. Maybe my search was something more spiritual. But I'm not religious, so discovering faith so near to the end smacked of hypocrisy somehow. Far better to make my peace in another way, pragmatically and emotionally. I began to realise it might be about balance, leave this world *ready,* with my life in order. That meant making my peace with our estranged and deranged father. Working on Jessica allowed me to make peace with him and myself. If I'd timed it right, Jessica would have carried me to my journey's end in Falmouth, where it all started. Quite fitting really. And that's as far ahead as I've thought."

Keith looked across the cab at me and nodded.

"I think you're ready now... for whatever comes next," he said in a neutral tone.

*

The Volkswagen's clattering air-cooled whistle died, leaving the cab in silence. I stared through the windscreen at Southampton General Hospital, large and imposing on the other side of the car park.

"Do you want me to come in with you, or..."

I glanced at Keith, taking a moment to collect my thoughts. After a long pause I slowly shook my head.

"No, I'll be okay thanks. It's nothing I don't already know, right?"

"Okay. There's a pub, half a mile away called the Malvern Tavern. I'll meet you there when you're done."

Keith offered his hand, which I clasped warmly.

"Thanks... for being here. I'm..."

"It's okay bro. It's long overdue."

I smiled and opened the door.

"I'll see you in the pub later," I said as I climbed out of the camper van and walked towards the hospital, my limbs shaking.

*

Professor Adams welcomed me with a warm smile and a firm handshake.

"Good to see you again, Mister Straight. Thank you for being patient. You're looking well."

"Not sure I share your optimism, Professor."

"That would be due to your recent bout of food poisoning?"

I held eye contact with him, my forehead creasing into a frown. He didn't look like a man about to deliver more bad news to a terminal cancer patient.

"Caused by listeria bacteria. Found in the blood samples tested by my colleagues in Falmouth. Which makes your other results… interesting."

I forced myself to hold eye contact with the Professor, despite the urge to leap up and run for the door.

"We've compared all the results today from your first visit, what was it… around eighteen months ago?"

He glanced down at the patient notes on his desk.

"We've also taken another look at the blood test results from Falmouth Hospital, to cross reference and make certain."

I waited for the Professor to finish reading the notes. He looked over at me and removed his glasses. He seemed to be studying me. I wondered if I should say something.

"Okay…" I offered, wishing he'd just get the bad news out of the way.

"So, results time," he said. "Ready?"

I barely nodded, my neck muscles tight and unresponsive.

"I deduced from your bloods that you've been drinking heavily. Given the history of liver disease in your family, I wonder if that's wise. What was it your mother died of…?"

"Cirrhosis."

"Yes, I remember now. Not particularly helpful for either of us if you carry on as you are. Although perfectly understandable, given your previous prognosis and your decision not to have any treatment. But you should probably think about the drinking, longer term. We can't have you spoiling my recovery rate statistics."

"Oh. Right. Sorry. I didn't think that would matter…"

I stopped talking, fixated on the smile developing on the Professor's wrinkled face as my brain re-examined what he'd just said.

"Recovery rate?" I stammered.

"Indeed. You, Mister Straight, represent the one in one hundred thousand who the medical profession doesn't really know how to categorize. 'Miracle' is often bandied about for cases like yours, quirk of nature is also used. Sometimes by doctors like me, but not publicly.

because we need to be black and white, put our faith in science to provide a definitive answer, do you see? So instead we use a fancy medical description: Spontaneous Regression. It's extremely rare, but it does happen. You're living proof."

"I don't understand. The diagnosis was…"

"The CT scans show your tumours have shrunk, massively. The blood tests concur. Congratulations, your cancer is officially in remission."

"No… how? I don't understand… a year and a half ago you tell me I'll be lucky to survive twelve months, but now…"

The professor's smile widened into a grin, illuminating his crinkled features.

"Fantastic, isn't it? So many times every week I have to give nice people bad news. So you'll forgive me if I'm seem to be enjoying this conversation. I rarely get the opportunity to smile when consulting."

"I'm not going to die…? I mean imminently, you know, the next few days or weeks…?"

"I'd still keep an eye out for rogue buses mounting the pavement, and you'll have to have regular checks. Six-monthly initially, then annually. But for now… no. You're very much alive."

I'd like to say I whooped and cartwheeled around the office at the fantastic news. But truthfully, I felt numb, unable to take it in.

"Don't worry, I've checked the date, it's not April the first. And these are definitely your results. That's why we kept you waiting and ran the tests a second time. Which brings me to my interest in your visit to Falmouth…"

"To see my father?" I whispered.

"No. To eat a tasty but no doubt very dodgy and extremely helpful kebab."

I stared through the Professor, my head swimming with random and pointless thoughts.

"The latest research, right at the cutting edge, is focussed on the theory that some lucky patients recover due to a spontaneous reaction by their immune system attacking the cancerous cells. There are patterns emerging of a link between those patients having suffered a fever, the high temperature they experienced actually stimulating the immune system to attack and destroy the cancer cells. In fact, there are currently studies underway where scientists are trying to harness the power of fever and infection in a controlled way to treat cancer patients. Researchers in the United States and Italy are using food-poisoning bugs salmonella and your friend, listeria, to provoke a tumour-killing immune system response. So that kebab, Mister Straight, may well have been the best bad food you've ever eaten."

*

I slumped down in the chair opposite Keith. He lowered his newspaper and regarded me through apprehensive eyes.

"I'm not sure I should ask, given your appearance, but… worse than you expected?"

I slowly shook my head.

"No. It's... weird."

"Bad weird, or..."

"Not bad weird. The opposite."

"Okay. Stay there. I'll get the drinks in..."

"No, don't, I... I'm not sure I should... but... scratch that. Yes, to drinks."

Keith squeezed my shoulder as he stood up, shooting me a concerned glance before he strolled off towards the bar.

A few minutes later he returned with a pint of Guinness, a large brandy and an orange juice.

"Your favourite, if I remember correctly?"

I nodded and eyed the Guinness and brandy glasses.

"I've been here before..."

"To this pub?" Keith asked, glancing around at the décor.

"No... got myself to the point of jacking in the booze."

"That bad?"

"Getting that way."

I continued to stare at the drinks.

"So... how'd it go?" asked Keith.

I sat up in my chair, lifted my eyes above the white frothy head on top of the pint of black liquid.

"It seems I might be around for a bit longer..."

"Oh. That's good news... isn't it...?"

I nodded slowly.

"It is, very good news... I just can't really get my head around it. Need a bit of time, to process. Give me a minute...."

I stood up and lifted the Guinness and brandy glasses off the table and carried them outside. Keith watched me leave.

It has to start right here, right now, I told myself as I exited the pub.

"Drink up, flower…" I said, watching intently as I poured first the Guinness, then the brandy into the shrubbery.

Keith stared at the empty glasses as I walked past the table and placed them on the bar.

"You didn't…?"

"It was important… to start immediately with the first conscious positive thought. Come on driver, let's hit the road. I'll tell you all about it on the way."

"Where to guvnor?" Keith replied as he stood up.

"To see a friend," I replied, already on my way out of the door.

*

Keith steered the camper van to a stop outside the veterinary surgery, but left the engine running.

"There's a car park in there if you want to come in and see Lacey."

"I'll see him some other time," he said, staring through the windscreen.

"Oh. Right. I thought…"

"I'm… not good at goodbyes. You take good care of Lacey, make sure you let him lead you into trouble, from time to time."

I nodded, reached out and hugged him.

"How long will you be gone for?" I asked as we parted.

"Hard to say. But I'll be there, if you need me."

"And me you," I said, stepping out into the car park between the door and the van. I turned to face Keith.

"There's something I need to ask you... about Dad's Will."

"Oh?"

"You didn't seem surprised that he left everything to me. In fact, I don't recall you being mentioned in it at all..."

Keith held my gaze.

"No. He was a funny old bugger."

"Almost as if he'd forgotten you existed at all..." I said.

"Almost," Keith replied, smiling at me. "You won't remember, but Mum used to say: *If you've got your health, you're rich...* so live a wealthy life, Harry. Live it like the last few weeks and let your soul grow a little brighter every day... don't sit still and ebb away. There's no fun in that."

Keith held eye contact, appearing to look through me, as if he'd silently challenged me to out-stare him. He grinned as I blinked. I stepped back and shut the door. Keith revved the engine and drove away, leaving me staring after the van.

*

"She had to nip home, the neighbours rang complaining about constant dog barking," said

Rose, lifting her eyes from the computer screen as I approached the reception desk.

"Oh. Is everything okay?" I replied.

"Your dog… has been a very naughty boy. Here…"

Rose scribbled on a post-it note and stuck it to my chest.

"…this is her address. I'd hurry round if I were you, before she castrates the little fella."

I nodded my thanks as Rose answered the phone, leaving me to scurry away, wondering what on earth Lacey had been up to.

*

"Your bloody dog…!" screeched Alice as she opened her front door.

"What's he done?"

"What dirty dogs do! Holly is in season… Lacey ran down the stairs at full pelt, then vaulted over the child gate, mounted Holly and frantically *took her* before I could intervene."

"Oh. That's… bad form…"

"Bad form?! It's a disaster! He's very likely hit the jackpot and got her pregnant!"

"That's not definite though, is it? I mean, it's actually not that easy, in humans I mean, so fingers crossed it won't…"

"It doesn't work that way in the dog world, Harry. It only takes one sperm at the right time and bingo, a litter of troublesome little Laceys…"

I felt sure I could see vapour being exhaled from her nose as she ranted at me, eyes bulging, cheeks flushed. I looked down at Lacey, laid out on the floor licking his paws, seemingly unconcerned. He paused, glanced up at me and whined.

"Come on Harry, you think you're the only one around here who likes a bit of rough and tumble? You wouldn't want your four-legged friend to miss out on all the action…"

Was that my imagination or did Lacey just wink at me? I couldn't help a chuckle. I tried to stifle it and fake a tickly cough, but I caught Alice's murderous look.

"And aside from that, what are you doing here? Yesterday we said goodbye for the last time owing to your 'alleged' terminal illness… so tell me straight, Harry, if that's not a contradiction in terms given your family's track record. What the bloody hell is going on?"

Forty One

Lacey arched his head back towards me, his chocolate-brown eyes finding mine.

"You are such a naughty doggy," I whispered in a playful tone.

I felt his tail twitch on my lap as I shook my head at his soft whining.

"Ahwr, but you still love me, right?"

Alice, sat opposite me, didn't share my amusement.

"Don't try and defuse the situation with Lacey's cute dog routine. Have you any idea how you've screwed with my emotions? It's not playing fair, Harry."

She clasped her hands around the mug and sipped coffee, blowing wisps of steam away from her flushed face.

"I'm sorry, it's unintentional… I didn't expect to still be here, honestly."

"So you're telling me that one dodgy kebab and you're okay?"

"Apparently so, yes. The professor told me it does happen. Just not very often."

"Luck? Is that what you're telling me? Terminal decline to remission in one night out. Come on… what makes you so special?"

I dropped my eyes, slowly shook my head.

"I don't know… but if Lacey hadn't dragged me away from the supermarket…"

I stopped myself, frowning. Lacey whimpered again. He shifted around on my lap and tried to nuzzle his wet nose into my face.

"And don't you forget it, bro. Took one for the team that night. That's gotta keep me in beer and sausages for years."

"Super dog saves the day... *Really?* You're no different to your brother, Harry. It's in the blood isn't it... you Straight men... You're a lying, cheating drunk. It's time to take yourself and that furry rogue out of my life.*"*

"But Alice, please..."

"No. No sweet talk. No puppy dog eyes. No more bullshit. Just go."

I stared at her for a few seconds, then sighed and edged out of the chair, lifting Lacey down to the floor. I stood and turned to leave, then stopped.

"We can't have you spoiling my recovery rate statistics," said the professor's jovial voice, echoing around inside my head.

Lacey barked, making me jump.

"Yeah Harry, you a man or a meow, meow?"

I slowly turned back to face Alice. She'd begun to blink back tears from her tired, red eyes. Her distress gave way to a flicker of unease as I took a step forwards, looming over her. I sank back down onto the chair and placed my palms face down on the table.

"No."

A confused and wary frown creased her brow as tears trickled down her cheeks.

"No, I'm not leaving without trying. No to

drinking anymore. No to wallowing in the past. No to walking out on a *possibility* for happiness... I want to try, to really live, without anything hanging over me."

I took a deep shaky breath.

"One chance, Alice. One opportunity to prove to you, and me, that I can make a fresh start. Please... I'll do whatever it takes."

Forty Two

I sat in the chilly church hall on the plastic chair
with Lacey on my lap, his shivering resonating
through my thighs. The frequency and intensity
of his tremors calmed as my body heat leached
through his fur. Twinges sparked and jabbed
deep inside my stomach, my nervous jitters even
more pronounced at being here, amongst these
people, than my visit to Southampton Hospital.

I glanced around the circle of friendly faces
as I stroked Lacey behind his ears, a nervous
fidgeting motion on my part rather than an effort
to calm him. I waited until the previous speaker
had finished and sat down and the clapping had
subsided. Then I glanced at the chap who'd
welcomed me to the meeting a few minutes
earlier. I waited for his prompting smile and nod.

There it is, Harry. Your turn…

I glanced to my left as a slender hand
squeezed my arm encouragingly. I nodded at
Alice's warm smile, then scooped Lacey up into
my arms.

*"Whoa, easy Harry. You never heard of
letting sleeping dogs lie…?"*

I ignored Lacey's grumbling complaint as I
stood up and glanced around the group.

"Hello everyone. My name's Harry Straight
and this is my best friend, Lacey. And we're both
alcoholics…"

*

I walked out of that first meeting feeling lighter on my feet, more positive than I can remember. Everything around me seemed to appear in slightly sharper, more vivid focus.

"Happy fortieth birthday, Harry," said Alice, as she offered me her hand.

"Thank you for the present. It's probably the most unusual and important gift I've ever been given," I replied, clasping her hand warmly.

"You're welcome. Stick with it, who knows where it may lead…"

She smiled and eased her hand away.

"Maybe I could buy you dinner sometime, you know, after…?" I replied.

"See how you go…" she said as she turned and walked away.

"I guess life really does begin at forty, eh Lacey," I said, glancing down at my four-legged friend, happily sniffing the pavement while he emitted whining doggy noises.

"Speak for yourself, sailor boy. I fancy a pint…"

Forty Three

Six long winter months later, I slid Jessica's hatch open and breathed in the warm spring air. I glanced around the boatyard at the other yachts, elevated on their stilt-like cradles, the morning dew droplets trickling down hazy white hulls.

"What a beautiful morning, Lacey. Ready for your walk?"

"You humans don't learn… tea and breakfast first, comprende?"

I chuckled. That dog, such a character.

"Launch day, boy. You know what that means… time to get those sea legs ready," I said, lifting the washboards out and stepping up into the cockpit to stretch.

Who'd have thought I'd be back here, in Poole, in the same boat yard that I'd been thrown out of the previous summer. Luckily Dave had negotiated with Barbara and after assurances that I'd never be visited by the police ever again, she'd relented. So I'd arranged for Jessica to be loaded onto a truck and brought back.

"Home…" I mumbled, scanning around the yard at the sailing boats, their masts rising skywards towards the heavens.

Somehow, after she'd calmed down and with

lots more pleading and assurances, I'd managed to persuade Alice to give me that precious second chance, albeit with some very strict conditions. An unblemished record of weekly visits to the Alcoholics Anonymous meetings had been top of her list. All she'd agreed to had been the possibility of friendship, after a prolonged period of my sobriety. So Lacey and I attended the meetings and we battened down Jessica's hatches for a winter of rebuilding. Me, this time. And to be honest, it took all of those long cold months to be clear in my head about what I wanted to do, which direction I wanted my new life, and Lacey's, to take me.

I glanced down into the cabin, watching him stretch out on the cabin floor in his doggy yoga 'salute to the sun' posture. After a leg-trembling stretch, he slumped back into a sitting position and yawned.

"What's the matter, Lacey... the kids keeping you up?" I called out, smiling as he let out a groan.

"Come on Harry, shake a leg, amigo. Lacey breakfast time."

*

I rang Alice's doorbell and glanced down to check my appearance: smart shirt, borrowed jacket and bunch of flowers. Not bad... fingers crossed.

Alice opened the door, surrounded by five excitable little Laceys yapping and tumbling around her feet, tails frantic, eager to see their dad.

"Weekly visitation rights. Lacey reporting for duty…" I said over the muted barking of the adorable fluffy puppies.

"And yet despite the normal routine, it looks like a special occasion…" Alice replied with a coy smile as she took in my appearance.

"Jim wouldn't lend me his car if I wore my boat work clothes…"

"Is that the only reason for scrubbing up smart?"

"That and the fact that the boat's back floating and I've remained dry for six months, as promised. Which in turn means…"

"A date. Yes, I remember."

"A date on board Jessica, no less."

Alice nodded and accepted the flowers, opening the door wider to let us in.

Lacey bounded in amongst the licking tongues, wagging tails and bouncing paws, embroiling himself in puppy play.

Be gentle on the old salty seadog…

"He's amongst his own age group at last," said Alice, with a raised eyebrow.

"Mmm… how's Holly?"

"Tired of Lacey already, I should think," Alice replied.

We left the puppies playing and I followed Alice through into the lounge.

"This is Martine, she's going to dogsit for us…"

I smiled at the trainee veterinary nurse,

wondering if she knew what a handful she'd taken on.

"Ready?" I asked.

"I am if you are..." Alice replied.

*

Alice placed her cutlery on the plastic plate and reached across the table to top our glasses up with sparkling water. She took a sip and sat back against Jessica's side, her eyes bright in the soft glow from a paraffin lamp.

"Thank you Harry, that was delicious. I'd never have guessed you'd be such a good cook."

"I try... I've been looking after myself a lot better since I gave up the booze. Just ask Lacey, he's turned his nose up at some of my more exotic creations."

She rolled her eyes.

"That doggy... mischievous rogue doesn't do him justice."

"No. But he does grow on you..."

We smiled at each other, a silence creeping across the cabin.

"So... what's next for you, Harry?" she said at last.

"In life?"

She nodded, watching me intently.

"I'd like to stay on the boat, for now... so I'm thinking of having Lacey chipped, get him a pet passport and take him across the Channel to cruise the French canals."

"Oh, wow. Sounds amazing. Are you and Lacey going on your own?"

"I thought I'd advertise for a crewmate."

"Right… do you have anyone in mind?"

Alice held eye contact with me.

"Maybe…"

She smiled and raised her glass.

"A toast, to you Harry. Here's to staying sober and a fresh start to our friendship."

I nodded and picked up my glass. We touched the plastic sides together and sipped the cool water.

"And on that note, Harry, it's time I got back. I'm working tomorrow and you need to collect Lacey before he corrupts those puppies. I can't find homes for them if they get too naughty."

*

I walked Alice to her front door and waited patiently while she searched in her bag for her key.

"Ah, I nearly forgot. Here, I guess you'll need this," she said, retrieving Jessica's logbook.

"I haven't seen this for months…"

I cradled the book in my hands and fanned through the pages.

"I read it, back in the summer… out of curiosity," she said quietly.

"Oh, right. Of course. That was the intention, when I gave it to you."

"Mmm… although slightly different circumstances back then…" she said, glancing away.

I nodded.

"Yes… of course…"

Alice smiled at me, then opened the door. I heard Lacey bark and scamper across the wood floor, closely followed by his puppies.

"Yo Harry, how's it hanging? You get lucky?!"

I saw Lacey launch himself at me. I caught him behind the shoulders in mid-air, holding his wriggling excited body away from my face.

"You Straight boys…" said Alice, shaking her head as she herded the pups back inside.

I clipped on Lacey's lead as I cradled him to my chest.

"Goodnight," I said to Alice, turning to follow the path away from the house.

"Thanks for dinner, Harry," she said, placing her hand on my arm. "Perhaps I'll cook next time, if you like…"

Alice took half a step closer as I turned to acknowledge her. She straightened out my jacket collar and held eye contact with me.

"That would be… lovely," I said, my heart rate increasing as she shielded her face from Lacey's tongue and stood up on tiptoe to kiss me on the lips.

"Woo-hoo!"

We both jumped back from Lacey's howl, but I couldn't let the opportunity pass and quickly lowered him to the ground, then gently pulled Alice towards me, kissing her again.

"Mmm, not bad for a dead man," she murmured as we eased a few inches apart. "But I'd better make sure…"

We kissed again. Tenderly, firmly, passionately.

I didn't think it was possible to regress to the sensations experienced as a teenager, but right there, at that moment, I felt everything I thought I'd forgotten. When we finally parted, I knew I wanted more of that addictive, stomach-twinging, fast-pulse euphoria.

"Be good until next week, Harry..." she said, drumming her fingernails on the boat logbook clutched in my fingers, "and you may get lucky..."

*

By the time I'd driven back to the boatyard and parked up, my face had begun to ache from grinning so much.

"Good night?" asked Jim, giving me the old raised clenched fist and exaggerated saucy wink routine.

"Big smile, Jim... big smile," I replied, tossing him his car keys.

"What does that mean?" he called after me as I wandered away, following Lacey as he sniffed his way towards a clump of grass.

"It means there are possibilities, Jim. Lots of possibilities..."

"Yeah, I'm still confused. Come on, I need details."

I shook my head, ambling away, breathing in hope and opportunity in the cool evening air.

Boatyards really are magical places, I

thought, as I wandered amongst the tapping halyards and twinkling stars with not a care in the world.

Pawnote

I swilled the last of my hot chocolate and took a final swig, conscious of Lacey's low whine and accompanying paw tapping on my leg.

"Save some for me, buddy."

"Chocolate's not good for you, Lacey," I said, placing the cup on the galley top.

Lacey took a deep breath and sighed noisily, turning away from me and slumping down on the floor to lick his paws.

"Spoilsport."

I smirked at his moody response and leant back against a pillow propped up against Jessica's hull. The electric heater thermostat clicked in over Lacey's paw-chewing noises, enhancing the cosiness of the cabin.

Something made me reach out and pick up Jessica's logbook from the chart table and flick through the old faded pages. Curiosity, perhaps.

"The next adventure awaits, Lacey… I think you'll like France…"

Lacey stopped licking his paw and lifted his head, a mildly inquisitive, enigmatic expression on his small face. His unblinking chocolate-brown eyes stared straight through me. We held our competitive gaze until finally he blinked and looked away.

I'd finally outstared him, go Harry!

I fanned through the other logbook entries, chuckling at my victory, until the last handwritten page remained. But it wasn't my father's final entry.

That's odd…

The new handwriting had a similar long swoopy elegance but it didn't sit lightly on the page, the black ink had been heavily pressed into the paper. The words had *prominence.*

I read quickly, then shifted my gaze to stare at Lacey, open-mouthed.

"You can't be…"

I dropped my eyes back to the logbook and read the entry again.

September 12th 2013 – Falmouth
Dear Harry,
I'm guessing that if you're reading this you've managed to pull your life around, or else Alice wouldn't let you have the logbook back.
That was your intention - give it to her when you dropped Lacey off?
I'm assuming it will have taken you a few months to prove to Alice your worth – after all, Straight men can be a little tricky to trust. But I'm sure in time, you'll win her over. I'm pleased that you decided to collect Lacey and adopt him properly, he's good for you. His mannerisms remind me of someone I used to know, a long time ago…
The funny thing about dogs is that they're immortal – did you know that? It's true, really. Unlike cats who are well known to have only

nine lives, dogs live on eternally. Not in the same body, it's different each time they visit. But their spirit is always around. They can be a blessing and a curse of course, but I like to think of dogs as little pieces of friendship, sent back to our temporary world to keep an eye on the people they care about, ready to liven up their lives whenever a little fun, laughter and mischief is required.

Have you adjusted to your spontaneous regression diagnosis yet? It'll take time, but always keep in mind the Straight family motto and you won't go far wrong: "If you've got your health, you're rich…"

You have a second chance now, Harry. So my question to you is this: what are you going to do with it? Will you squander or savour the time you have left, however long that may be…?

We'll see you on the other side of the water. Until then, look after the little monster and your family will always be there, faithfully by your side…

I laughed nervously and shook my head, staring at Lacey. He lifted his head and held my gaze, letting his lower jaw relax into a pant. It almost looked like he was smiling at me.

Dedication

This book is dedicated to Poppy Baxter-Green. The most mischievous, naughty and adorable four-legged friend you could ever wish to share time or your dinner with.

Also by Mark David Green

The Travel Auction

It should have been their trip of a lifetime. But with just days to go, Jonathan Cork is dumped by his girlfriend. Unable to change the name on the spare ticket and fast running out of time, Jonathan decides to take desperate measures. He advertises on eBay for a travel companion with the same name as his ex-girlfriend.

UK Charity Row 2015

On 2nd May 2015, I will be joining three full time crewmates and two support guys to row a 26 year old Australian surf boat around Britain.

We anticipate this 2,500 mile circumnavigation will take approximately three and a half months to complete. We are doing this to raise funds for two fantastic charities:

**The Royal Marines Charitable Trust
and Wessex Cancer Trust**

If you'd like to find out more about the UK Charity Row 2015, or would consider supporting this epic challenge in any way at all, please visit our website and 'Like' our Facebook page:

www.ukcharityrow2015.com

www.facebook.com/ukcharityrow2015

Thank you from the Cheeky Chaps in Speedos!

Printed in Great Britain
by Amazon

60516306R00220